HUGE

A NOVEL

BRENT BUTT

DOUBLEDAY CANADA

Doubleday Canada and colophon are registered trademarks of Penguin Random House Canada Limited

Library and Archives Canada Cataloguing in Publication

Title: Huge / Brent Butt.
Names: Butt, Brent, 1966- author.
Identifiers: Canadiana (print) 20230206352 | Canadiana (ebook) 20230206360 | ISBN 9780385688321 (softcover) | ISBN 9780385688338 (EPUB)
Classification: LCC PS8603.U8656 H84 2023 | DDC C813/.6—dc23

This book is a work of fiction. Names, characters, places and incidents are products of the author's imagination or are used fictitiously. Any resemblance to actual events or locales or persons, living or dead, is entirely coincidental.

Cover design: Matthew Flute
Cover art: (man) breakermaximus, (mic) Anton Eine / EyeEm, (wall) Jostein Nilsen / EyeEm, (neon type) Tetiana Lazunova, all Getty Images; (lightbulb type) piai / Adobe Stock Images

Printed in Canada

Published in Canada by Doubleday Canada, a division of Penguin Random House Canada Limited

www.penguinrandomhouse.ca

10 9 8 7 6 5 4 3 2 1

Penguin
Random House
DOUBLEDAY CANADA

For Nancy
(who I happen to be in love with)
and Oliver
(who can't even read)

1

Most people passed under the sign without giving it a second thought, but it always bothered Nick. *Why did they write RED CACTUS in blue neon? Did someone screw up? Was someone trying to be funny? If they were trying to be funny, Jesus, they really screwed up.*

Recently, someone suggested it may have been done with a deeper psychological purpose, a clever marketing move designed to "pit the mind against itself to draw extra attention." Nick had scoffed at that eggheaded idea. The Red Cactus was not the type of establishment that wanted extra attention.

From inside the old brick building, Nick peered out a window up at the rusting metal sign to make damn sure it shut off when he hit the switch. The wiring was thirty years old, installed when the tavern opened in 1964, and had become unreliable. If the signal didn't send properly and the neon remained glowing, there would always be some drunk staggering up to kick at the door, howling for one last drink.

The thin blue tubing spasmed briefly, then went to sleep.

Nick smiled and lit a cigarette. He enjoyed this time of night. The pain-in-the-ass customers were long gone, the last of the staff had left to go party at some after-hours club or grab a late-night bite at Sal's, and it left him alone in the stale, smoky quiet with nothing but his thoughts and some questionable porn. He double-checked the front door locks, rattled the side doors to the alley, then headed to the back of the club to secure the rolling door in the loading bay.

He found the space strangely dark. Usually a bare low-watt bulb burned inside an ancient socket at the end of the storeroom ramp, throwing just enough light to see where you were going but not enough to draw customers into the area, which was off-limits. Nick flipped the switch a couple of times, but that did nothing to fix the situation. *Whole goddamn place is falling apart.*

He pulled his dented copper lighter out of his vest pocket and sparked it up, giving him enough visibility to navigate down the ramp, which creaked and sagged—weakened by thirty years of heavy beer kegs rolling up and down it. Holding his lighter high to extend the reach of its dim flickering, he shuffled along, sliding his feet instead of picking them up to minimize the risk of stepping on something and going ass over elbows—which he had done before. Prophetically, his right shoe banged into a loose booze bottle, and he heard the thick glass skidding and clattering loudly across the concrete until it came to rest somewhere in the darkness. Then quiet again.

"Jesus Christ," Nick whispered, "that coulda killed me."

He slid his left hand along the cinder-block wall to guide him as he continued toward the back, farther into the gloom, deeper into the dark—"Fuck!" he yelped as the flame burned his thumb, and he dropped the lighter to the floor, returning the storeroom to blackness.

Nick had spent a thousand nights alone in this old dump, and never a minute of that time scared, never worried about being robbed—this place was protected, that was well known. But something felt different. Felt off. An instinctual alarm prickled his neck and a sudden dread knotted his guts. He crouched quickly to his knees, floundering blindly for his lighter. The only sound was his breathing, rapid and choppy now, and the clammy *pat-pat-pat* of his panicked palms across cold concrete.

Then another sound.

K-tink.

Nick froze in place on all fours. His breathing ceased. His eyes widened, desperately scanning the void. Every cell in his brain ratcheted focus to his ears, straining to hear the sound again. Hoping not to. Because it sounded a hell of a lot like an empty booze bottle being lifted off a concrete floor.

He heard nothing for a few moments. Then—footsteps? A chuckle? *Jesus Christ, is someone chuckling?* "Who's in here?" Nick shouted in the deepest voice he could muster. There was definite chuckling. "I have a gun!"

From the dark came a low reply. "Not on you."

Nick was rigid with fear, yet almost relieved to hear a man's voice—a human's. His imagination had caught wind in the darkness and sailed to ghosts and demons. A man, he could deal with. The smart move would be to get the man talking. Track his voice. Draw him near. Hope he was alone.

"What the fuck do you want?" Nick hollered, with failing ferocity. No response. "You know who owns this place, asshole?"

"I do."

"Then, you know you're a dead man." Nick was gaining courage, fuelled by adrenalin. He remained crouched low, a smaller target, his right hand sliding down his leg toward the knife strapped above his ankle. "Dead meat. Unless you get the fuck out of here right now."

Then he heard sniffing.

"What was in this bottle?" the voice asked. "Rum?"

"Wait—I know your voice," Nick said. "Who are you?"

"If you know my voice, why are you asking?"

"I've heard it before. And when it comes back to me, you're as good as dead." He had his hand on his knife.

Sniff sniff.

"Rum, for sure. Still some in the bottom, too. Feel that?"

Pain exploded on the side of Nick's skull as the thick glass bottle pounded into his head. Shards of coloured light ripped across his vision and he sunk fully to the floor. His ears whistled and the room took on a thick woolly tone. He heard the voice saying, "See what I mean?" Slow and distorted. "At least half a cup in here." He felt cool liquid pouring into his hair and over his neck before his consciousness let go of the situation and drained away.

Nick half woke as he felt himself rising, but only in the middle— hoisting up in the centre like a tent as the rest of him sagged limply to the floor. Next, the sensation of drifting—half-carried, half-dragged by the back of his belt across the smooth concrete, with a wide set of rough knuckles dug into his lower back. His mind found it all too much again, and he vomited once and slipped back out of reality.

He next woke with a sudden snort, his eyes wide and searching. He lurched to get his feet under him, but his pant legs were caught on something. He kicked to free them before seeing his legs were not caught but rather tied to a wooden chair. No—a stool. He was sitting on a wooden stool with each of his ankles tied to one of its legs. Confusion matured to terror as he realized his arms were also bound, cinched tight against his body by a thick black cord wrapped around his torso multiple times and around his neck, feeding into the bottom of a microphone tucked up and pointed at his chin.

"What the fuck is—" Nick was startled to hear his voice amplified over the house sound system. "Hello?" Zero ferocity was being mustered now. "Who's there?" Only fear.

A white light bloomed to life in front of him, hammering Nick with a harsh brilliance that stabbed his eyes and he recoiled, hitting the back of his head against a brick wall. He screamed, "What the fuck? Untie me!"

"Relax."

"Who are you?" Nick bellowed, sending a squeal of feedback through the speakers.

"Me? I'm just a critic. Like you."

"What are you talking about? I'm not a fucking critic."

"Everyone's a critic. But you're a harsh one. Rude and shitty."

"Hang on . . . I know who you—"

"You don't know a goddamn thing!" the voice rumbled. "And yet you sit back and pass judgment anyway. Even though you've never been onstage yourself. Until now, that is."

Nick swung his head around and realized he was in the main area of the bar, but higher. Elevated. He was on the stage where the bands and strippers performed. He looked down at the worn, stained carpet beneath him and saw a half-dozen empty bottles lying spent on their sides around his feet. Then the smell hit. Overpowering. He was drenched in rum.

"Jesus Christ. Jesus Christ. What the fuck is going on?"

"It's comedy night, tough guy," the voice replied.

Nick sat silent, trying to digest the pieces as they came.

The voice continued, "I know, I know, you stopped booking comedians in here, but look at this as a 'one night only' type of deal. One final show . . . for all the marbles."

"Get me down from here, you fucking psycho!"

"Sure, I'll do that, Nick. I will absolutely get you down and let you go. If you can do one small thing."

"Do what?"

"Make me laugh."

"What? Is this some sick fucking joke?"

"*This* is not a joke. But you better come up with some. I'm giving you a five-minute spot. Five minutes to make me laugh once. Just one honest laugh, Nick. How hard can it be?"

"But . . ." Nick was almost too terrified to ask. "What if I don't?"

"Same as any other comic. When you've done your time, you get the light."

Nick heard a sharp metallic scratch and saw a small flame spark to life and hover in the darkness. He watched the flickering reflected in the dented copper casing beneath it, then reflected again off something below that. He focused hard to bring that lower, shimmering image into view and determined it was a liquid. A narrow line of liquid snaking across the barroom floor to the foot of the stage, seeping up the fabric attached to the filthy carpet on which he sat, tied to a stool and soaked in rum.

The reality of his predicament hit at once—stark and horrifying. Any strength that remained in Nick shrank to nothing. His words crawled weakly from trembling lips. "Come on . . . Come on, man, you can't just—"

"Make me laugh!" the voice punched through the darkness, heavy and grave. "If I laugh . . . you live."

2

301 . . . 303 . . . 305 . . .

One small overnight bag dangled from Dale Webly's shoulder as he made his way down the long, beige hallway of the Journeywide Inn. Managing five days away from home with only one small bag was a skill cultivated over seventeen years on the road.

. . . 307 . . . and . . .

He slid the plastic key card through the brass slot of room 309, leaned against the door and pushed inside. A faint but distinct tang of bleach, or some other chemical cleaner, hit his nostrils. When he first started getting booked on the road as a stand-up, the smell of disinfectant made him nauseous, but he had grown to appreciate it—or at least what it meant. You never knew who was in your room two hours ago, or what they sneezed on, or coughed on, or sat naked on. *Hose the whole place down with Clorox, I'll wear a nose clip* had always been Dale's unspoken motto, and he eventually became almost immune to the smell. Almost.

He tossed his bag onto a credenza, which was built of pressed wood and cloaked in a chipped cherrywood laminate that wasn't fooling anyone. Aside from the bed, it was the main bit of furniture in the room, comprising a small writing desk, three dresser drawers, several cigarette burns, a TV stand supporting a twenty-inch Zenith, and a coffee station. *There's the first order of* "—business," he half thought/half muttered. Years of solitude in bland hotel rooms had seen Dale develop a form of self-communication that blended inner and outer dialogue. He often caught himself saying the last part of a thought out loud. He might think *I wonder if there's a place to* and then utter audibly "—do laundry nearby." Or *There's only about two days' worth of toothpaste left* "—in this tube." More than once it had caught his wife, Brandy, off guard. The first time, he had come home after a five-week run of shows and the two of them were sitting in their apartment, watching TV, when Dale suddenly blurted "—just lazy." Brandy had looked at him strangely and said, "Who're you calling lazy?" He laughed at the time, tried to explain that he had been thinking that the guy who invented crunchy peanut butter was probably just lazy, and he laughed even harder trying to explain how he must've said the first part in his head and the last part out loud. He smiled now at that memory, recalling the concerned look on her face as she wondered if her husband was coming unhinged. A lot of Dale's comedy material had been born from that kind of half-thought/half-spoken germ of an idea, which he would flesh out later in a notebook and eventually onstage in front of an audience. That's how the act grew.

He pulled the slightly warped plastic basket from the lip of the coffee maker—a Morningmaster 200, according to the stencil on the front—and tore open a foil packet of ground coffee. He filled the four-cup glass carafe in the bathroom sink, after rinsing it very very very very thoroughly, filled the tank, hit the switch and waited to hear the spittle and hiss that meant the machine actually worked.

Success.

He glanced at the digital clock on the nightstand, which read 4:27 p.m. Showtime was set for eight o'clock, so he'd head downstairs about a half-hour early to check out the stage and the showroom. That gave him roughly three hours to relax and absorb all the splendour the Journeywide had to offer.

While the Morningmaster burbled softly, Dale moved to the hotel room's window and yarded back the off-orange curtains to soak in the view. Alley, parking lot, car wash, pawnshop, half a bicycle, 350-pound guy in a tank top, old-style family ice cream stand with a FOR LEASE sign propped in a broken window. Probably not the parts of Saginaw, Michigan, you'd see on a postcard. Then again, if you got sold on the idea of coming to Saginaw because of what you saw on a postcard, you're probably not used to the high life.

Dale's eyes were drawn back inside to the corner of the window-sill, where a dramatic scene was playing out. A grey beetle was trying to wrench free of a dusty cobweb, as a pudgy spider approached menacingly from above. It strangely mirrored a human scenario shaping up on the street beyond, and Dale's attention was pulled back outside to where an elderly woman walked stiffly across the alley behind his hotel, while a young man in pants six sizes too big followed her slowly. The woman held a single plastic shopping bag in one hand, and a clasp purse draped from the crook of her other arm. The young man's head swivelled around as he methodically closed the gap between himself and the woman.

Yeah, I see you, you "—sack of shit." Dale flicked the metal latch on the frame and slid the window open. "Hey, lady!" he hollered. The elderly woman and the young man both stopped dead and looked up at him, equally startled. "You know that dude behind you?" She turned back to look at the young man. "That your grandson?" Dale continued loudly. "Hey, man, how come you're not carrying your gran's groceries?

That's not cool. Or hang on—maybe you're not her grandson." Dale's booming voice had caught the attention of some other folks on the corner, who now looked over. He hollered to them, "Any of you folks know this saggy-assed kid? Is he this lady's grandson or just some shitty mugger? Help me out here, I'm from out of town."

The young man backed away, flipped the finger to Dale in the window, then hustled across the street and disappeared behind a record store.

The lady looked up to Dale and gave him a wave. He waved back and slid the window closed. He looked down at the spider, nearly on top of the wriggling beetle, and pulled the window back open. "Nope. New sheriff in town," he said, and separated the two creatures with a cardboard coaster. He scooped up the beetle and set it on the ledge outside and slid the window closed again. The beetle shuttled over to the wall and crawled up and away.

Dale raised his shoulders and rolled them forward, then stretched his neck side to side. His back was tightening up from the travel, and he was grateful this was the last show of the run. It had started with four shows over two nights at the Tickle Bar in Detroit, two of which had gone really well, then three one-nighters: Comedy and Chicken Wing Night at a pub in Livonia, Comedy and Trivia Night in Midland, then backtracking to Saginaw for Comedy and Who-the-hell-knows-what tonight. The one-nighters never seemed to be just comedy anymore. Every gig had some other angle tacked on as a promotional afterthought. Maybe comedy was the afterthought. It certainly seemed like comedy alone wasn't drawing the crowds it used to. Perhaps the notion of a night out watching strangers try to be funny for ninety minutes was losing its lustre. It had a good run, though.

Dale had gotten in at the right time, learning his craft in the late 1970s, so by the time the comedy boom hit in the mid-eighties, he was an established headline act. A solid one too, that bookers could rely on.

He didn't do drugs, beyond a bit of weed now and then. He could manage his own travel without someone holding his hand, got good laughs and didn't cause trouble. That was the sweet spot. There were lots of comics working who weren't particularly funny but got gigs because they never trashed a room or got weird with a waitress. Conversely, there were a few comics who were brilliantly funny, but absolute flakes that would miss flights or not show up because they wrote the show info on a napkin then blew their nose on it ten minutes later. Hilarious, but hardly worth the inevitable headaches. Dale straddled the line as a guy who could deliver good laughs with original material and never a complaint from the clubs. That was gold to a booker back then. But it was 1994 now, and audience tastes had turned elsewhere. Grunge, maybe? Whatever that was. Stand-up gigs were fewer and farther between, and still paid basically the same as they had a decade earlier. That was increasingly hard to swallow, especially for someone in his forties, and lately Dale had found himself thinking a thought he couldn't bring himself to say any portion of out loud: *It might be time to look for a future outside comedy.*

He stepped away from the depressing thought and the depressing window and poured a cup of the freshly brewed coffee. He took a sip and his face puckered so tight he pulled a muscle in his cheek. Dale was no coffee snob, but that was legitimately awful. Tasted like a blend of moss and ear wax filtered through a sock. He shuddered and bent down to retrieve the foil packet from the trash, looking for a brand name so he could make a mental note to never buy it for home. The silver packet had green lettering that read Seven Pines Medium Ground Coffee.

Why would you grow coffee beans in the same dirt you grow pine trees? It goes against nature, like "—Arabian beavers."

He set down the cup and reached for his notebook.

3

The sun in the Los Angeles sky was temporarily masked by a single cloud that was so puffy and white it looked like it had been cut out of a cartoon. It was the only cloud visible in a ridiculous sea of powder blue and the temporary relief it offered from the ultraviolet onslaught was very much welcomed by Rynn Lanigan. She felt a little stupid wearing the large, floppy hat she had purchased from a street vendor on Fairfax for nine U.S. dollars, but her milky Irish skin demanded the investment. The two-minute reprieve provided by the solitary cloud gave her a chance to take the hat off and stroll for half a block looking a bit more like a local, if such a thing existed. She hoped, at least, it would make her look less like a tourist. It did not.

Just as the sun slipped free of the cloud to continue hammering the pavement, Rynn slipped inside the air-conditioned lobby of the Carlaw Professional Building and took the elevator to the fifth floor, fixing her hair on the ride. She wondered if becoming rich and famous would require living an increasingly incognito life under a series of ever-floppier hats. On the fifth floor, the elevator dinged and released her into the reception area of Beering & Brady Talent Management, where she checked in for her 2 p.m. meeting.

"You look good," Gail Beering said as she walked Rynn to her office. "You got some sleep, didn't you? I can tell."

"I did, yeah," Rynn replied in her lyrical Dublin accent. "I thought I might be too excited about everything, but the jet lag caught up, I guess. I went down for a quick eleven hours."

"Wow. You must've been tired."

"Yeah," Rynn replied, "or drunk, who can say? I'm not a doctor."

They sat down, not at Gail's desk but on the tan sectional in the corner of her office. Gail asked, "Do you like what I did in here? Redesigned it since you were in last."

"Looks great," Rynn said. "Stark yet opulent. Didn't even know that mix was possible, so well done you." She smiled a bit too wide, hoping that remark hadn't been insulting. "It really is gorgeous."

"The way you talk, I can't tell when you're being sarcastic," Gail said, "so let's just press on to business. Avenue Media Group has definite and serious interest in signing you to a development deal."

"Feck, that's great!" Rynn shouted.

"Come on," Gail said, "I told you to practise talking without the F-word, to clean it up."

Rynn cocked her head. "The F-word is 'fuck,' isn't it? I said 'feck.' Feck *is* cleaned up."

"Not here, it's not," Gail said.

"Okay, well . . . for now, fuck, this is good news, yeah?"

"It's very good," Gail said. "We've even started discussing what the potential terms and conditions might look like. And I promise you, they would not waste their time feeling us up if they weren't keen to bang."

Rynn chuckled. "Hey now, who needs to watch their language?"

"You're the one practising to be on TV every week, not me." Gail grinned. "I can talk however I want."

"Wait," Rynn said. "Avenue Media? Are they the ones that wanted me for that afternoon show, with the flowers and the cookies and shite?"

"No," Gail assured her, "that was Arling Entertainment, and I told them you were a bit too skanky for an afternoon audience."

"Bless you."

"Avenue is looking at you to host a late-night show," Gail explained. "It would be a mix of stand-up and sketch and interviews."

"Holy fuck! I mean, holy . . . moly, mother of Murphy, are you serious?" Rynn said, her eyes twice the diameter they were a moment ago. "That would be my ultimate dream come true. Jesus, how do we make this happen, Gail? This needs to happen."

"Well, first," Gail said calmly, "we act like it doesn't need to happen. We want it to happen, but we can walk away."

Rynn closed her eyes, took in a deep breath, and began slowly. "Gail, I love you. I mean I don't, really, I've only known you three months, but I do like you. And I think you're incredible at what you do." Her eyes opened. "But if this doesn't happen, be advised I will kill one or both of us in horrible and violent fashion."

Gail smiled. "I'm glad we've reached the death-threats stage of our relationship. Now we can really get to work." She leaned forward. "Okay, I told you the Cinderella part of the story, here's the ugly stepsister part. It's between you and one other person."

"Who?"

"You don't know him. Some handsome, toothy, corn-fed kid from Nebraska or Wyoming or one of those places."

"Shit," Rynn said.

"Relax. He's not as funny as you," Gail said. That calmed Rynn's mind a little, until Gail added, "But he really is handsome—it's sort of breathtaking."

"Shit." Rynn looked down at the carpet, her mental wheels turning. "Well, can we get a meeting with the execs at Avenue? Today? Or lunch tomorrow? I'll try and wow them or woo them or whatever."

"No," Gail said. "The person making the final decision is the president of Avenue, Vic Zayne, and he's out of town. He's gone to New York for a couple days, and from there he's going right to Montreal for the Just For Laughs festival."

Rynn considered. "Okay . . . um . . . I can get to Montreal. I'm already booked to do a club in Canada next week. In Winnipeg, right? Is that close to Montreal?"

"Nothing in Canada is close to anything else in Canada," Gail said, "but yeah, you're playing Whispers Comedy Club in Winnipeg. And why you got a work visa for Canada and not America is beyond me."

"I applied to both countries and one of them didn't spit on me. Guess which."

"Our lawyer is working on that. In the meantime," Gail said, "I found a comedy booker up there that has a run of shows heading east from Winnipeg toward Montreal. So you go do your week at Whispers, and then you work your way toward Montreal, emceeing that run."

"That's fantastic," Rynn said. "But why emceeing?"

"Because you're out of practice, and it's a two-bit dump-ass run through rural Canada, entertaining lumberjacks and sled dogs and whatever the hell else lives up there. They'll be hard shows and that'll sharpen your skills. Because I also called Just For Laughs to do some long-distance ass-kissing and guess who's now emceeing the show that Vic Zayne will be at."

"Me?" Rynn beamed.

"You. So all you have to do is get there and show Vic how good you are at hosting a show—how fast on your feet you can be, how quick off the cuff." Gail leaned back. "Give him no choice but to send Handsome back to the corn patch."

"You're brilliant, Gail. Utterly, wondrously, stunningly—"

"Oh just say it your way."

"You're fecking brilliant."

4

By seven thirty, people weren't exactly flooding into the showroom in
Saginaw. Although, calling it a showroom was a little misleading. It was
basically a bar with two pool tables, and the few people in the place were
there to shoot pool. It didn't even have a dedicated stage, just a small
plywood riser covered with a nasty chunk of burgundy carpeting and
crammed into the corner by the women's bathroom. If you were a singer
or a band or a comedian or a magician or a monkey juggler, it was all
the same set-up: *Ladies and gentlemen, Doolen's Roost off the lobby of the
Saginaw Journeywide is proud to present someone in the corner making noise
while you drink.* But it was a room and there were sometimes shows, so
the term wasn't an out-and-out lie.

Usually when Dale played a place for the first time, he'd step up to
the bouncer or whoever was collecting the cover at the door and introduce himself. He was well aware that performers like him who played
joints like this weren't exactly famous faces. Ideally there would be a

photocopy of his headshot stapled up somewhere nearby that he could point to and say "I'm the comedian" so he wouldn't get shaken down for the five bucks. When Dale stepped inside Doolen's, there was no one at the door taking money. No cover—not a good sign. It was the second not-good sign he had encountered on his way into the place—the first being the fact he saw no poster, no banner, no sheet of paper, no anything to suggest there might be a comedy show tonight.

Dale made his way about six feet farther inside, then stood with his back against a wall where he could survey the situation. There were several more not-good signs. He couldn't see anyone anywhere who looked like a bouncer, which meant crowd control would fall entirely on him. A few TVs were on, mounted at various heights and angles around the room to provide the patrons with an option to his face. There wasn't even a microphone on the riser. Only one spotlight pointed at the stage area and it had a red bulb in it. Not a red gel that could be removed, but an actual red bulb. *Shaping up to be a hell gig anyway, the lighting may as well* "—reflect that." No seating near the stage. There were some chairs parked around several small tables, but they were on the other side of the dance floor, at least twenty feet from where he'd be performing. A lot of factors working against him. Time to find the bar manager.

Dale stepped up to the long, chest-high stretch of Formica and waited for the bartender to come over. It was calculated patience. It paid to keep the staff on your side in these types of rooms, and barking for the bartender as soon as you stepped up was a good way to piss her off. It was less than a minute before she headed over to him anyway.

"What can I getcha?"

"Looking for the manager, actually. I'm the comic tonight."

"Aw shit, is that tonight?" She turned and hollered over to a mullet-headed man with thick-rimmed glasses. "Is it comedy tonight?"

Mullet strolled over in no great rush. "Oh yeah. I guess it is. Every second Tuesday and there wasn't none last Tuesday, so yeah." He extended a hand to Dale. "You the comedian?"

"Yeah. Dale Webly." They shook hands.

"Jake," the man said. "Just you?"

"Far as I know."

"Usually two guys. Opener and headliner."

Dale wondered why anyone would agree to do this gig if they were splitting the money with another act. Barely worth it potting the whole nut. He shrugged. "Not sure what to tell you."

"Supposed to be an hour show," Jake said. "Can you do an hour by yourself?"

Dale nodded.

"Then it's no skin off my ass."

Dale asked if there was any chance they could shut the pool tables down during the show.

Jake laughed. "Hell no. We tried that once and goddamn near had a riot. Some guys ain't in here for jokes. They want to shoot pool and you're better off without them being pissed off. Trust me."

Dale said they'd have to at least kill the music when he went onstage. He was firm on that.

"You bet," Jake said, like it was some terrifically benevolent gesture on his part. "Anyway, Nina will set you up." He turned to the bartender. "He gets two free drinks." Then he smiled back at Dale. "Usually costs me four, two per comic, so I guess I should be happy."

"Well, don't force it," Dale replied.

"What's that?"

"I said is there a microphone?"

Jake wrenched his head toward the riser. "Oh yeah. I should get that set up," he said. "I'll turn the spotlight on too."

"Are we starting at eight?" Dale asked.

"Yep. Eight sharp. On the dot. Or ten after, the latest. Maybe eight thirty. Might want to wait to see if any more people show up. You good with that?" Jake asked, already walking away.

The bartender—Nina, apparently—was smiling now. She had overheard the "don't force it" comment and liked it. She asked Dale what he wanted. He took a pint of local lager and drank it over the course of the next half-hour, chatting a bit with Nina whenever she stopped by his end of the bar, which was often enough. During that time, he looked around casually, making mental note of a few odd items in the room. Like the stuffed animal—a bobcat, maybe?—mounted in a ridiculously un-animalesque pose on the wall, high above the pinball machine, which looked mercifully out of order.

By twenty past, a couple dozen more patrons had arrived, and some of them were even seated in the chairs, at least sort of facing the stage area. Encouraging. Mullet Jake wandered over to Dale and asked if he was ready to go up. Dale said he was, and asked Nina for his second beer. Then he asked Jake, "You going to introduce me from stage or offstage?"

"Jesus Christ, you need an introduction, like you're friggin' Pearl Jam?"

"Yeah, but don't say I'm from Seattle."

Nina snort-laughed as she was pouring his pint.

"Well shit," Jake moaned, "I don't want to go up there. We don't got a DJ either, so . . ."

"Don't worry about it." Dale clapped a friendly hand on Jake's shoulder as he rose off his stool. "I can probably make it work better without one anyway."

The sharp *crack* of a cue ball being drilled into a fresh rack split the air as Dale headed to work. The music died abruptly, causing some of the grislier patrons to protest mildly, but their attentions soon went back to their games. In short order Dale stepped onstage, both hands high and open, welcoming, unthreatening, right to the microphone.

"Hey, everybody. How you doing?" He started off loudly but casually. In control. A few heads turned his way, but most turned right back to whatever they were doing two seconds earlier. He pressed on as though he didn't really care, he just had a job to do. "Now, you all know every second Tuesday is comedy night here at Doolen's, and this second Tuesday is no exception. So I'm just up here to introduce your comedian, and I'm telling you, you are in for a hell of a good time."

Over at the bar, Mullet Jake was gawking at the stage with equal parts panic and confusion. "What the hell's he doing?" he asked Nina, "I thought *he* was the comedian." They both watched as Dale continued.

"I got a chance to meet this fella earlier," Dale said, "and he had me pissing myself. Maybe the funniest son of a bitch I've ever come across. Funniest and smartest, if he doesn't mind me saying so. And I mean this in a totally straight, heterosexual way—he's a drop-dead gorgeous hunk of man meat that I would love to see naked and maybe have sex with. So, give a huge Doolen's welcome for the man of the hour, all the way from Chicago, it's Dale Webly!" Dale began clapping like the most enthusiastic maniac that ever hosted a cable game show and headed off-stage grinning like an idiot. Most of the patrons joined in half-heartedly but every eye was on the stage, curious to see exactly what kind of man deserved such a grand buildup. Two seconds later, Dale stepped back onstage holding his fresh pint in one hand and grabbing the microphone with the other.

"Well thank you, everybody, and thanks to that guy for a hell of a nice introduction." Everyone chuckled at the blatant charade and began to begrudgingly applaud. It was just stupid enough to be a little charming. Most of the crowd was at least partially on board after that. One deep gravelly voice hollered a half-hearted "fuck you" from back by the pool tables, and Dale fired back, "Maybe, sir, but let's see how this goes first."

He was getting laughs early and that was everything. An audience decides within seconds if they think you're anything or nothing, and it's nearly impossible to turn them around if they land on "nothing." Dale didn't let up, either. Crowds are often partial to local material, so he started riffing on the room. "This is my first time here at Doolen's. Nice place. I mean, I'm a little creeped out by that thing on the wall"—he gestured toward the animal mounted by the pinball machine. Everyone turned to look at it as Dale went on. "I don't even know what the hell that is. Any guesses? It's like what would happen if a bobcat knocked up a possum." That got good laughs, because a tenured professor of zoology couldn't have picked a better combination of animals to sum up the look of that creature. Big laughs on a topic meant *stay on topic*. "That thing's a nightmare. I think I saw it in the opening credits of *The X-Files*." That reference didn't quite land. *Maybe not a pop culture crowd, up on the latest shows*. But Dale was savvy enough to know the thing on the wall was going to be what got this gig rolling, so he stuck with it. "Seriously, is that thing even an animal? I don't think the taxidermy guy was convinced. That's why he mounted it upright." More laughs, because the creature did have an odd, almost bipedal pose. "It's like a guy walking home from his job as the mascot for the Saginaw Possum-Cats." That brought it all together with a roar of laughter from every person in the place, and Dale was rolling for the rest of the hour. An hour and fifteen, actually.

When he wrapped up and said good night, there was a terrific round of applause from the audience, made up of about thirty percent who were there to see comedy, thirty percent who couldn't care less, and thirty percent who were flat out against the idea but were won over by his show. The remaining ten percent were passed out. Dale didn't let on as he stepped down from the stage, but he was relieved. He was a veteran comic who knew what he was doing in almost any situation, and he knew rooms like this could easily go sideways. They usually did. The vast majority of working road comics would have bombed up there, or at least really struggled, and Dale hadn't. He allowed himself a moment to appreciate that truth. It might not have meant much in the whirling machinations of the world, but it meant something in here tonight and he swelled a bit inside as he sat back up at the bar.

Nina glided over with a frosted pint glass. "This one's on me," she said. "That was really funny."

"Thanks," Dale said. "Wasn't sure how it would go, but it went all right."

"More than all right," she said. "It was amazing. Really. Especially compared to how the comedians usually do in here. Are you that good, or are they that bad?"

"Well, if I say they're not that bad, it'll sound like bragging," Dale said.

Nina smiled and fixed her eyes on him for a long, warm moment. "So, what now?" she asked. "You want to get a drink or something when I'm done?"

Dale smiled back. She was a very attractive woman, with an effortless backyard sexiness about her. Their eyes danced a slow dance, holding each other close without touching. He knew she wanted him, and he allowed himself a moment to appreciate that truth as well.

"I'm married," he said.

Nina pushed out a pouty lip and shrugged, to let him know it didn't much matter to her. But it mattered to him—even if he wasn't sure why—so he said good night and headed over to the mullet man to get paid.

5

Remember, old bones break easy, the big man cautioned himself as he pulled his pickup truck over to the curb and killed the engine. He was smart enough not to park right in front of the house, instead stopping around the corner about halfway up Trueman Avenue, in a dark dead zone beyond the reach of the dim yellow streetlights.

He sat in the gloom of the quiet cab for a full minute, scanning the sidewalks and boulevards for potential witnesses. A full minute wasn't really necessary, and he knew that. This was a quiet part of town at high noon, so he didn't hold much concern that anyone would be out for a stroll at two in the morning. Still, he wanted to be thorough, and he wanted to finish his cigarette, and he wasn't in any hurry to hurt old Merlin. *The guy must be seventy, at least. Probably weighs a hundred and thirty pounds.* That would put him at less than half the mass of the big man.

The last drag of smoke was pulled in deep, then exhaled long and slow. The truck door popped open with a metallic groan, and the big man lurched his bulk out into the night air. *Work work work.*

Merlin's house was a small, faded, yellow-and-white bungalow on the second lot from the corner. There was a front door facing the street, but the door at the back of the house was the principal entrance, which would help the big man conduct his business in the shadows. He crossed the rear lawn, stepped up to the back door and raised a fist the size of a toaster.

Bang bang bang.

Inside the bungalow Merlin snapped awake. He lay there with his face half-buried in a grey pillow, blinking, as cold streams of terror trickled up his back. *Was that a real knock or did I dream it? Please be a dream please be a dream please be—*

Bang bang bang.

Oh shit.

The very last thing Merlin wanted to do was get out of bed and head toward that sound. But he knew the door was opening one way or another, and if it was booted in off its hinges, the next five minutes would be infinitely worse than if he unlatched it with a calm smile. He slid his feet into a pair of ratty corduroy slippers, wrapped his bones in a greenish robe and shuffled into the hall.

"Where are you going?" a thin voice asked from beyond a partially open door opposite his.

"Nowhere. Just getting some water. Might watch some TV."

"Is someone knocking?"

"I doubt it, but I'll check. Go back to sleep." He pulled the door closed with a soft click and headed down the hall, through the kitchen, toward a world of pain.

Merlin flicked on the bare bulb outside. "Who is it?" he whispered through the door.

"Kill that fuckin' light and get out here."

The porch light died. He clunked the deadbolt, pulled the door open about four inches and peered out at the grim brute. "Oh, hey . . . heya, Bull. What's going on?"

"Come outside. We need to talk."

Merlin began what he knew would be futile negotiations. "It's the middle of the night. Can we talk tomorrow?"

"Would you rather I come in there?"

Merlin stepped out onto the porch, pulling the door closed behind him. "Probably better out here. Mary's sleeping. Not feeling well."

"Chemo is a bitch," Bull said flatly. "Won't catch me doing that. I'll eat a bullet first. You should do her a favour. Seriously."

Merlin had no response to that. The coldness of the words sank him, and his chin settled slowly onto his chest. Only seconds before, his mind was nimbly scrambling through a dozen lies and deflections and excuses. But now, seeing Bull here in the flesh, at his own back door, and hearing the callous comments about his only sister as she lay dying inside, he knew no words were going to fix this. He stopped hoping and just waited.

"You cold, Merlin?" Bull asked. "I can hear your ribs rattling." Bull paused for a reply, got none, so continued. "How about I make this quick? You know why I'm here, and you know what happens when people don't pay what they owe. You know how this works—hell, you were probably already a degenerate gambler before I was born, right?"

Merlin was trembling more but found his voice. "Probably."

"How old are you?" Bull asked suddenly. "Seventy?"

A single spark of hope awoke in Merlin's mind. Maybe this was the angle. Maybe Bull was reluctant to hurt someone older.

"Seventy-two," Merlin said. He was sixty-three but they had been hard years.

"I knew it," Bull nodded proudly. "Seventy-two. And most of those years you spent chasing a game, so you wouldn't sit down at a table without knowing who owns the cards. That means you knew my guys were running the game. That means when you don't pay, you know who you're not paying. Me. Is that supposed to not piss me off?"

"I can pay," Merlin blurted.

"You can pay?" Bull snapped back, pretending to be aghast at the notion. "Shit, Merlin, don't tell me that. Bad enough if someone doesn't pay when they can't, but not paying when they can—that's just slapping my face."

The ember of hope began drifting away on the wind. Merlin's mind raced to get it back.

"I mean I can pay soon. And to make it up, because I know I fucked up, I'll pay double. Double what I owe."

"Double? Where are you going to get ten grand?"

"I owe four. Double would be eight."

"Where are you going to get twelve grand?" Bull glared.

Merlin realized he needed to shut up about the numbers. This was about buying time and mitigating punishment. "I'm booking a new run. Good clubs," he said.

"Run? Oh, are talking about your little comedy shows? The fuck do those make you?"

"Normally not much. Bit of commission is all. But this time it's a longer run, and I'm not just pocketing commission. The comics are all working for nothing because they owe me."

Bull chuckled. "Jesus, how low would someone have to be to owe you?"

"Favours. They owe me favours," Merlin explained. "I help a lot of young comics when they're starting out. This run is payback, so the comics are working for free. That means I pocket the whole fee from every show. It'll give me enough to clear with you and make amends."

Bull studied Merlin with hard eyes. He was angry and tired and the thought of being played by this scrawny, shifty weasel made him want to sink a crowbar into that spotty skull. But the more he studied Merlin, the more he saw an angle. An idea formed in Bull's mind and it calmed him a little. Yes, there could be some good business here, with some personal benefit on top. He stood thinking, formulating a plan to best execute the notion that was taking root.

Merlin knew he should keep his mouth shut, but fear and desperation pushed words out anyway. "If I could—" The sales pitch was cut short by a thick thumb and finger digging deep around both sides of his windpipe as he was pulled close to Bull's wide, red face. Hot tobacco breath forced its way up into Merlin's nostrils.

"Here's the deal, old man," Bull said through grinding teeth. "Ten days. Ten thousand. If you don't pay me ten grand in ten days, you're going to sell this fuckin' shack and give me the money from that. All of it. I mean . . . I might let you keep enough to buy your sister a half-decent coffin. Because business is business, but family is family, right?"

Tears bubbled from the corners of Merlin's bulging eyes, channelling down the wrinkles of his face and dropping onto the faded green robe.

Bull continued. "Ten days. Ten grand. Plus, speaking of family . . ." Bull turned Merlin's head like he was working a puppet, then whispered into his ear. "You're going to do something else for me. And not ask any fucking questions about it."

Bull let go of his throat and Merlin sank down to his knees, sucking great gasps of cold night air into his chest, coughing and wheezing on the brink of blacking out. Bull watched him, letting him sputter back into some semblance of life, then began explaining in detail exactly what he wanted Merlin to do.

When the conversation was over, Merlin nodded. Bull reached down, extending a huge right hand. "Deal?"

Merlin stared up weakly, then raised a thin arm and placed his frail hand into Bull's. The crunch was sickening. Merlin's jaw stretched wide in a twisted blend of horror and agony, but no sound escaped, like a scream in a silent movie. The pain was more than could be processed. He shuddered and passed out face-first onto the dark wet grass.

Bull looked down at the scrawny frame sprawled in a half-conscious heap, and chuckled. "Jesus, they really do break easy."

6

The door to 309 opened and Dale pushed his way back inside, dead-bolting and chaining the door behind him, more out of habit than any security concerns. It was symbolic. The chain meant *I'm done for the day and in for the night* and it helped him sleep. He needed sleep, even though he had come to dread it.

He used to look forward to sleep. When he was starting out in comedy, he looked forward to every element and every aspect of the life. The shows, the writing and crafting of material, the camaraderie that came from touring with other like-minded misfits, the drinking, the laughs into the middle of the night, each of these gems was treasured. Even the greasy fast food and filthy truck stop bathrooms held wrinkles of romance for Dale. But sleeping late—sometimes into the afternoon—was easily the most prized luxury in that sea of half-baked blessings. And each blessing was a tactile reminder that he was on an adventure, in the middle of pursuing his dream—something few people in this world actually get to do. Only, he wasn't in the middle anymore. The midpoint of his adventure was a long way back in the rearview mirror. Somewhere along the line, he wasn't sure when, the sheen had faded and then tarnished, and he now mostly looked forward to each road trip coming to an end so he could go back home.

He turned on the TV but hit the mute on the remote. It would be an hour until Letterman, and he wanted to make a call. He grabbed the receiver off the phone on the nightstand, dialed a Chicago number, then punched in the digits from his long-distance calling card and waited. After two rings, a young woman picked up.

"Hi, Daddy."

"Hi, baby girl. How'd you know it was me?"

"Who else calls this time of night?" Vanessa said.

"Fair point," Dale replied. "You miss me?"

Vanessa's shrug was almost audible. "It's only been five days."

"Ouch. Right in the heart," Dale said, holding one hand to his chest even though she couldn't see the dramatic move. "I guess you're a grown-up college fancy-pants now, too cool to miss your old man." He heard the slightest half-chuckle from Vanessa and it filled him more than any audience could. "But guess what, college kid. If you know the number of days I've been gone, it means you miss me."

"Fine, maybe a little," Vanessa said. Dale could hear the smile in her voice now and it warmed him like the sun. There had been times over the past few years when he feared he would never feel warmth from her again.

He had been away for too much of Vanessa's childhood, trying to carve a living out of the road, and missed some milestones that were truly important to her. Each one of those disappointments caused a thin, jagged fissure in their relationship, but it managed to hold together for the most part. For all but two occasions. Twice he had messed up bad enough to fracture that bond and see it shatter.

Once, when Vanessa was thirteen, he had promised to take her to a New Edition concert but called from the road to say he couldn't make it because he had been offered a run of five shows and he needed the money. He had tried to courier the tickets back to her, but they didn't arrive in time. Vanessa was devastated to miss the concert and cried all night. The next day she learned that her friends who went were selected as part of a group that got to go backstage for a meet-and-greet with the band. She would have been with that same group had her dad kept his promise. It was almost impossible to pick up the pieces from that one, and it had taken over a year to get back to where Vanessa would speak to Dale in complete sentences.

Then, when she turned sixteen, he was supposed to take her for her driver's test in the family car. Again, he stayed on the road to take some added bookings and didn't have the car back in time. She missed her appointment and had to wait four months to schedule another test. An extra third of a year without her driver's licence was, to a sixteen-year-old, the greatest betrayal imaginable. Without intending to, Dale had made Vanessa feel utterly unimportant—an inconvenient afterthought—and the event was like a hammer dashing her confidence in him, and in them. He was gutted to see how his actions had made her feel and vowed he would never let that happen again. It took almost another full year of subtle prodding and flat-out bribery, culminating in the gift of her own second-hand car, to get the pieces of their relationship swept up and glued together. As relieved and grateful as Dale was to be back on speaking terms, he was also gravely aware of how brittle their bond had become.

"I'm back off the road soon," Dale said into the phone. "Can I take you out for lunch?"

"Maybe," she said.

"I'm talking about Filmore's," Dale said. He was pretty sure that would seal the deal. Vanessa loved going to Filmore's Diner. The burgers were excellent, but it was all about the milkshakes. Filmore's milkshakes tasted like they were spun in Heaven and chilled by the flapping of angel wings. He also suspected it held a special place in her heart because it's where they used to go as a family when he still lived with her mom.

"Well, if it's Filmore's . . . ," Vanessa said.

"Then it's a date, fancy-pants."

"I'll see you when you're back, Dad. Mom wants to talk to you."

"Okay. I love you," Dale said. He hoped to hear the words returned, but the phone was handed off and Brandy came on the line.

"Dale?"

"Yeah, how're you doing?" Dale said.

"I'm trying real hard not to be pissed off at you, that's how I'm doing," Brandy said, in a hushed but stern voice.

"Doesn't sound like it's working," he replied. "What have I done to almost piss you off?"

"You said you'd get the money to me this week."

"I sent it to you," he said. "I looked at my account and you cashed the cheque."

"Not the child support—I mean, thanks for that—but I'm talking about the tuition."

"I thought I had two months to get you that."

"No, Dale," Brandy said, frustration rising. "Vanessa *starts college* in two months. But we have to pay her tuition first."

"Oh shit. Okay. Um . . . shit. Well, when do they want it?"

"They want it now."

"Right, and I want a flying donkey that pisses cold beer, but when do they *need* it? Like, when's the official cut-off?"

"Deadline is the last of the month. If they don't have it by then, she can't attend orientation, and it will absolutely break her heart, Dale. I won't let—"

"That's not going to happen," he said firmly. "I'll get you my half before the end of the month. I'm playing a club up in Canada, it's a full week and it pays great." There was silence on the other end. "I promise. My half is three grand, right? I will wire you a thousand tomorrow and I'll have the other two when I get back. Whatever has to be done, I'll make it happen. I will not hurt Vanessa again. I will always be there for her."

Brandy was calmer now. "I know that."

"Well, that's cool," Dale said, "but I need *her* to know that."

They talked for another minute, formalities and niceties, then said goodbye. Dale sunk onto the edge of the sagging Journeywide mattress, stared through the wallpaper and did some math in his head. There was just no way to tumble the numbers that didn't end up confirming what he already knew. The club in Winnipeg would pay okay, but not enough to cover what was needed. He had to find another run of shows. Any run.

7

Rynn folded some clothes neatly and laid them flat inside a blue rolling suitcase. She wadded up some other clothes and tossed them in on top. The folded were for on stage, the wadded for everywhere else. She had come to dissect her entire wardrobe into two distinct teams: the foldies and the waddies. They would all be waddies if she didn't hate ironing so much. That was probably the thing that surprised her most about this business. When she was a teenager, alone in her room, listening to comedy albums and watching comedy specials, dreaming about getting into stand-up herself, she imagined the spotlight, she imagined the hotel rooms, she imagined the laughs, she imagined exciting, meaningless one-night sexual adventures, but she never once thought, *I bet there'll be a fair amount of ironing involved.* She grinned at the notion, but the memory pulled her mind back to that time in her life and the smile slid from her lips.

School had been brutal for Rynn. The middle grades had been bad enough—that's where the teasing started—but by the time she turned fifteen, it had ramped up to another level. Teens are true artists in cruelty, equally adept at splashing paint in wide, garish strokes as they are at applying microscopic subtleties that stain the psyche on a strictly subconscious level. Rynn encountered all forms and genres, and each day of school became a nightmare in which the main lesson learned was how insignificant and worthless she was. She never understood why she was being teased. The bullying didn't seem to focus on any particular point, changing day by day. One day they'd make fun of her hair, the next her clothes, the next her voice—it could be anything. It was so confounding that she even once asked the mean girls straight up, "Why are you doing this to me? Why have you all decided to hate me?" But the reply was only cackling laughter echoing away down the hall. It ground Rynn down in time, and by her sixteenth birthday she was earnestly contemplating suicide. It never progressed beyond the hypothetical, however, because fate intervened to provide her with a new level of pain that would put school-hall taunting into proper perspective.

Rynn loved and idolized her father. He was her hero in a thousand regards. He was a simple, down-to-earth man in the way an oak tree is a simple, down-to-earth plant, and in the same way an oak could be climbed as an escape, sat under for shade or swung from for a laugh, her father provided all that and more.

He certainly provided more to Rynn than her mother could. Not that her mother was a bad person, but to the degree a mother should provide comfort, sympathy or encouragement to her children, she fell notably short. Even at an early age, Rynn knew that the shortcomings in those areas were the result of her mother's own history. She never knew much about that history, so never blamed her mother, but a natural distance swelled between them all the same. Rynn found herself sharing little with her mother, because any wounds were regarded as wee scratches to be ignored, and any pain was a reflection of weakness. Dreams and aspirations were childish nonsense to be discarded as quickly as possible and replaced with practical pursuits that could better lead to the comforts of normalcy. The idea of taking a run at show business would certainly be something to smother or drown or stone to death, so it had been a goal shared exclusively with her father. Even then, Rynn had only shared it because he asked if she had any plans for after school. The moment she told him was one she would always remember.

"I'd like to try doing stand-up comedy," she had said quietly, her eyes on her shoes.

"Well now, that's something you don't hear every day," he exclaimed with a broad smile and a slap on the arm of his chair. She looked up with a smile of her own as he leaned toward her with a serious expression. "So, are there schools for that, or would you just dive in and learn as you go type of thing? You'd have to get a day job in the beginning, I suppose, one flexible enough to let you do shows when they come up. I know they have those comedy clubs, but where else would you perform? Do other clubs hire comedians?"

Each of her father's inquiries was answered by Rynn, to apparent satisfaction, and each of his comments was weighed and discussed sensibly by the two of them, and the entire conversation had been as grounded as if she had suggested a career in accounting or veterinary medicine. His genuine interest and lack of derision varnished her dream with a gleaming layer of validity. That had made all the difference.

"I don't think Ma will look at it the same way you do," Rynn had said to her father, and he chuckled.

"No, I believe you're right about that," he replied, and then turned a little more serious. "But it's only because she is a worrier, your mother, and that's in her soul. It's not because she doesn't want you to be happy, you understand. It's because she doesn't want you to be *un*happy. There's a difference."

"I know," Rynn said, "but they sort of feel the same on the receiving end."

"They can at that," he nodded, before brightening. "At any rate, no need for this to go beyond the two of us for a while yet." He smiled and winked. "Maybe I can work on her in the meantime."

The warm recollection of that conversation triggered the next memory—the unwanted memory, the memory that kicked its way into Rynn's head whenever it was given any sliver of opportunity. In that wisp of the past she could see her teenaged self, almost as if she were watching television—a grainy rerun of the darkest episode in the worst season of the show of her life. There she sat, preparing for school that morning, brushing her hair, hearing the telephone ring downstairs. She could hear her mother come in from outside, where she had been watering potted tomato plants. She could still hear the dull, hollow gong of the tin watering can being placed into the sink, then hear the phone ring a second time. Hear her mother's voice say hello. Hear the silence. Feel the silence. Then the scream. Rynn could hear her own footsteps then, thundering down the stairs, could hear her mother's terrible, primal wailing. She could still see her mother crouched on the floor, back against the wall, the receiver dangling, swaying on the end of its stretched coiled cord and a thin electric voice nattering her mother's name and the words *sorry . . . sorry . . . I'm so very sorry*. Rynn recalled her own mind whirling and calculating—always too fast for its own good—stitching together the fragments of that collage quicker than it should, before her gut could prepare, and the abruptly assembled truth hitting like a sledgehammer.

When the accident at work took her father's life, the effect on Rynn was incalculable. No graphs or meters or scales had been invented to measure that depth of grief. Mathematics were designed to decipher smaller things, like the weight of the universe or the distance to infinity's edge. Yet the effect went beyond the heart-crushing sadness and the tor-rential tears. It seemed to change Rynn on some molecular level. The magnitude of loss stood like the Great Pyramid of Giza, trivializing by comparison all other misfortune. From that point in her life any other sour stroke of chance seemed like the slightest bump in the road.

It also changed how she looked at the future. Having seen how instantaneously your world can be shredded and scattered into oblivion on any given Wednesday morning, Rynn began to see her time on earth as both precious and nebulous, a tenuous gift that was not to be wasted by sitting out the dance. It was also not to be wasted worrying about what others thought, so the snotty opinions and cruel comments of a few girls at school became exceptionally unimportant, and Rynn began countering any taunts with cutting jibes and razor wit that often drew big laughs from other students.

"Look at Rynn's shite-brown shoes!" the leader of the mean ones had blurted loudly in front of the entire class one day. "Why would you pick shite brown for a shoe colour?"

"Well, they were pure white when I bought them," Rynn said, "but I had to cut through your yard on the way to school." The class had roared with laughter.

As the weeks passed, and the mean girls saw their superficial assaults being casually swatted aside, they tried to cut deeper. "At least my dad is still alive," one had hissed.

"Have you asked him?" Rynn fired back. "I'm not sure he'd call shagging *your* ma *living*." The class roared.

For the mean girls, targeting her had become a stark lesson in dim-inishing returns.

Rynn's relationship with her mother changed as well. They would never be particularly close, but the chasm was bridged a little by the shared trauma. As different as her parents were, Rynn had always been aware of their deep, true love, and she knew her mother was shattered by the loss.

In the following year, especially during difficult times with her mom, she thought often about that surreptitious discussion with her father regarding comedy and her mom's inclination to worry, and had therefore staved off relaying her plans for as long as possible.

As graduation drew nearer, however, with Rynn never speaking about university or a trade, her mother naturally became curious about her daughter's intentions. Rynn was absolutely going to chase her dream with the one life she had, regardless of what her mother thought, but she had still dreaded the inevitable conversation.

Her plans for a career in comedy were received with the anticipated lack of enthusiasm, but also with a notable absence of negativity. It seemed they had both been changed by the loss. In a glaring effort to seem as supportive as possible, her mother had managed to say, "I always enjoy that Stephen Fry." It was a bigger gesture than the brevity of words would imply, and Rynn wore the sentence like a comforting cloak ever since.

Her mind rolled back to the present, and she finished packing her suitcase. All except her toiletries. She'd need use of those in the morning before heading to LAX to catch a flight north to Vancouver, connecting to Winnipeg.

8

A freckle-faced woman sat smoking a thin cigarette and reading a supermarket tabloid, which, according to the headline, unfurled a sordid and exclusive tale about Julia Roberts being pregnant by Wesley Snipes. Every now and then, she'd set the cigarette in the ashtray and lift a can of Dr Pepper to her lips. Her motions were slow and methodic, so her eyes never strayed from the page, and her expression changed only once: a dramatic lifting of her brows as she mouthed the word "twins?"

The desk Shirley sat behind was not actually a desk but a small kitchen table. It fit nicely within the office, which was not really an office but a rundown studio apartment. Behind her, the phone/fax machine sat on the kitchen counter, partially obstructed by a toaster oven. Hanging beside her head was an oversized whiteboard calendar, its date squares populated by names and dollar amounts written in various colours of erasable marker. The phone half of the machine rang with a harsh electronic warbling, and Shirley lowered her tabloid and reached for the receiver.

"Laughing Gas Entertainment," she said. She listened. "He's not in at the moment. Can I take a message?" She listened some more while jotting information down on a pink sticky note. "Okay, I'll have him call you as soon as he gets in." She hung up and lit another slim cigarette, then cursed herself when she realized the other one was still burning.

The door to the office/apartment opened and Merlin stepped inside, turning back to lock the deadbolt behind him.

"Well, look who finally comes rolling in," Shirley said. "Did you get drunk last night and have to sleep it off? It'd be nice if—" Her eyes widened. "What the hell happened to your hand?"

"It's fine," Merlin said, trying to pull the arm of his denim jacket over the thick white cast. "Can you help me with this?"

Shirley hustled over to assist but was not about to let this be glossed over. "It's not fine, Merlin. They don't put casts on hands that are fine."

"It's broken. A few small bones. I was changing a tire last night and the jack wobbled and—It's not a big deal."

"You were at the hospital? You should've called me," she said. "I didn't know what to tell people."

Merlin whirled around to her. "Who called?" he snapped, the blood rushing away from his cheeks.

Shirley picked up a couple of sticky notes and handed them over. "A few people. The phone company wants the bill paid," she said. "Oh, and there was a message on the machine from Dale Webly. Called last night. He's on the road. Seemed sort of urgent."

The orangish curtains refused to close completely, and the mid-morning sun knifed its way into the hotel room, across the carpet and onto Dale's face. It didn't wake him right away. He was deep in a dream in which he had gone back downstairs to Doolen's and had another beer with Nina. The dream started pleasantly enough, but then morphed into Dale facing off against some jealous local dude. The next bit of the dream had Dale saying some tremendously clever things while easily winning the fight by way of some badass kung fu, and it was just at the part where Nina removed her top and rushed over to have her lustful way with him when the phone rang.

Dale groaned and wrestled his eyes open one at a time. He cursed himself for saying no to Nina and couldn't understand why he still instinctively declined when these situations—rare as they were—came up. Why he always—or almost always—still said no, a full year after the divorce. The ringing phone wouldn't let him ponder the puzzle any longer, so he rolled over to answer it. "Hello?"

"The Journeywide? La-dee-dah! You're moving up in the world."

"Merlin, how are you doing? Thanks for calling me back," Dale said.

"No problem," Merlin said. "What's this area code I dialed? You in Alabama or something?"

"Michigan," Dale said. "Livonia. No . . . Saginaw, I think. But I'm headed up your way soon. Playing Whispers in a couple weeks, so I just thought I'd call to see if you had any one-nighters I could tack onto the front end of that."

"Your timing is impeccable. I do have a new run of shows, good gigs, some around here, some in Ontario," Merlin said. "Six in total. Interested?"

"What do they pay?"

"Seriously?" Merlin countered. "You're going to try grinding me on the money after calling me in the middle of the night to beg for gigs?"

"I'm hardly begging. I have some time before Whispers," Dale said casually, "so I just thought I'd fill it up. But I'm just as happy to go back to Chicago and hang with my daughter."

"Okay. Say hi to her for me. Let's get a beer when you're in Winnipeg."

"Whoa, hold up," Dale said. "Just give me the details on the shows."

Merlin smiled and reeled him in, relaying a list of dates and town names, and what each would pay. Dale asked Merlin to fax him a copy of the show information and a contract.

Merlin huffed. "You need a goddamn contract? You called me, I didn't call you. I have a dozen other comics hounding me about this run, meanwhile I'm over here giving it to a guy that thinks I'm going to cheat him."

Dale's gut told him not to agree to the run without something in writing, but his heart and his head were louder. *Shut up and take the gigs. You need them. Vanessa needs them. He's going to pay you. He can't afford to rip you off, you'll rip his reputation* "—to shreds," Dale blurted.

"Two sheds?" Merlin asked.

"I said . . . touché. Fine, I don't need a contract. If you rip me off, I'll hunt you down and kill you, deal?"

"Absolutely," Merlin said, pretending to take the threat seriously. In the current context of Merlin's life, Dale was like a chihuahua growling at him while a pride of lions circled.

Dale hung up and immediately called his travel agent to book the cheapest flight possible from Chicago to Winnipeg.

Merlin slumped into the folding chair across from Shirley, his eyes locked in deep thought. She craned her neck up at the whiteboard.

"You just double-booked," she said. "You already have Hutch headlining that run. With that Irish chick."

"I know. I need you to call Hutch and cancel him for me."

"Oh Merlin, it's too short notice. He'll be super pissed off. Don't make me—"

"Just do it!" he barked. Then he softened. "Please. I can't explain it all, but Hutch lives here in the city and I can't have that. Not now.

Whatever goes down on this run, when it's all over I want the comics heading back far away from here."

Shirley didn't say anything else. She had known Merlin long enough to recognize his drowning face—she had seen it many times—and this time he looked like the water was a mile over his head. She picked up the phone and started dialing.

"When you're done with Hutch," Merlin said, "grab your address book. I have a bunch more calls to make."

9

Rynn had performed here once before. The first time she'd played Winnipeg, a rare metropolis on the yawning Canadian prairie, she knew little about the city. She never told anyone as much, but she'd never even heard of it, honestly, growing up in Ireland, so didn't know what to expect. She had not, however, been expecting to find the audiences so hip and supportive.

"Hell, Winnipeg's been an entertainment hub since vaudeville," the manager of Whispers Comedy Club had explained. "All the big theatrical circuits from California and New York would send their big-name stars up here to either begin a new run or switch from an eastern run to a western run, and vice versa. We were sort of a showbiz testing ground. If an act didn't do well in Winnipeg, it never went anywhere else. Shit, Bob Hope learned how to golf while playing a theatre in Winnipeg. Groucho Marx, Charlie Chaplin, we had 'em all here before they made it big in Hollywood, so live entertainment is pretty much woven into the fabric of the city."

Whispers had opened in November of 1979, just in time to host several corporate Christmas parties and ring out the old decade, poised presciently to profit from the sudden popularity live comedy would enjoy in the decade to come. It had an entrance off the front of the Viscount Plaza and benefited greatly from that visibility among the associated foot traffic streaming into the shiny new shopping mall to buy their Rubik's Cubes and Strawberry Shortcake dolls and everything else the eighties had to offer. Now, in 1994, Whispers was still going strong and drawing good, steady crowds who loved to laugh.

An almost full house was laughing loud and lots on this particular Thursday night as Rynn Lanigan delivered her whimsical and personal stand-up material about growing up in Ireland and the things she found strange about Canada. In truth, a lot of that material had been written about the things she found strange about America, but it was fairly easy to transfer the vast majority of it, and the locals were eating it up with a spoon.

She was also able to sprinkle in some new bits that were about Canada specifically. These were in relation to things she had noticed back on that first trip, the previous winter, and the insertion of those jokes gave a lustre of authenticity to the whole package. *Boy, she sure has us nailed!*

"I honestly don't think I could have grown up here," she said, before taking a sip from her beer. "Maybe if I'd been born in the late spring, I could have made it into early October, but the first time that thermometer hit minus forty I would've curled up in a pale, freckled ball and shut down. 'Nope, this is not for me!' Even if my parents were able to wrap me in moose wool and dangle my crib over an open fire to keep my blood moving, I'm sure they'd still see the thought in my wee baby eyes:

47

'What the feck are we doing here, honestly?' I mean, I thought it got cold in Ireland. We have some pretty thick sweaters—you may have seen photos—Van Morrison in one of his knobby turtlenecks, maybe? But here's the difference between Irish cold and Canadian cold: you'll never be sitting down to watch the evening news in Ireland and have the fella end the night's reporting with a casual reminder about how long it takes for exposed flesh to freeze." The crowd was pounding the tables as she continued. "First time I heard that on a Canadian newscast I was gob-smacked. I thought I must've missed the first part of the story where the Earth had broken out of its orbit and was hurtling away from the sun."

As well as the prepared material was being received, Rynn never lost sight of the grander prize at the end of the string. She needed to practise her off-the-cuff skills so she would arrive in Montreal as sharp and as fast as she could be. To that end, she began working the audience.

"You're a fun crowd. You seem like you're having a good time, sir." She gestured to a man at a table up front. "Are you from Winnipeg?"

The man replied, "Kelowna, but originally Saskatoon."

"Oops," Rynn said, "this one doesn't speak English." The crowd laughed heartily. "Am I supposed to know what Kajona and Sakaplook means? Or did he just cast a spell on me? Am I going to go back to my hotel room tonight, strip down and find a tail?" She shook her head in feigned confusion as she moved along to another member of the audience. "Sakatooga, he says. How about you, ma'am? Which one of Jupiter's moons are you from?" The crowd was loving her. Her comedy was bent and sharp, the accent was infectious, and the whole package was charming as hell.

At the arrivals level of Winnipeg International, Dale held his passport and his work visa in his fingertips, consciously keeping the documents propped away from his moist palms. He wasn't outwardly nervous—there wasn't much reason to be—but crossing international borders was never a completely comfortable affair. It was an inherently tense situation purposely designed to generate suspicion both ways—the idea being that such a scenario would serve to keep agents in a focused state and travellers off balance. In theory this would increase both the chances of an illicit visitor tripping up and the likelihood of that trip-up being observed. In practice it just made everyone sweaty. Even with everything in order there were always a dozen opportunities for things to go sideways, for information to be miscommunicated, for an eye movement to be misinterpreted, and it only took one snap decision by one border agent, justified or not, to send your ass home at entirely your own expense with some kind of red flag electronically gouged into your permanent digital record. Such thoughts, of course, did nothing to decrease Dale's perspiration. *Just don't talk too much. That's the key.*

"Next."

Dale stepped up and handed his passport over to the agent, open to the picture page—a move he hoped would be subconsciously appreciated while implanting the subliminal message: *This guy knows the deal, he's cool, does this all the time, wave him through.*

"What are you doing in Canada?"

"Bit of work," Dale said. "I have a visa here." He handed the paper to the agent, who perused it with no special interest.

"What kind of work?"

"Comedy. I'm a stand-up comedian."

The agent's eyes drifted up to Dale, then submerged to the passport photo for comparison. "Great," he said flatly. "Like we don't have enough of those up here."

"We get quite a few of yours down south, too," Dale said. "Jim Carrey, Norm Macdonald, Mike MacDonald . . ." *I'm talking too much.*

"You're early," the agent said.

"Pardon?"

"This visa doesn't start for a week."

Dale hadn't even considered that. *Goddammit, is that going to sink this? This is the only shot I have at getting Vanessa's tuition. I can't go home. Make something up. No, don't, he'll smell it. Your top lip is wet. Goddammit. Make something up. No, don't. Just explain. Wipe your lip, no don't. Don't let—*

"Why're you coming up early?" the agent asked.

"Fish."

The agent furrowed his brow. "Did you say fish?"

Did I say fish? "Yeah. The guy who books the comedy shows wants me to go fishing with him," Dale said with an easy smile, "and that's about third from the bottom on my list of fun things to do, but . . ."—he felt the agent scanning his face for trip-ups—"he's the boss."

"Sort of a kiss-ass move," the agent said, perhaps testing to see if a slight push would topple the man in front of him.

"I know," Dale chuckled. "And I got into comedy because I thought I wouldn't have to kiss any more ass. That's how stupid I am."

The agent looked like he was right on the fence. Dale calculated a sidestep and a parry. "I didn't even know you had lakes up here, I thought it was mostly farmland."

"Any lakes up here? Are you kidding me?" The agent visibly swelled with national pride. "You know how many lakes Minnesota says it has?"

"Ten thousand?"

"Yeah, they're so proud of that they put it on their licence plates," the agent smirked. "You think we have double that up here? Double that many?"

Dale knew it was a hell of a lot more than that, but he also knew this was the time to *not* know it.

"No way. You don't have twice that many."

"You're right." The agent bobbed his head cockily. "Try ten times that many. Over a hundred thousand lakes in Manitoba."

"Well, damn. I guess my American public-school education is showing," Dale said.

The agent chuckled and stamped his passport in triumph. "*I* didn't say it. Enjoy yourself. Don't fall in."

Dale smiled, got his papers back and headed into Canada, more than a little pleased with himself. He had faced a stern customer there and still—

"Hold up!"

The agent's voice hit Dale like a slap in the head and his stomach dropped. He turned back.

"I think you forgot," the agent said.

"Forgot?"

"Yeah. John Candy. Canadian, and the funniest of 'em all." The agent looked like he might actually burst into tears.

"Just passed away, too," Dale added. "Breaks my heart." *But I didn't forget him, I specifically said I was talking about stand-up comedians and John Candy wasn't a stand-up comedian, was he, you smug maple-sucking dipshit, even if he was* "—genuinely brilliant."

The agent gave a wave and turned back to the lineup. "Next!"

10

This time Dale's dream didn't entail kung fu kicks and appreciative damsels. This time it was a nightmare. No vampire scratched at his window, no wolfman charged snarling from the woods, no stick-limbed bug-man crawled across his roof looking for a way in. It was something more terrifying. A truth haunted his sleep.

That's all Dale knew about the dream—or rather, *felt* about the dream. He felt it was a truth. He couldn't actually know it on an intellectual level, because the dream itself made no sense to him, even after all this time. For the last year or so, at least four nights a week, it had been some recurring variation of this:

He was always in or on water—floating or swimming or in a small boat . . . once he was bobbing around on an inner tube—and the water was always a deep, rich green, like some kind of veggie smoothie you might see blended up at a mall kiosk. And it always pulled at him, the green water, called to him. In the dream he always found himself tempted by the idea of diving down deep and never coming up. But before he ever got to the point where he had to make the choice, he would see them, whatever they were, coming for him. Blue, bulbous heads, more like dolphins than sharks, but with rows of gleaming white teeth chomping through the water on their approach. And he would turn his back and try to paddle away, but it was always that weak, powerless pushing that everyone has felt in their dreams—the futile flailing of rubbery boneless limbs—so he could never move through the thick green water and inevitably he would feel the sharp fangs clamp onto his leg.

The ring of the phone ripped Dale free of the dream, gasping, so soaked with sweat it looked like he *had* been swimming. He stared wide-eyed into the dim grey light of his hotel room. *Where am I?* The phone rang again, and he leaned to answer it.

"Hello?"

"Hi, is this Dale?" the voice asked.

"Yeah."

"It's Rynn Lanigan. I'm doing this run of shows with you," she said.

"Right . . . okay . . . great." He was slowly pulling himself into the waking world. "What, um . . . what, uh—"

"It's eleven a.m.," Rynn said. "We're supposed to head off at two this afternoon, so I thought maybe we'd have some lunch first. Or breakfast, whatever."

"Yeah. Sounds good," Dale said. "Meet in the lobby at noon?"

"Good. See you in an hour," Rynn said.

Dale hung up and rolled over onto his back. He thought about the images in the dream and began to cry.

Sharply at noon he stepped out of the elevator and into the lobby of the Grainwood Hotel. He saw a young woman sitting in a lavender wing-back chair reading a copy of the *Winnipeg Free Press*. As he walked over to her, she looked up, folded the newspaper and stood.

"Dale?"

"You're Rynn?" he said, as they shook hands.

"I am, yeah. So the easiest thing is to just get a table in there," she said, gesturing toward the Gold Sheaf restaurant off the lobby. "Food's not bad. I've been here all week and I've eaten about nine meals in there. Only got sick once."

"Decent odds," Dale said, and they headed into the restaurant.

The waitress motioned for them to take a seat anywhere, and they settled into one of the vinyl booths against the window wall, so they could look out onto the street if conversation got difficult or tedious. It was always a crapshoot, meeting new comics on the road. It was a bit like closing your eyes at the zoo and reaching into a cage to pet an animal, not sure if you were about to ruffle a koala or a cobra. In the comedy zoo, they keep the koalas and the cobras in the same cage. Either way, there wasn't much you could do about it but buckle up and do the run.

Right off the bat Dale had a good feeling about Rynn, though. She seemed like someone who shot pretty straight, without a lot of extra babble. He could tell she was naturally funny, not someone who had to try hard. Try-hards were exhausting. Of all the X factors you could meet up with in your travels, the most tiresome was the one who felt the need to stuff every waking moment chock full of wacky takes or snappy banter that was usually about as snappy as boiled lettuce. Rynn didn't seem that type; she already had her attention back on the newspaper.

The waitress stepped up with a metal carafe. "Coffees?" she asked.

Dale and Rynn turned their cups right side up and pushed them toward the waitress with alarming synchronization.

"Did you guys rehearse that?" the waitress asked as she poured the coffee.

"Hell of a team," Dale said.

"And that's after two minutes together," Rynn said. "By the end of the run we'll have our periods harmonized."

The smile dropped off Dale's face. "Don't," he said. "I don't like that."

Rynn straightened. "Oh, sorry," she said, leaning back as if distancing herself from the apparent faux pas.

"I don't like to discuss a woman's menstruation until I've known her for at least five minutes," he said earnestly.

Rynn furrowed her brow a moment, then laughed out loud. "Oh, ya prick," she said. "You had me going there. I almost shit. Day one, piss off the headliner. Smooth move."

Dale smiled as he lifted the large laminated menu. "Takes more than that to piss me off," he said.

"No worries. I'll figure out how, I'm sure."

Dale ordered a club sandwich with a side Caesar salad, and Rynn ordered a cheeseburger with fries and gravy. One of the things she had been enjoying about Canada was their automatic assumption that people wanted gravy on everything. You had to talk them out of it. The waitress left to put in their order.

"So, you're from where," Rynn asked Dale. ". . . Chicago?"

"Yeah. And 'Rynn Lanigan' . . . What's that—Polish?" he asked.

"Polish, yes, yes," she said with pseudo seriousness, "the Irish part of Poland. Little Corkski, they call it."

"What're you doing in Canada?"

"I'm settling in Los Angeles, actually, but I don't have the papers to work in the States yet. I do for here, though," she said, "and hey, a girl's got to make a living."

"How long have you been doing stand-up?" Dale asked.

"Eight years," she said. "Started when I was eighteen. You?"

"Uh . . . let's see, I started in my early twenties, and I'm forty-two now, so . . ."

"Forty-two! Jesus," Rynn said, then feigned politeness. "I mean, you look good. Like, for your age."

"Oh, so you *are* committed to pissing me off."

"Hey, age is only a number," Rynn said with a dismissive flip of her hand, then added, "accompanied by rapid physical decline, of course."

"And a reduced tolerance for young punks," Dale said. "So." He took a sip from his cup. "An old American dude and an Irish wise-ass meet for lunch in Canada. Sounds like the start of a bad joke."

"Well, here's hoping it's a few laughs, at least," she said, raising her coffee and taking a sip. "Hey, what's this new guy like?"

"What new guy?" Dale asked.

"The guy who's middling the run," she said.

"I thought it was just you and me," he said. "I didn't hear anything about any middle act."

"Yeah, some local kid from here. Just starting out, but the booker fella, what's-his-name—"

"Merlin," Dale said.

"Yeah, Merlin the comedy wizard is sending this new kid with us. I'll emcee, open the show, warm 'em up, loads of hilarity bordering on too funny probably, then I'll bring up the kid, he'll do twenty or a half, and then I'll bring you up for however long you do."

"That pisses me off," Dale said. "Merlin could've run that past me. I'm only closing the goddamn show." He stirred his coffee, lips puckered. "And the kid's money will come out of ours, too. So that's money from our pockets."

"No, the kid is working for free, apparently," Rynn said. "He's really new and just wants experience. Not only is he not getting paid, he's agreed to do all the driving and pay all the gas money himself. Can you imagine what it must be like to be that stupid? Feckin' bliss, probably!"

"Oh. So then . . . this kid coming along is actually going to make me money?"

Rynn shrugged and nodded simultaneously.

Dale considered for a moment, then said, "I like this kid. He's a good kid."

After eating, they sat back for another cup of coffee while the table was cleared. The conversation had been relatively easy, considering their differing backgrounds. It reminded Dale of something he had heard Bob Newhart say in an interview when asked why he enjoyed the company of other comedians so much. He said something to the effect that no matter where you're each from or what your histories are, the moment you realize you're both stand-ups you have a thousand shared experiences that most other people could never understand. That had stuck with Dale. It made comedy feel personal, even though the same sentiment likely applied to about seven hundred other occupations. Newhart was talking about *him* and the things that people who *weren't* him didn't understand. That's what it was like with Rynn. She got it and she was living it. Newer to the game than he was, but with enough shows under the bridge to legitimize her. After an hour's conversation—even before that—Dale felt they were peers, and that was something that didn't always happen when he was chatting to a younger comic.

"So," Dale said, "tell me why you got into comedy."

"Well, I was fascinated with it pretty early on, as a teen," she said. "Made the decision that I was going to at least take a swing at it after school. Had no notions of university. No interest in anything else, really. Who knows what I'd be doing if I wasn't able to do this? *Her* job, I suppose," Rynn said, as the waitress drifted past a few tables away with a smile and a bus pan full of dirty dishes. "She seems happy enough." She certainly did. "How about you? How did you start all those many, many long years ago?"

He shrugged. "I always liked stand-up, wondered if I could do it," he said. "I started going to a club in Chicago called the Rebound Room. It was originally some kind of folk music place in the sixties, but then they started having open mic nights where people could do whatever they wanted, and a lot of comedians started going there and brought crowds with them. By the mid-seventies it was all comedy all the time. Late seventies I started going regularly to watch and finally found the guts to go up. I got some laughs and was hooked. Next thing you know I was living the dream." He looked out the window. "But now . . ."

The thought died in the air, like it had flown into a cloud that was too thick and sticky to punch through.

"But now what?" Rynn asked.

"I don't know. All feels different now. Feels like it's changed. Or it hasn't changed enough. Or maybe I've changed too much."

"Jesus Christ, Grampa," Rynn said, "that's sour as hell."

He chuckled. "Yeah, that was pretty sappy, wasn't it?" he said. "I'm just in a weird place. I had an opportunity put to me and I don't know what to make of it."

Rynn brightened. She was keen to talk about opportunities. Her chance to host a new TV show was dangling on a gold string just out of her reach, so close she could taste it, and Dale might be able to give her some veteran advice about how to grab for it without falling on her face. "Now *that* sounds a bit more uplifting," she said. "What opportunity?"

"To get out of the business."

"Oh, for Christ's sake," she moaned and dropped her head onto the table.

"I don't know if it's a bad thing," he said defensively. "Not at this stage. Wife and kid. Ex-wife, but still . . . that's not exactly cheaper. Daughter's heading to college, and not one of the sensible colleges above a sandwich shop where they teach hair weaving or VCR repair, she's going to one of the big ones, with books and everything. Anyway, an old buddy of mine has been into commercial real estate for a long time and he owns some warehouses. Told me he needed someone to run one for him. Regular hours, steady pay, know where I stand. There's at least a part of me that doesn't hate that."

"Get out of show business?" Rynn said, like it was the stupidest thing someone could do.

"I could work during the day and write at night," he said.

"Write what? Books, like a pompous arse?"

"Scripts. Movies, TV, whatever I wanted," he said grandly, trying hard to sell them both on the idea.

"And how long ago did this tremendous opportunity come your way?" she asked.

"About a month ago."

"Well, there it is," she said. "If you were going to take it, you wouldn't be here in fecking Canada waiting to haul your tender American arse across a thousand kilometres of frozen bushland to tell jokes to people in their igloos."

"Wow. That was a lot of stereotypes crammed into one sentence. P.S., you know it's July, right? Anyway," Dale said, "enough of my dour bullshit. What about you? Moving to Los Angeles. You got any interest from anyone? Agents? Managers?"

Rynn fiddled with her spoon on the tabletop, then shook her head. "Nothing to speak of. I mean, I do have a manager and she says all kinds of wonderful things are bound to come my way, but that's what they have to tell you, isn't it?" Rynn figured Dale maybe wasn't in a place where he needed to hear about someone younger—a foreigner, no less—getting a shot at hosting a national TV show while he was considering pulling the plug and taking a warehouse job.

Dale nodded. "They can blow smoke, that's for sure. But I wouldn't be surprised if she's right."

"Well, thanks," Rynn said, genuinely moved. That was nice to hear.

They both sipped their coffees quietly. Dale watched a dog take a leak against a mailbox on the sidewalk. Rynn went back to her newspaper.

"You're right, you know," she said, "I did have some preconceived notions about this country and her people but I'm well off the mark, apparently. Look at this." She pushed the newspaper across to Dale.

"BRUTAL MURDER AND ARSON AT RED CACTUS TAVERN," the headline blared.

"You don't think of Canada as having murderers, do you?" Rynn said. "If someone says *Canada*, I think hockey players and polar bears."

"Those are two of the most dangerous creatures on earth," Dale said.

After they had paid for lunch, Rynn took the elevator up to her room to pack her bag, while Dale headed out to find a bank. They agreed to reconvene in the lobby just before two and wait for the new kid to pick them up.

11

Dale was first in the lobby and sat in the wingback chair earlier occupied by Rynn, although unlike her, he wasn't reading anything. His eyes stared emptily at a potted fern, with half his mind trying to determine if the plant was real or fake and the other half stewing over how little he had in the bank after seventeen years on the road. Having wired $1,000 to Brandy to go toward Vanessa's tuition, Dale had exactly $9.53 in his account to get him through today. He'd be getting paid cash after the show tonight, and after each subsequent show, so he would squirrel away enough for a few small meals on the road and save the rest. If his math was right, when he was done this run, he would be able to wire the other two thousand to Brandy and have enough left over to pay almost half his rent.

The work-to-reward ratio of this business was tilting the wrong way, further every year, grinding him down physically and emotionally.

He wondered how many more rough runs like this he would do. How many more *could* he do? He closed his eyes and mumbled a muted prayer to the road gods for an easy, pleasant run with no hassles and no drama. He jumped when a blue bag landed with a thump at his feet.

"Keep an eye on this, will ya, while I check out," Rynn said as she made her way to the front desk. As a general rule in comedy, the room charge and taxes were taken care of by the venue—in this case, Whispers—but any incidental charges were the responsibility of the performer. To that end, there was a brief dispute between the clerk and Rynn as to why there were two charges for the same movie on her bill. She conceded that, yes, she had indeed watched *Encino Man* on the in-room Spect-o-Flik system, but only once, and she defied the clerk to give her any half-rational reason on God's green earth why anyone would need to see that movie twice in their lifetime, never mind twice on the same day. The clerk, unable to provide any such reason, deleted one of the movie charges from the bill and the rest was settled civilly. Rynn made her way back to Dale.

"I guess I showed that apple-faced dimwit who can and cannot be trifled with," she said, stuffing a receipt into her purse.

"Some kind of ruckus outside, too," Dale said, straining his neck to see where the shouting was coming from.

The front door of the old hotel was flung open wider and faster than it probably had ever been as a towering, powerfully built young man strode into the lobby, gawking around the room.

A portly bellman hustled along after him. "But that laneway has to remain clear," the bellman was saying.

"Hold your water, buddy, I told you I'll be two fuckin' minutes," the large man grumbled, without looking back, then his eyes landed on Dale and Rynn. A toothy smile sprawled across his face as he shot a finger right at them. "There they are!"

"Aw shit," Dale said under his breath, already exhausted by the big kid's energy.

"It would seem our chariot has arrived," Rynn said.

In three steps the grinning giant had crossed fifteen feet of royal blue carpet, with a large open hand outstretched the entire journey.

"I'm Hobie! Great to meet you both," he boomed, and shook their hands like they had just been elected mayor. "I'm parked right out front, as this yappy knob will happily tell you." He tossed his head toward the winded bellman, whose face had blossomed into a dangerous shade of rouge.

"We should get going then," Dale said, as any hope of a calm, leisurely run drained away.

"Let me grab your bag, pardon my French!" Hobie said, stooping for their luggage.

"I got it," Dale said, lifting his duffle onto his shoulder.

"Okey doke." Hobie looked to Rynn. "How about you?"

"A gentleman!" she declared.

Hobie smiled, snatched up her blue suitcase—in his paw it looked more like a child's lunch box—and the two of them hurried to catch up to Dale, who was already out the front door.

Hobie and Rynn stepped outside and almost bumped into Dale, who was stopped on the top step, staring at the vehicle looming before them.

"Is this your ride?" Dale asked.

"Pretty sweet, eh?" Hobie beamed.

"It's got character, for sure," Rynn said, wide-eyed.

Hobie strode proudly to the back of the beast and opened the rear door to deposit Rynn's luggage, while she and Dale continued to absorb the vehicle's "character." It was a 1984 Chevy van bathed in a deep metallic shade of purple that was as dark as anything could be before crossing the threshold into black.

"What colour would you call this?" Rynn asked.

"Paint code is G20-B," Hobie said, slamming the door closed, "but they call it Midnight Curtain."

Rynn barely stifled a laugh. Dale nodded. "I was just going to ask, 'Is this Midnight Curtain?' And did you manage to get all this done locally?" He pointed to the dreamy mural that swept up like a fog from the rear wheel well and splayed its way across the sliding side door, depicting a dramatic and formidable entity that seemed to be the hybrid offspring of a storm cloud and a warrior princess, complete with blood-soaked sword and two tiny triangles of armour shielding two very un-tiny breasts.

"You bet," Hobie said, stepping up to the driver's door. "I used to work with a guy who's a killer airbrush artist, so when I was getting the van tricked out, I told him to just open up his imagination and paint whatever he thought was in my head."

"Yikes," Rynn blurted. "How close was he?"

"So close it scared the shit out of me," Hobie said, as he swung himself inside and closed the door.

"And now we're all a little scared," Dale said for Rynn's benefit, and they both piled into the van.

"You have to move that, right now!" the crimson-faced bellman shouted from the top of the steps.

"The fuck's it look like we're doing, Matlock?" Hobie hollered back and roasted the tires as he roared from the laneway into the open street.

"Wow. You know how to make an entrance *and* an exit," Rynn said, sitting shotgun.

"Damn straight," Hobie said, hunching over the steering wheel as he drove.

He truly was a remarkably sized young buck, at least six foot five, maybe more, with broad, hulking shoulders anchoring a hell of a wingspan, and those long, muscular arms cradled each other across the top of the wheel in front of him, showing off an elaborate patchwork of tattoos. The ink crawled all the way up under his shirt sleeve and poked out above the collar, culminating halfway up one side of his neck.

Behind the driver's seat, Dale was stretched out on a velvet captain's chair that was bolted into the floor through a thick grey shag. The carpeting only ran a short way back from the cab. The bulk of the rear space was more industrial, with a hard rubberized floor and steel strapping running up the walls with various attachment points for securing loads. It seemed to be a working van as well, not just a ridiculous showpiece.

"Party in the front, business in the back?" Dale asked.

"Yeah," Hobie said, glancing up to the rearview mirror. "I'm always hauling one thing or another, for work or for friends, so I keep it nuts-and-bolts back there. Nothing to damage and easier to clean."

"What kind of work do you do, when you're not doing comedy?" Rynn asked.

"Lift and carry, lift and carry. Car parts, machinery, lumber, rocks, furniture, whatever . . . I grew up strong, so most people look at me like I'm a mule, basically. No one wants to see the creative side in here," he said, tapping his forehead, "or they might have to give me something more intelligent to do."

"Hey, what did you say your name was?" Dale asked. "Sounded like you said 'Hobie.'"

"That's it," Hobie said proudly.

"Right, and now tell him your last name," Rynn said, then looked back to Dale, smiling. She had been made privy to the full name earlier in a fax from Merlin.

"Huge!" Hobie said. Only he drew it out long, like the *u* in the middle was one of six.

"Your name is Hobie Huge?" Dale asked, although it came out flatly and not like a question at all. He repeated it to make sure it sounded as stupid outside his head as it did inside. "Hobie Huge."

"Yeah," Hobie beamed. "What do you think?"

"Depends," Dale said. "If it's your real name, it's swell. If you made it up, you're a goof."

"No fuckin' way," Hobie bristled. "I mean, of course it's made up, but it's not goofy."

"I didn't say *it* was."

"My real name's Howie. Howard, really," he said, "but when I decided to get into comedy I realized there's already a famous Howie, and I don't want to be just some other Howie, I want to put my own stamp on the biz. So I changed a letter."

"And what's your real last name?" Rynn asked. "Let me guess— Little? But you realized there's already a Rich Little, so you just yanked that one inside out and turned Little into Huge. Right?" She raised her arms triumphantly.

"Wrong," Hobie said, then asked, "Who's Rick Little?"

"Rich."

"Whatever, it wasn't that. I chose the name for one simple reason. Because that's exactly what I'm going to be. Fucking HUUUUUUGE!" and he fanned his broad, open hand across the windshield like it was a marquee ablaze with his name in lights.

"Oh," Dale said, "I didn't know it worked like that. Now I feel like an idiot for not changing my name to Millionaire Banglotz." That cracked Rynn up.

"I know you're laughing at me," Hobie said, with a smile that looked just a little forced, "but positive visualization is real, you know. If you want to live it, you have to see it."

"Great," Dale said, "thanks for the tip."

"Take it or leave it, I don't care," Hobie said, a slight sourness seeping under his words. "But the name Webly didn't exactly put you on a rocket ride to the top, did it?"

"Excuse me?" Dale said, leaning forward. "Say that again?"

Rynn saw where this was headed and hauled it off the tracks immediately. "Okay, settle down, both of you," Rynn said. "Christ's sake, we're not even out of the city yet and you're going to get into a goddamn fight?"

"It's not a fight," Dale said, a little louder than was necessary. "Just not sure I heard him right."

"You heard him fine," she said. "He took a shot at your name, but only after you took a shot at his, yeah?"

Dale just stared out the window.

Rynn turned back to Hobie. "Dale says no hard feelings."

The three of them sat in a cold clump of silence as the van headed toward the off-ramp that would take them onto the highway south of the city. It seemed a lot of folks were heading south, maybe to spend the last day of the weekend at one of those ten zillion lakes. The traffic increased block after block, with trucks and cars merging into the mix, weaving and jockeying to make sure they didn't miss their exits. Space grew tight while the relative speed increased.

Without warning Hobie yanked the wheel hard right and the van lurched out of its lane, cutting off a red sports car that screeched its tires and swerved left. Rynn screamed and Dale tumbled out of the captain's chair. Behind them a pickup jammed its brakes to avoid hitting the van, then dove into another lane, almost hitting a station wagon as Hobie veered his vehicle farther right and brought it to a stuttering stop on the shoulder. Horns blared as drivers roared past with middle fingers sprouting up like dandelions.

"What . . . in the thundering Christ . . . was that?" Rynn said, both arms braced rigidly against the dash.

"What the fuck is wrong with you?" Dale shouted, his ass still on the shag floor.

There was no reply from Hobie. He sat with his head down, eyes squeezed shut. The palms of his large, callused hands began to slide rhythmically and heavily up and down the length of his thighs, from his knees to his pockets, pockets to his knees, the rough skin hissing against the denim. Rynn and Dale watched him, unsure what was happening. Rynn could see the muscles in his jaw flexing and flaring, like burrowing animals tunnelling under his skin.

"Are you okay?" she finally asked. "Hobie?"

He stopped rubbing his legs. His eyes relaxed but remained closed for another few moments. Then the lids lifted, slowly. He shifted deliberately in his seat, turning toward her. His right arm flung up and over his headrest, so he could better face them both. "Sorry about that," he said.

They waited for more. It didn't come.

"Sorry?" Rynn said. "You almost kill us in a twelve-car pileup and just say 'sorry about that'?"

"Pileup?" Hobie looked genuinely confused, then shook his head. "No, no, I'm not sorry about pulling over," he clarified. "That was no big deal, had it under control the whole time. I'm sorry for what I said." He twisted further and looked directly at Dale. "It was out of line. It was a stupid thing for me to say and I sincerely apologize. You're a veteran guy, been on the road a long time, and I'm just starting out, so I should shut the fuck up and know my place. I do know my place. Honestly, I do. I just messed up there."

Dale looked intensely at Hobie. He didn't know how to respond. The apology felt genuine, but the insanity of the circumstance was equally real. The context was fractured and felt unsteady. Pushing it now would be pointless. Or worse. Besides, he was too preoccupied with the sound of his heart kicking his ribs loose to say much of anything. The best he could do was shake his head and manage to spit out, "Sure. Fine. Okay."

"Forgiven?" Hobie asked.

"For now," Dale said, clambering back into the captain's chair.

"That thing does have a seatbelt if you like," Hobie said. "Just dig under the cushion there, you'll find it."

Dale did exactly that and buckled himself in.

"It swivels, too," Hobie said proudly.

"Jesus Christ."

"We'll call that round one, then," Rynn offered. "Now, can we get back onto the road—when it is clear and safe to do so, yeah? We still have a show tonight in, feckin' . . . wherever. I can't remember the name."

"Horsewater," Hobie said.

Dale and Rynn broke into laughter, which ripped a hole in the tension and released a flood of neural chemicals that stoked them both into higher and higher fits of hysterics. Soon they were laughing at how hard each other was laughing, and that grew into alternating waves of shrieking and silent shaking, and the whole thing snowballed until they could barely breathe, wiping tears from their eyes.

Hobie watched them for a while, perplexed, then put his van into gear. "You should hear some of the town names in Saskatchewan," he said. He checked his side mirror and pulled back onto the highway.

Dale and Rynn spent the next few miles getting their heads back and then a few more gathering their breath. Hobie pulled out and passed an eighteen-wheeler that was hauling pigs, and Rynn made eye contact with one of the animals that was peering out through the slats of the trailer. If she harboured any lingering laughter, that snuffed it out in short order, and she leaned her head back as they rolled on in silence.

In time, Dale leaned forward with a hand on the back of Hobie's seat. "Listen, I'm sorry too," he said. "I've been in a pissy mood because of some personal stuff at home, so I was being unnecessarily shitty."

"No hard feelings here," Hobie said. "I'm on this run to learn and I'm getting schooled early. I hope you'll still let me pick your brain a bit."

Well, you're already picking my ass, so "—why not?" Dale said.

12

Railside Salvage Ltd. was aptly named. At least a dozen times per day a great, belching locomotive would rumble past the mountainous stacks of twisted car frames that lined the yard's perimeter and rattle the walls of the trailer that served as the office of the operation. Inside the office, Bull Henski sat behind a metal desk scratching figures onto a notepad with a pencil. Intermittently he would flip the pencil upside down and use its eraser to push buttons on a calculator—his fingers being too beefy to hit just one button at a time—and then he'd scribble more figures onto the notepad. He barely even noticed the train engines. The sounds from beyond the fence meshed with the sounds of the heavy machinery working inside the fence, and over the years it all blended into one droning gnash of metallic muscle that didn't even register in his head anymore. The noise simply became background music for his business dealings—legitimate and otherwise. Still, his instincts for survival always perked up at anything new, no matter how small, so when he heard the slam of an unfamiliar car door it cut through the regular ruckus like a cannon shot. He raised his head and listened. The dogs in the yard all erupted simultaneously into a raging chorus of barks and growls. Bull slid open a desk drawer, pulled a handgun and walked to the window.

"Fuck," he grumbled. "They didn't waste no time."

He tucked the handgun into the back of his pants, lifted his leather vest over the butt end and walked outside to greet his visitors.

As Bull made his way down the three wooden steps from his trailer, four large, menacing men walked his way. One of those men strode two steps ahead of the others. This was Stacker, and he was not someone to be taken lightly. As Stacker and his men drew closer, a half-dozen other men, every bit as menacing, rallied from various areas of the salvage yard to flank Bull protectively, while the barking dogs continued to test their chains.

Stacker came to a stop about ten feet from Bull. "You and I should talk," he said.

"You should have called first," Bull said, "out of respect. Showing up out of the blue like this is a little insulting."

"I didn't want to catch you at a busy time and have you blow me off," Stacker said. "That's happened before, and it's more than a little insulting."

"I'm a busy guy. I'm busy now," Bull said, "so what is it we need to talk about?"

"Someone hit one of our clubs a couple nights back. Killed the manager."

"Uh-huh."

"Yeah," Stacker said. "Only they didn't just kill him. Tied him up and lit his ass on fire. Roasted the fucking guy alive, near as we can tell."

"Uh-huh."

"That's all you got to say, 'uh-huh'?" Stacker shifted his weight and cocked his head. "Doesn't feel like any of this is news to you. Makes me think you must have some thoughts on the matter."

"Thoughts about what? About who? Or why?" Bull said. "Nope. Thanks for dropping by."

Stacker didn't let anger cloud his process. "Used to be a time when nothing like this could go down without you knowing something about it," he said, "so basically, you're telling me you're not on top of things as much as you used to be. That's good to know."

"You can figure it tells you whatever you like," Bull said, taking one step forward, testing Stacker's resolve, "and if that makes your balls grow a couple sizes, good for you. But I wouldn't advise whipping them out any time soon."

Stacker's eyes never blinked. He took one step toward Bull. "I'm not looking for advice. I came here to see if you'd own up to what I already know."

"What do you think you know?" Bull sneered.

"I know who killed my guy at the Red Cactus," Stacker said.

"And you figure it's got something to do with me?"

"I do, yeah. Maybe indirectly," Stacker said, "but that still puts it on your plate to make right. And if it doesn't get made right"—he took another step forward—"you and me aren't going to have much choice but to put our balls on the table."

Five years ago, Bull would have reached out and crushed Stacker's throat for taking a stand like this. And his guys would have slaughtered Stacker's guys, and all four of the visitors would've been stuffed into the trunk of a rusted-out sedan and compacted into a four-foot cube, never to be heard from again. Problem solved. But Stacker and his gang had grown considerably, in smart and brutal fashion. If it came down to it,

Bull had no doubt that his own gang could and would still win an all-out war with Stacker's. But it would not be a one-sided beating that was done in an afternoon with a clear message sent to everyone watching. No, it would be a long and costly war with heavy losses on both sides. Life, money, turf, reputation—it would be far too high a price to settle such a stupid bill. A thoughtless, needless bill garnered as the result of something that never should have happened in the first place. Bull didn't need his pencil for this kind of figuring. He calculated the scenario in his head and determined that the best way for him to stay on top of the mountain was to raise Stacker up a step. Yes, it would require a personal sacrifice, but for the greater good.

"You can keep your knickers on," Bull said. "Let's talk in my office."

13

At some point during the drive, Dale and Rynn had begun referring to Hobie's van as Midnight, and Hobie liked it. He said it was the first time, for whatever reason, that he hadn't given a name to his primary vehicle. There had been a '76 Trans Am he called Ace, a '75 Dart Sport he called Roxy and a green '81 Silverado he called Gator, and it was high time his new ride was christened. So Midnight it was, and Midnight just passed a road sign that read HORSEWATER 10.

"Ten more miles," Dale said.

"Kilometres," Rynn corrected.

"Oh right," he replied. "So, another . . . six hundred miles?"

"Be there in five minutes," Hobie assured them, but it was less, since the Horsewater Tavern was on the nearest edge of town as they pulled in.

It was one of the classic flat-faced two-storey wooden structures that housed a tavern on the ground floor and several hotel rooms on the upper level. Such cookie-cutter buildings could be found in almost every town and small city across the country because federal law once mandated that no establishment could legally sell liquor unless they also offered rooms to let. So beer and whisky parlours cropped up throughout the land, with grand, varnished oak bars, ornate stained-glass mirrors, lush patterned wallpaper and the very barest minimum effort put toward the rooms above: a squeaky spring bed and a copper piss-pot to satisfy the local constabulary.

Midnight was pulled up to the side of the building and the trio hauled out their luggage and headed inside, following the hand-painted arrow that said HOTeL DeSk.

It took some doing to rouse any attention at the front counter, but finally a woman built like a steamer trunk stepped up wearing a dirty apron, apparently from the kitchen, and said, "Whattayaneed?" The trio explained that they were the comedians on the show tonight and there should be three rooms here for them.

"Oh yeah," Steamer said, "I was told about that. All right." She sighed and pulled down three keys, each attached to its own diamond-shaped orange plastic fob that featured a number scratched into the silhouette of a horse's head. "I'll give you one, two, and four," she said. "Room three has a weird smell."

"Which of these is the best room?" Hobie asked. "That should go to Dale, he's the headliner."

"Doesn't matter," Dale said, a little annoyed at the kiss-ass comment.

"No, it don't matter," Steamer said. "They're all the same." They each filled out their photocopied registration forms and headed up the stairs.

The hallway was narrow and dark, barely illuminated by two weak bulbs that were suffocating under dust. What feeble glow did radiate off them was thirstily absorbed by the dark brown carpet and dark brown walls and dark brown ceiling. Rynn mused that if the doors weren't painted a lighter shade of brown, someone could spend a month trying to find their room. She imagined the housekeeper showing up on one of her biannual tours of duty and stumbling across a decomposing skeleton clutching its abdomen in hunger.

"Goddamn," Rynn finally blurted, "this is like spelunking." She stopped in front of a door and rubbed her fingers across the number screwed into it. "Feels like a four. This must be me," she said. "What time do you want to head down?"

"Show starts at nine," Dale said, "but I'm going down an hour early to see how they have the room set up. Might give us a chance to straighten out any catastrophes."

"Want me to come down, too?" Rynn asked.

"No," he said. "It'll just take a few minutes to scope it out, make any tweaks, and then I'll come back to my room until eight thirty or so."

"Knock me up at eight thirty, then," she said. "That means something different where I'm from, by the way," and she went into her room, locking the door behind her.

Dale stopped in front of room 1, and Hobie stopped at room 2.

"Can I come down with you at eight?" Hobie asked. "I'd like to learn what things you look for in a room's set-up."

"Sure," Dale said. "Until then, enjoy the palatial splendour of room two, high above the Horsewater Tavern."

"Bet your ass I will," Hobie said with a wide, honest smile. "This is awesome," and he went inside.

Dale smiled too. It had been a good long while since he felt that kind of enthusiasm on the road, and a small part of him was jealous. He stepped inside his room and locked the door. He flared his nostrils and pulled in three quick breaths. He did not smell any disinfectant. *Damn.*

He left his shoes and his clothes on and lay on top of the scratchy crocheted bedcover. The nightstand was draped in a greyish doily and was home to a small desk lamp. The lamp had an off-white paper shade rimmed with lines of red and blue, and the base showcased a small bronze figure of a man doing some kind of activity that seemed to involve squatting. *Curling, maybe? Yeah, they do that goofy* "—shit up here." Next to the lamp was a cheap digital clock radio. Dale set its alarm for forty-five minutes, then lay back for a nap. He could hear music, faintly, but was far too tired to let that stop him from drifting off. He closed his eyes and crossed his fingers, even though that only kept the dream away about half the time.

In her room, Rynn stepped out of the shower, towelled off and brushed her hair straight back. She pulled on a T-shirt and sweatpants—both properly wrinkled, like a good couple of waddies should be—and turned on the fourteen-inch RCA television that was, much to her surprise, connected to a cable coax. She began flipping through far more channels than she expected to see and stopped when she heard the theme song to *Entertainment Tonight*. "Ah, let's see what's in the news," she said to herself, and lay back on the bed to watch.

Down the hall, in Hobie's room, a CD boom box was kicking out Slayer as he banged off two hundred and fifty push-ups.

14

At five minutes to eight there was a knock on Dale's door. Hobie, it seemed, was keen to get the evening under way. The two men headed down to the bar.

"So, what are we looking for?" Hobie asked.

"The main thing we need is focus," Dale said, "so first we look for anything that might pull focus."

Hobie saw a TV mounted high on the wall above the corner of the bar. "TV's on," he said. "I'll go tell them to turn it off." He took a step, but Dale grabbed the tail of his shirt.

"Whoa. It's an hour until showtime," he said. "We don't want to turn the place into a mausoleum. We want them to switch off just a couple minutes before the show starts. That'll make the show more of an event. It's like a gearshift. TV and music suddenly go off, something must be happening, so they check it out."

"Got it," Hobie said. "I'll tell them to kill it at two minutes to nine."

"Don't tell them to do anything," Dale said. "If you tell them what to do, they get their noses out of joint. This is their place, not ours. So we just explain what can help create a good show in their place. They want the show to be good, same as us."

"Right, right." Hobie was nodding. "Use psychology."

Dale shrugged. "I don't know if I'd call it psychology. It's just logic."

"Everything is psychology, man," Hobie said. "Some people say everything is sales, other people say everything is sex, or everything is survival. And maybe all that's true. But guess what? Boil all that shit down and you'll see the psychology behind it."

"Maybe," Dale said, "but boiling takes a long time and we're only here for one night."

They heard a gruff voice behind them. "I suppose you two are the comedians?"

They turned and saw a middle-aged man strolling their way. Both Dale's and Hobie's eyes dropped involuntarily to the man's middle, where a prominent belly jutted from an otherwise average frame. It pushed forward so independent of its person it not only warranted attention, it demanded it. The fellow behind the belly appeared to be an after-thought, like something hauled along out of obligation. Dale and Hobie looked up to the adjacent face. It was plenty round itself, although much less impressive. A pale, pock-faced moon trapped in orbit. The main crater opened and spoke.

"Name's Mickey. I own the place." He extended a hand and Dale shook it.

Hello, Mickey Moonface. "Nice to meet you," Dale said. "I'm Dale and this is Hobie. There's one more of us, Rynn. She'll be down in a bit."

"The woman takes longer to get ready, eh?" Mickey said smugly. "Big surprise."

That comment told Dale roughly ninety-eight percent of every-thing he needed to know about this guy. He looked around the room one more time, pleasantly surprised by how things were set up. The stage looked decent. There was even a stool by the microphone. The lighting looked fine. There were seats facing the stage in fairly close proximity, and each table was adorned with a small tea candle with a twinkling flame, lending the space a deceitful elegance. "The room looks good," Dale said. "Should be a good show."

"Friggin' better be, for what I'm paying. Jesus, wish I made what you make for an hour's work."

Even though their entire relationship to this point had consisted of a few hours together in a van, Dale immediately knew Hobie's hackles would be ruffled by Mickey's comment, but he did not expect to see Hobie stepping toward the man.

"If you think it's so—" Hobie started.

Dale slid in front of him. "Yeah, we're all millionaires, clearly. Are you charging a cover tonight?"

"Six bucks at the door," Mickey said, warily eyeballing the enor-mous young man.

"Then we'll give 'em at least seven bucks' worth of laughs and everyone leaves happy," Dale said, turning Hobie around with him and starting to walk away. He called back over his shoulder, "We'll be down in a half-hour," and they headed for the lobby, with Hobie still stewing.

"Like that tub of shit has any idea what a day's work looks like."

"Oh, I don't know," Dale said. "Must take at least eight hours of hard labour to do up his bottom button." He felt a pang of guilt at taking such a cheap shot, but that was snuffed quickly by the cackle that exploded beside him.

Hobie's laughter was abrupt and louder than normal. Louder than natural. Then his mouth slowly tightened into a darker, sicker smile, and he suddenly threw a punch at nothing—a fast overhand right drilled into the empty space before them. Dale veered a little and, looking over, saw Hobie's face ratchet into a twisted snarl, his teeth clamped together behind curled lips. The big kid threw another hard punch into empty air—a sharp, violent left hook. As he reached the bottom of the stairs Hobie bent his enormous frame forward and propped one foot up onto the second step as he recoiled his right arm. A series of heavy punches began to hammer downward into nothing. A malevolent pantomime— methodical, mechanical, but unquestionably violent. Breathy, guttural noises escaped him with each manoeuvre, bits of spittle popping past his teeth, and his eyes projecting a malice that Dale hadn't seen before.

Then, as quickly as it had come over him, it faded. Hobie straightened upright and smiled at Dale, and started up toward their rooms.

Dale waited a moment before following a few steps behind, unsure of what he had just witnessed and choosing not to ask.

15

By quarter to nine the room was looking full. Dale's quick estimate had it at a hundred people or close to it. The crowd had a definite rural vibe, which was no surprise, considering where they were. A hell of a lot of plaid was settling into those seats. The gender mix was about eighty/twenty men-to-women, and of the roughly eighty male heads out there, Dale counted three that weren't covered in a snapback ballcap. The crowd was loud, but that wasn't necessarily a bad thing. It could just be a sign of life. If a crowd's excited for the show, that's a good thing, provided they're excited for the right reasons.

Dale and Rynn settled onto stools at the back of the room, as far away from the stage as possible, with Hobie standing beside them. They saw Mickey the moon-faced manager meandering around, and Dale gave him a slight wave that said, *Hey, we're here, ready when you are.* Mickey strolled over and peeled off six little red tickets from a roll he had in his pocket.

"All righty, here are six drink tickets. Two each or however you want to divvy them up, I don't care." Mickey turned his attention to Rynn. "Hi, I'm Mickey, I own the place. We didn't meet earlier, you were busy getting yourself all sexy, and sister . . . it paid off," he said with a crooked grin that highlighted a couple spots where teeth used to be.

"Oh. Thanks, I guess?" Rynn said pleasantly enough. "But in future, Mickey, try not to use 'sexy' and 'sister' in the same sentence. Bit of a red flag."

Mickey took a moment to scrounge up a comeback, but didn't really have the tools, so he settled on a half-wink and turned back to Dale. "Full house. Everyone's pumped to see some live comedy, so you ready to kick things off?"

Before Dale could start a reply, Hobie barked out "Let's do this thing!" with far more enthusiasm and volume than was appropriate to the situation. The three others all looked at him flatly for a clunky second, then Rynn said, "Sounds like we're good to go."

Unlike Mullet Jake in Saginaw, it didn't take any convincing to get Mickey Moonface to go up onstage to introduce the show. It was his idea.

"I'll pop up first and welcome the folks, get them settled in," he said, "and then I'll bring you three up."

"Just bring Rynn up," Dale said. "She'll do the rest." Then he turned to her and asked, "Anything specific you want Mickey to say in your intro?"

"Just let them know I'm from Ireland, so my accent doesn't throw them for a loop," she said.

Mickey gave a nod and another wink and followed his navel to the front of the room.

Hobie watched his departure with disgust. "How the fuck is he going to get up onstage?" he asked. "Forklift?"

Mickey managed to get up all right, leaning an unwelcome amount of mass onto the shoulder of a man sitting at the side of the stage, and the spotlights came on as he stepped to the microphone. Mickey tapped the mic like a goon and blew into it like he was calling bingo at a church picnic.

"Thanks for coming out to the Horse, folks," he said. "For anyone who don't know me, I'm Mickey, I own the place." There was a low, long boo from the middle of the crowd. Mickey capped his eyebrows and looked out past the lights, then said, "Oh screw you, Les. Heckle me and you're cut off and you can go drink alone in the woods. You want to heckle, heckle the comedians."

"Oh thanks, idiot," Dale muttered.

Hobie looked sideways to Dale, unsure why that remark had upset him.

Onstage, Mickey continued with some general bar business, mentioning next week's prime rib and pasta night and promoting the fact they would be showing the upcoming Lennox Lewis versus Oliver McCall fight at the bar. "We all know Lewis will beat the crap out of McCall," he said, "but hey, that'll be fun to watch. Okay, now it's time to get the comedy started, and we're starting things off a little different here, a little unusual, because our first comedian is actually a little lady!"

"Are you fecking kidding me?" Rynn said, and she lowered her head and started walking to the stage.

"She's here all the way from Scotland," Mickey continued, "so give her a big Manitoba welcome, it's . . ." He looked at a piece of paper in his hand. "Rene Langdon."

The crowd began applauding as Rynn stepped up onstage and shook hands with Mickey. She took the microphone out of the stand and looked over as Mickey started leaving the stage.

"Thanks, Mickey, for that lovely and nowhere near accurate introduction," she said as Mickey leaned onto the man's shoulder again and cautiously began a protracted descent from the stage. Rynn watched for a moment, then asked the crowd, "How long does he usually take to get offstage? Should I sit down for this?" She leaned against the stool and watched Mickey manoeuvre himself until both his feet were firmly back on the bar floor. "And we have splashdown!" she announced and stood again to address the audience. "All right, well not that it matters a great deal, but my name isn't Rene, it's Rynn, like Lynn with an R. And Lanigan, not Langdon. And more importantly, what matters a hell of a lot, is that Scotland isn't Ireland and never fecking will be!"

That didn't get the response she thought it would, but she also knew why. She had heard the words coming out of her head and they sounded angry. She was trying not to sound angry, and thought she had it covered, but something in her delivery betrayed her. The crowd could sense it, and they were unsure now. She had about five seconds to get them back or it was going to be a long night for her.

"And I'm not your little lady, Mickey, although any lady that didn't have a bell around her neck and a pail under her jugs would seem little next to you." *Oh I've fucked it up good now*, she thought. She was right. The crowd murmured and shuffled in their seats as she took a deep breath and dug in her heels to start the long hard climb.

At the back of the bar, Dale raised his eyebrows. "Woof," he said, half to Hobie and half to himself, "that's a bad start. Is she trying to Campbell them? That's risky."

"What does that mean?" Hobie asked.

"There's a comedian named Colin Campbell—or was, sadly. Died a couple years back. One of the strongest acts I've ever seen. He was such a good stand-up that sometimes he'd open his show by saying a bunch of deliberately horrible things to purposely make the crowd hate him, just to see if he could win them back. To challenge himself."

Hobie grinned. "That is badass. Did he ever get them back?"

"Always," Dale said. "But I don't think that's what we're seeing here."

Rynn was trying the same local material that had worked so well all week at Whispers, but the crowd wasn't on board. She was getting a few small laughs here and there, but the good folks of Horsewater were certainly not ready to forgive and forget just yet. In fact, one fellow took it upon himself to fire back.

"Are you new at this?" he shouted from the darkness.

"Now, now, sir," Rynn said, smiling, "we stumbled out of the gate, but we won't get our stride back if you start throwing rocks, now, will we?"

"Then bring up a comedian," the heckler said.

Dale got off his stool, craning his neck to see if he could tell where the voice was coming from. Hobie got up and moved beside him, just because.

"We got an asshole," Dale said. "Do you see who's heckling?"

Hobie looked into the crowd. "No, I can't tell."

"Keep your eyes peeled, I want to know," Dale said, continuing to scan the room. Hobie kept looking, but his eyes drifted back and forth from the audience to Dale, who seemed genuinely angry.

"You look kind of pissed off," Hobie said.

"Yeah, I'm pissed off if we're going to have to deal with a heckler all night," Dale said.

"Hey, hecklers are a part of comedy, that's just how it is," Hobie said in a manner that was casual enough to make Dale even more pissed off.

"Okay, first of all, you've been in the business a minute and a half," Dale said, "so don't tell me 'how it is,' and secondly, yeah, hecklers are a part of comedy—the same way bird shit is a part of vehicle ownership."

Hobie had to think about that. Dale drilled it home.

"You spend a bunch of time painting and polishing Midnight, and then some pigeon drops an oily deuce right on the hood," Dale said. "How's that make you feel?"

"It pisses me off," Hobie said, starting to understand. Dale went on a brief rant, talking in detail about the craft of comedy, of honing the idea, polishing the phrasing, of working a bit and moulding it and trying it again and again and tweaking it each time, shaving off words, adding tags, adding a pause, removing a pause, should I look down or look up? Art and craft weaving together to fold a hundred experiments into a thousand decisions to make two minutes of decent comedy, and then some thick moron decides he should cram his dim dribblings into your work uninvited. The words and the passion that Dale spoke were setting off fireworks in Hobie's head. He was idling high and hot.

"Fuck that thick moron!" Hobie said, straining his neck in a more eager and focused hunt than before. He wanted to see the heckler's face. Smash it. He was pacing and searching and seething. It was a few moments before Dale realized that Hobie was getting too worked up. He saw the fists clenched and the teeth gritted. He moved over and put a hand on Hobie's back. Hobie whirled around and glared with an animal's eyes, and for a split second Dale thought Hobie was going to punch him.

"Whoa, okay," Dale said calmly. "I'm pissed too, but there are ways of handling this."

"Yeah," Hobie said, "like ramming my fist down that prick's throat."

Dale knew with absolute certainty Hobie meant what he said. He knew if that local dipshit happened to stroll back this way, Hobie would break his jaw. Dale didn't like where this was headed and felt at least a little responsible. His rousing speech about respecting the craft had baptized a frighteningly righteous disciple, and it was time to temper the sermon.

"That's not what we do," Dale said. "Comedians use our minds and our words and our wits, right?"

Our.

Hobie's eyes were softening. "Yeah. We do," he said.

Dale kept it inclusive. "Why use fists when our words are knives?"

Hobie smiled at Dale and nodded slowly, as if deeply appreciating that sentence. He rolled it around in his head a few times, liking it more and more. *Our words are knives. Our words are knives.* Then he burst loose with a single "WOOOO!" that turned every head in the room back their way. Dale slipped behind a pillar in the darkness to avoid their eyes. Hobie stood where he was, still bobbing his head, apparently unaware of the people trying to see where that sound had come from.

Onstage, Rynn said, "I'm not sure if that was a heckle or if someone accidentally sat on their beer bottle." That was her biggest laugh to that point, and she seized the moment. "Well, on that strange note, what say we bring up your next act?"

The crowd applauded. Everyone was keen to see this evening taken in a different direction, Rynn included, so she began to introduce Hobie. As she spoke, he started doing deep knee bends and high kicks in the dark accompanied by strange grunting and huffing. Dale watched him from the shadows with confusion and concern while Rynn finished the intro.

"So please welcome, sort of a local lad from up the road in Winnipeg, one of your own, Hobie Huge!"

The crowd offered up a large round of applause as Hobie carved through the audience like a torpedo, bounding onstage so dramatically it took Rynn aback, and she held up her hands as she walked off.

As Hobie began his portion of the show, Rynn made her way back to where Dale was seated. He opened his mouth but she spoke first, "I'm better than that."

"I have no doubt," Dale said.

"That Mickey prick got me madder than I realized," she fumed, "which is understandable, sure, but I let it affect my show and that's on me. 'Splashdown'? Comparing him to a cow because he has a big belly? Fuck me. Easy, ignorant shite any half-wit could—. I need to be better than that. Fucking—*fecking* unprofessional is what it was."

"Don't worry about it," Dale said. "Maybe he won't pay us and that'll take the pressure off the 'professional' part."

Rynn hung her head. "Jesus. I'm sorry about this. Maybe our boy Hobie Huge will save the day."

"Wouldn't hold my breath," Dale said, eyes locked on the stage. Voices from the audience were rising and grumbling en masse, some heckling, as Hobie's voice grew louder and more strained.

He was strutting around onstage like a pompous professor trying to impress his students with his mighty intellect, which would be bad enough, but it was exacerbated by the fact that he was clearly a substitute teacher fresh off the bus and the audience could smell it. They weren't there for a lecture from some green kid.

"You know comedy is a two-way street," Hobie stated into the microphone, "and some of you folks were jamming the brakes before the show even started. I could see you."

"Fuck off!" someone hollered.

"Sit down, Junior," another yelled.

But Hobie had points to make and he was going to make them. At the back of the room Rynn and Dale watched the calamity unfold.

"Has he even tried a single joke yet?" Rynn asked.

"Nope," Dale said. "He's too busy relaying what I told him ten minutes ago."

"You told him to do this?" Rynn asked, surprised.

Dale shot her a look. "No, I did not tell him to do this. I told him that hecklers were bad, so now he feels the need to spank the bad people."

Rynn smiled. "I think he feels the need to impress you. The puppy's showing off for the tall dog."

"I wish that was all it was," Dale said, "but I think this weirdness runs a lot deeper than that."

Onstage, Hobie apparently thought he could just slide from his rant into his brilliantly prepared stand-up material and have that wrap everything up with a bright red bow.

"Okay, now that you know where I stand, I'll tell you a bit about myself," he said, holding the head of the microphone within his hand, like a rapper. "I like to cook."

The crowd moaned and Rynn doubled over in laughter.

"Wow! Talk about a sharp left," she said to Dale. "Spend five minutes making the crowd hate your guts and then, 'A bit about me—I'm a whiz in the kitchen.' Sweet baby Jesus. Can you picture our big lad cooking up a lovely turkey dinner with all the trimmings?"

Dale's eyes remained fixed on stage. "I can picture him killing the bird."

Hobie was trying to tell the audience a lighthearted story about the first time he made an omelette, but they could not be less entertained. He ploughed ahead, unfazed.

" . . . and I figured a few eggshells in there would be all right, make it crunchy. I like crunchy," he said. "And then it hit me—potato chips! Yeah, I'll crunch some potato chips into the omelette . . ."

A voice shouted, "Nice shitty tattoos, greaseball."

Hobie stopped abruptly. "What the fuck did you say?" he growled, not sure where the voice had come from at first, until several audience members turned to look at the same face in the crowd—a smirking face on a narrow head with big pink ears sticking straight out like a couple of open car doors.

"You don't like my tattoos?" Hobie sneered. "Well, good thing I didn't get them to impress some scrawny hayseed in Fuckwater County. Maybe I should tattoo your fucking face with my fucking fist and we'll see if you like that any better."

The show wasn't just off the rails, it was halfway into a cornfield and sinking into the mud.

"I'll be honest with you," Rynn said to Dale, "I have no idea how I'm going to get the crowd back now. They weren't fond of me, but they're ready to kill him."

"That's how," Dale said.

"How's what?" she asked.

"Use their dislike of Hobie to make them like you by comparison. If you're on their side about him, they might get on your side about everything else."

"Throw him under the bus?" she asked, just to be clear.

"He threw himself under the bus," Dale said. "You just need to point it out."

Rynn considered the advice. Sounded like a solid strategy, actually. Besides, they were all leaving town in the morning, so who cared? *Let's get this shit show behind us.*

Up under the spotlights, Hobie continued tanking and the crowd was growing increasingly agitated and angry. Moonface Mickey rumbled up to Dale and Rynn with a face as purple as a plum and hissed at them, "Get this shitty punk off my stage right now and get this show back on track or I'm pulling the plug on the whole fucking thing!"

"He's getting himself off the stage," Dale said, pointing to Hobie, who was planting the microphone back into the stand. Rynn hustled up to the stage, where Hobie stood with arms outstretched, as though he were absorbing the crowd's energy. His face was awash with a giant smile.

"Thank you, and you're welcome!" he said, then bent deeply at the waist into a sweeping, dramatic bow, rose up, blew a kiss and left the stage.

Rynn stepped into his place. "That was Hobie Huge, ladies and gentlemen! Making friends wherever he goes!"

16

Hobie made his way through the unhappy crowd to the back of the room. Dale said dryly, "I didn't get a chance to watch. How'd it go?"

"That was a rush," Hobie said, absolutely beaming. "Every eye in the place was riveted on me."

"Okay . . . guess that's one way to look at it," Dale said.

"What do you mean, *one way*? That was it, man. That's everything!"

"Not exactly," Dale said. "There is the small matter of getting laughs."

"Some things are more important than laughs," Hobie said.

"Not on a comedy show."

"What's comedy without a point of view?" Hobie challenged.

"What's comedy without the funny part?" Dale said. "That's what that was. 'Ladies and gentlemen, welcome to the Horseshit Inn for Point-of-View Night.'" Hobie looked a little bit wounded, so Dale tried to smooth it over. "Look, having a point of view is great. And you're right, the best comedy has a point of view. But if it's *just* point of view, it's not comedy. It's a speech. Or worse, a goddamn lecture."

"But they never gave my comedy a chance," Hobie said. "You heard them—they heckled the material."

"No, they heckled *you*. It was you that never gave your comedy a chance. And now we may not get paid."

"I'll get our fucking money," Hobie snapped.

"How? You going to beat it out of Moonface? That'll go over great with the locals . . . and the local cops."

Hobie was beginning to pace again, feeling cornered, edgy. He hated this feeling—not knowing who his real friends were. Then he heard his name from onstage, coming from Rynn's lips.

"Whatever you thought of Hobie, you have to admit it takes a pretty big set of stones to blow a kiss after bombing like that," she said. "Stones in his sack or rocks in his head, not sure which." The crowd was starting to laugh again. Dale looked over and saw that even Moonface was smiling a little.

Hell, we might pull this off yet, he thought.

The laughter didn't feel like salvation to Hobie, however. He watched, slack-jawed, as Rynn roasted him, getting bigger and bigger laughs at his expense. He moved from the back wall slowly, drifting almost, as though her words were magnets drawing him forward. Dale looked at Hobie and saw a face he hadn't seen before. Anger? Not really. Pain? Maybe. It was hard to tell. His mind rifled through a dozen words to describe what he was witnessing, then he said one softly, out loud.

"Disconnected."

That was the closest he could come up with. Whatever was happening behind those eyes, it wasn't good. Dale moved up beside Hobie. "You might save our asses yet, pal."

"What?" Hobie said in a hollow, drawn-out voice, eyes still fixated on Rynn.

"This was my idea," Dale said. "I told her that if she poked a bit of fun at you, it might get the crowd back."

Hobie turned slowly to face Dale. "You told her to do this?"

"Yeah. She didn't want to, but I told her it was okay," Dale said. "Told her you were strong enough to take it."

Hobie seemed to wince a little, but his gaze was still distant. Not yet reconnected. "Take it," he said simply.

"Right. You know, take one for the team. It's a move we have to do sometimes on the road in bad situations, but still," Dale said, "some guys I wouldn't want to do this with. They'd be all pissy about it. But I knew you'd get it."

Hobie stared at Dale for what was likely three seconds but felt like eleven minutes. Dale kept his eyes toward the stage, nice and calm. *Don't say anything else. He'll come around.*

"Aw hell yeah," Hobie said. "I get it."

Dale looked into Hobie's eyes and saw he was back from whatever trip he had taken. And he was smiling. A flood of hot relief washed over him, but he played it cool. "I knew you would."

The crowd was in a much better mood by the time Rynn finished her last bit, and the room was a lot lighter. There was comedy on the stage and laughter in the air and all was as it should be. It was time to bring up the headliner to knock the whole thing out of the park.

"Please welcome to the stage, all the way from Chicago, Illinois, the hilarious Dale Webly!" Rynn said, her voice rising to a crescendo. Dale stepped onstage to hearty applause, pulled the microphone from the clip and moved the stand to the back of the stage.

"Thanks, everybody, thank you, and keep that applause going for your emcee Rynn Lanigan," he said, and the applause swelled. Earlier transgressions were erased, a few more drinks had been swilled, and it was time for some fun.

Dale launched into seven straight minutes of local material, starting with what he thought of the name "Horsewater" for a community. "Makes me wonder what names were voted down," he said, "Pigpuddle? Goatsoup? Come on, that would've been a better name. 'I'm off to Goatsoup, Manitoba, for the weekend!'" They were loving it.

At the back of the room, Rynn was watching Dale. Studying him, really. Dale had a smooth, no-bullshit manner that put everyone at ease. Watching him was watching a person who was clearly in control, and the audience crawled into his hand. And when he took a few lighthearted jabs at their beloved Mickey—"So after you opened a tavern in Horsewater, how long did it take you to come up with the name Horsewater Tavern? That is a creative genius right there, folks!"—the folks fully submitted to his charms.

Rynn recognized the high level of skill and experience on display and was realizing how fortunate she was to have this opportunity. She could've been saddled on this run with some pedestrian hack of a headliner who would spend each night telling forty-five minutes of dick jokes. Instead, she was going to spend six nights watching and learning from this guy. Invaluable. His advice on how to turn the room around and get the crowd back was brilliant. As she sat counting her blessings, Hobie loomed out of the darkness to stand beside her.

"Oh, hey," Rynn said. "Where've you been?"

"Getting a beer," Hobie said, raising a bottle. He plopped down heavily in a chair next to her. "You took some pretty good shots at me up there."

"Just taking the piss," she said. "No hard feelings, I hope."

"You think I can't handle it?" he said, slow and low. "You think I can't take it?"

"Um . . ." She wasn't quite sure what was happening. "We sort of just met, so I have no idea what you can or can't take," she said. "You'll let me know, though, yeah?"

A patch of dead air hung between them as they eyed each other. Then Hobie's gaze moved down to the table.

"You'd be surprised," he said, hovering his hand just above the table-top. "People are always surprised at what I can take."

"Oooookay," Rynn said warily. "Well, I don't really like surprises, so let's just leave it there."

She waited for a response, but Hobie said nothing, still staring at his own hand. Her eyes followed his focus downward until she saw what he was doing. And smelled it. The meaty pad on his palm was beginning to smoulder above the flickering flame that danced on the tea candle. "Jesus Christ, Hobie!" She yanked his wrist back. "What the fuck are you doing?" Hobie turned his palm up to examine the small roasted patch, the centre of which was almost black, then tilted his hand to show Rynn.

"Ta-daaah," he said in a semi-melodic drone.

"I'm getting you some ice for that," Rynn said. "And don't do anything that fucking stupid around me ever again."

Hobie grinned at her. "You can't take it?"

She stood and headed for the bar. She asked the bartender for a glass of ice and shot a stern look over her shoulder back at Hobie. *Stupid macho arsehole, why on earth would*—Her thoughts stopped short as she noticed Hobie seemed to be having a discussion with someone, despite the fact he was sitting alone. His lips danced in mute conversation and his arms gesticulated. The bartender set the glass of ice in front of her, but she didn't move, continuing to stare at Hobie.

"Will there be anything else?" the barman asked.

"I feckin' hope not," Rynn said, and took the glass.

Onstage, Dale rocked the Horsewater Tavern for forty-five minutes with a masterful blend of written material and off-the-cuff commentary, then said good night to a roar of applause. Rynn hopped up onstage for the extro and thanked the crowd for coming out and supporting live comedy. She threw a thank-you Mickey's way as well and got the crowd to give him a big hand for bringing the show to town. *Couldn't hurt when it comes around to getting paid.* Mickey glowed with pride and waved to the audience.

After sitting and having a beer with Rynn and Hobie for fifteen minutes or so, Dale stood up. "Time to talk to Mickey," he said. "You guys want me to get all the cash and we can settle up ourselves, or you want to go in one at a time?"

"Doesn't matter to me," Rynn shrugged.

"I need to come with you," Hobie said.

"What?"

"I want to, I mean," Hobie said. "Learning the ropes."

"Not a great idea," Dale said. "You really shit the bed up there, and Mickey was plenty pissed about it."

"No, I talked to him already. Apologized and all that," Hobie said. "We're cool."

"Oh? Well, I guess we'll see how cool," Dale said. "Let's go."

"Come in," Mickey hollered when Dale knocked on the office door, and they stepped inside. Mickey was seated behind a cluttered desk. Dale moved up and took a seat, while Hobie stood behind, near the door. "You pulled it out of the fire, didn't you," Mickey said. "The show was swirling in the shitter for a while, and I was about ready to go ballistic."

"I could see that," Dale said.

"Anyhoo, all's well that ends well." Mickey smiled and leaned forward with an open hand extended. "Thanks for making the trip. Have a good rest of the run." Dale shook Mickey's hand and said thanks, but remained in his seat. Mickey looked at him oddly. "Is there something else?"

"We have to get paid yet," Dale said casually, not accusatorily, giving Mickey the benefit of having maybe just forgotten, even though a bad feeling was starting to rise in his stomach.

"Oh. Well, I don't pay you," Mickey said. "I paid the whole fee up front to your man in Winnipeg. Marvin."

"Merlin?" Dale said. "You paid the whole thing in advance, to Merlin?"

Mickey nodded, rather emphatically, and looked up at Hobie. Hobie stared back with cold, unblinking eyes.

Dale tightened his lips. "Un-fucking-believable," he said. "That is some low-grade bullshit."

"Sorry," Mickey said, putting his hands up. "That's just how it was arranged."

"Really. How come nobody told me this?" Dale asked. "Because it's—"

Hobie took a step closer to Dale. "I think I do remember Merlin saying something about that," he said. "About the fee being paid up front."

Dale looked at Hobie, even more confused. "And the fucking opening act knows about the money while the headliner sits in the dark," he said. "Jesus Christ, what an operation." He stood up, then turned back to Mickey. "All right, well . . . Sorry to be pissy about this, but it's news to me and it throws a wrench into my plans."

"Understandable," Mickey said. "Hope you get it all squared away."

"You're fucking right I will," Dale said, heading out the office door. Hobie lingered behind, giving Mickey a long, dark look. He didn't like that goddamn moonface one little bit. Mickey could see that, too, and sat waiting to see what was going to happen.

Rynn was still sitting at the back table when Dale threw himself down in a chair.

"Bad news," he said.

"No. No no no. You better not be telling me that smarmy bastard won't pay, because I will go back there right now and walk out with our money and his last four teeth."

"Says he paid already. The whole thing went to Merlin in advance."

"Oh. So we'll just get it from Merlin, then, on the tail end after the run?"

"I suppose so," Dale said.

"That's not so bad," she said. "Feck, you had me worried." She took another drink of her beer but could see this news was hitting Dale harder than would be expected. Before she could follow up on the matter, Hobie yanked out a chair and sat down.

"First show done, five to go!" he said, raising his beer bottle in a toast.

"I'm going to head up," Dale said, standing.

"Whoa, no, it's the first night of the run," Hobie said. "We got to have some drinks, pal!"

"Sorry, man," Dale said, "just not in a mood for celebrating. And I'm tired. We'll have some drinks after tomorrow's show. Meet in the lobby at eleven."

"Think I'll turn in as well," Rynn said as she stood up and slid her chair under the table.

"No way," Hobie protested. "This sucks. And it looks a little suspicious, too, you guys going up at the same time. Huh?" He smiled coyly. "You two aren't already playing slip-n-slide, are you?"

"Jesus Christ. Good night," Rynn said and walked away.

"I was just joking," Hobie said. "Did it come out wrong?"

"It came out gross," Dale said. "If that's what you were going for, you nailed it."

"Well, fuck," Hobie said, sinking lower into his seat. "Didn't mean to piss her off. I'll apologize tomorrow."

"I'm heading up, then," Dale said. "You?"

"Nah. I'm going to hang around here for a while. Have a couple drinks."

"Don't start any trouble," Dale said, turning to walk away.

"Zero," Hobie said, raising his beer to Dale's back. "Zero trouble."

Hobie sat alone at the round wooden table in a dark corner at the back of the room. He took a long pull from his beer and swallowed hard. He looked out toward the main area of the tavern, where a dozen or so locals remained, finishing up their drinks and having a few last laughs for the night. One of them in particular caught Hobie's eye—a ropy beanpole of a man with a pinched face and protruding pink ears, who was loping his way toward the exit. Hobie began slowly twisting the neck of the beer bottle in his hands. As the man pushed open the door and disappeared outside, a sneer wrestled a smile across Hobie's lips and he whispered to himself, "You don't like my tattoos? Maybe you just need to see 'em up real close."

He stood and followed after the man.

17

The next morning, Rynn and Dale stood in the lobby with their bags. They had checked out and were waiting, with diminishing patience, for Hobie to come downstairs.

Rynn checked her watch. "Quarter after now."

The same woman who checked them in the day before came out from the back and started sifting through a stack of envelopes. Dale stepped over to her.

"Hi. Would it be possible for you to ring up to our friend's room? We're afraid he might have slept in."

"He checked out already," she said without looking up. "Long before you two."

Dale and Rynn exchanged panicked glances, then headed for the door. Things hadn't ended on great terms with Hobie last night, but surely to God he wouldn't have—

No. The dark purple van sat out front, shaded partially by an old maple and partially by the facade of the hotel, and sitting in the driver's seat with the window down was Hobie, fast asleep.

"You think we should sneak up and scare the bejeezus out of him?" Rynn asked with a devilish twinkle. "He did some weird shite to freak me out last night, so maybe I'll return the favour."

"Better do it from a distance," Dale said. "He strikes me as the wake-up-swinging type."

Rynn scanned the ground around her and spied a long, spidery tree branch with a half-dozen leaves still attached to it. She picked it up and crept slowly forward until she was close enough to dangle the branch above Hobie's face. She smiled and let a leaf tickle his nose. His arm shot out like a viper and ripped the branch through Rynn's grip before his eyes were even open. She screamed and grabbed her hand. A ridge of blood rose up in a jagged line across her palm. Hobie's eyes were open wide now.

"The hell's going on?" he asked, blinking.

"You tore my fucking hand open!" she snapped at him. Dale hustled over to look at the wound as Hobie popped the door open and jumped down.

"Shit, I'm sorry! Sorry! How did I do that?"

"She was just joking around," Dale said. "Why did you freak out?"

"I didn't mean . . . I didn't . . . What did I do?" Hobie stammered.

"You lost your shit for no—"

"It's all right, I'm okay!" Rynn shouted, then added more calmly, "It's not his fault. It was a stupid thing for me to do. You even warned me not to joke around with him."

Hobie turned to Dale. "You said that?"

"And look how wrong I was," Dale fired back. "You sure you're okay?" he asked Rynn.

"It's not deep. It'll be fine," she said. "Let's just go."

The two of them put their bags in the back, then climbed into their respective positions—she in the passenger seat, Dale in the back. His eyes caught something and he bent for the floor.

"This a first aid kit?" Dale asked as he grabbed at a small metal tool-box against one wall.

"Leave that alone!" Hobie hollered.

Dale pulled his hands away. "All right, shit. Relax."

"Sorry, I'm just . . . no. No first aid kit." Hobie climbed into the driver's seat.

"It's fine," Rynn said. I have a tissue on it. Let's just go. Get to the next feckin' town and put Horsewater behind us. What is the next stop, anyway?"

"Thickhill," Hobie said.

Dale shook his head. "Where the hell are they even getting these names? Goatsoup wasn't far off. How long a drive?"

"About three hours," Hobie said.

Rynn perked up. "Good. That means we have time for a proper breakfast. I'm starving. Keep your eyes trained for a diner."

They rolled south for about ten minutes before spotting a truck stop restaurant on the highway.

"Perfect," Rynn said. "Let's see what these wild moose-people will put gravy on this morning. I can probably get a bandage for my hand, too."

Hobie eased into the exit lane and swung Midnight into the lot.

As the three of them entered the outer alcove of the restaurant, Dale stopped. "You guys go ahead and get a table," he said. "I'm going to use the bathroom." Hobie and Rynn pressed on into the place, and when they were out of eyesight Dale reached for the pay phone on the wall under the WASHROOMS sign. While he dialed, he wondered, *How many trips north will it take before I get used to the term "—washroom?"*

"They're right behind you, young fella," an elderly woman said as she passed.

"Thank you," he said, smiling—partly to be polite, partly amused by the misunderstanding, and partly because he enjoyed hearing "young fella," even if it came from a 110-year-old.

The phone/fax in Merlin's office warbled and Shirley answered. "Laughing Gas Entertainment."

"Hi, can I speak with Merlin? It's Dale Webly."

"I'm not sure if he's in yet—I just got into the office myself. Can you hold a moment?" She held the receiver to her chest as she looked over to Merlin and mouthed the words *Dale Webly*. Merlin scowled, shrugged and mouthed back *Who?* She repeated the manoeuvre with exaggerated and pronounced facial contortions until he understood.

Merlin's eyes went distant. He rubbed his bottom lip while his brain quickly ran through several scenarios, each playing out in his mind like a mini movie scene on hyper fast-forward, but none had a clear outcome. None told him what he needed to know: *Am I here? Do I take this call?* The process only took five seconds and he landed on a decision: the smartest play would be to gather the data and formulate a plan according to where the situation sat. Merlin took the phone from Shirley.

"Hey, Dale," Merlin said in a rushed manner, "sorry, I have to be quick, I'm on another call. How's the road?"

"So far so shitty," Dale said. "The creepy bar owner in Horsewater didn't pay us."

"Was there a problem with the show?" Merlin asked.

"No—well, yes and no—but it all ended great and he was happy as a clam," Dale said, "but he says he already paid you. The whole fee up front. Said we had to get our cut from you. That's news to me."

"Shouldn't be," Merlin said. "Pretty sure I mentioned that on our phone call."

"Oh, are you? Because I'm damn sure you didn't," Dale said, getting good and heated. "I have a tendency to remember being told I won't get money after my shows. Sort of important to me."

"You'll get it. I pay at the end of each run," Merlin said.

"Since when? You never used to," Dale said.

"So? I never used to take ten minutes to chuck a piss, either. I never used to have an answering machine, and I never used to call back comedians who left a message in the middle of the night begging for work. Things change, we roll with it."

"I never begged for—" Dale stopped himself. This was not the time. The words he wanted to say—and many others—would be more wisely delivered after he had been paid in full. "I'm going to see every dime, right? Swear to God, Merlin," Dale demanded. "No, fuck that, swear to me."

"You have my word," Merlin said sombrely, as though he were advising a pope.

Dale massaged the bone between his clenched eyes, trying hard to keep his composure. He knew Merlin's word carried as much significance as a fart in a hurricane, but a promise was all he could cling to at the moment.

"Whatever. So, when the run is done, do I just come into your office, or should—"

"I gotta hop off," Merlin interrupted. "On the other line, like I said. Travel safe." Click and dial tone.

Dale hung up and raised a middle finger to the face of the pay phone.

Inside the restaurant Rynn and Hobie had taken a booth. She was applying a bright, almost neon yellow bandage from the box she bought at the counter, while the waitress poured coffee into their cups. When she walked away, Hobie stirred some non-dairy creamer into his and spoke to Rynn without looking at her.

"Sorry again about your hand. And for what I said last night."

"Which?" she asked.

"The slip-n-slide thing," he said. "I was just trying to be funny. I don't actually think—"

"Forget it," Rynn said casually. "We were all tired and punchy. And if I do shag anyone on this trip, I'll be sure to let you know." She pressed the corners of the bandage firmly on her hand. "There. Now we have matching war wounds."

"Whattaya mean?" Hobie asked.

"You know, your little self-immolation routine last night."

"Imitation?"

"The candle!" Rynn said, frustrated at his thickness. "Roasting your own fecking hand over the candle."

Hobie's expression puckered slightly, and with mild confusion he looked down at his hand. A sickly purple patch of flesh between this thumb and wrist had blistered.

"Huh," he said flatly. "That's nothing to worry about." He set his wide paw back on the table.

Rynn's eyes narrowed. "You act like you don't even—" She noticed a pair of open red sores marring two of his knuckles. "What happened there?"

"Ah, I just scraped them on something. Anyway . . ." Hobie looked around, then pulled a small wad of tinfoil from his pants pocket and began unfolding it. Rynn watched with a blend of interest and trepidation as he bent back the edges of the foil to reveal a tiny plastic baggie containing a fine white powder.

"I hope that's Sugar Twin," Rynn said.

"Something like that," Hobie said. "A sweet little boost."

"Are you seriously pulling out cocaine at the breakfast table?" she said.

"Got it off a guy last night after the show," he said.

"Didn't look like you made any friends last night."

"I didn't say he gave it to me."

"So, you just buy coke off a total stranger?"

"Didn't say I bought it either. Want some?" He held his hand out to her, palming the baggie like a boardwalk magician.

"No, I've never really been one to get coked up before I've had my toast," she said.

"It's just a stimulant. No different than coffee."

"Right, right," she said, and took a sip from her cup. "I'm always hearing about some poor bastard losing his house and family 'cause he couldn't kick the Folgers."

She watched him snort a small pinch, then fold it all away neatly into its wrinkled silvery pouch and slip it back into his pocket. He massaged his nostril with a thumb, smiled at her and double-pumped his eyebrows.

Dale joined them, plopping into the booth beside Rynn. She slid her menu his way.

Dale slid it back. "I'm just having coffee."

"That's no way to start your day," Hobie said.

"Yes, ask Hobie how he likes to start his day," Rynn said. Hobie glared at her.

When the food came, they ate in mostly silence. Dale looked through a newspaper and did concede to having one of Rynn's pieces of toast when she offered. With jam. Then it was time to get back on the road.

As they walked toward the exit, Rynn said she was going to grab a bottle of water for the road, and maybe some sunflower seeds.

Hobie said, "You two get your snacks. I'll whip Midnight over to the pumps and fill the tank before we head off," and he headed outside to the van.

"Not to be a snitch," Rynn said to Dale, "but just a heads-up that Hobie does blow."

"Really? Oh," Dale said. "That's actually, weirdly, a bit of a relief. Sort of explains his behaviour last night."

"Only it doesn't," she said, opening a clear cooler door. "He didn't have any coke until after the show."

"Jesus. So that was him being regular?" Dale said. "I don't want to know what he's like when he's bumped up."

"You might get a peek soon," she said, taking down three bottles of water. "He had some with his pancakes."

Fifteen minutes later, the gaudy van was roaring down the flat, open highway, with the comics in their regular seating arrangements. They weren't talking a great deal, certainly not as much as Hobie would've liked, so he asked if they'd mind if he put on some music, and the rest of the ride was scored with an incongruous soundtrack consisting of late-eighties hair metal and mid-century country standards. Hobie's head thrashed just as much to Def Leppard as it did to Conway Twitty. Rynn leaned against her door, intermittently spitting sunflower seed shells out the window, while Dale sat in his captain's chair, seatbelt buckled tight, intensely watching Hobie's every move.

They arrived in Thickhill—a thriving metropolis of almost nine thousand people—a good half-hour earlier than anticipated, thanks to Hobie's foot being a little heavier on the pedal than the law would allow. They rolled down Main Street, with the van drawing more than a few curious looks from locals. One group of teenage girls pointed and laughed. Dale noticed, and thanked his stars that Hobie had not.

"There's the gig," Rynn said, motioning toward a single-storey stone-faced structure that had the words Vega's Tap & Grill hand-painted in gold and green letters across the width of a large square window.

"What's the hotel?" Dale asked. Rynn consulted her faxed information sheet.

"Your Merlin has shitty handwriting," she said. "Looks like Oaf Lips. Do you see any hotel called the Oaf Lips?"

"There's the Oak Line Motel," Hobie said, pointing to another single-storey structure that took up half of the next block.

Rynn sighed. "Yeah, that's probably it," she said sadly. "Was excited to see what an Oaf Lips Inn would look like."

Hobie parked the van near the office, and they were soon headed to their rooms with a plan to meet out front at eight twenty for the block-and-a-half walk to Vega's.

In his room, Dale pulled back the orange shower curtain and started running the water as hot as he could get it. He stretched and twisted and rubbed his kidneys. He wondered what sitting at a warehouse desk all day would do to his back, comparatively speaking.

In her room, Rynn pored over the notebook containing her material. The night before, when the crowd was not liking her, she had shortened and streamlined some of her usual bits, and the truncated wording felt better. Sharper. More efficient. She had made the mental note then, even in the midst of bombing, and was committing the changes to paper now. She pulled out a small tape recorder and checked the batteries. She would record her set tonight and listen to the tighter versions of the bits to hear how they play. *The old saying really is true*, she thought. *You don't learn anything from a good show.*

In Hobie's room, he stood staring silently into the mirror. He held his palm up to the glass so the blistered burn reflected back at him, well lit by the lamp on the dresser. He examined it closely and scowled as a voice rumbled inside his head.

Take it. You take it, boy. Not a fucking sound. Show me you can take it. Show me your mettle, boy. Shut up and show me your mettle.

18

The crowd in Vega's was much better behaved than at the Horsewater Tavern the night before. Although, to be fair, the show did not get off to the awkward start it had there. At Vega's there was no creepy manager dropping a sexist turd onstage to start the show. There was, instead, a pleasant-looking (sort of hot-looking, if you asked Rynn) young DJ who gave her a terrific introduction, and she parlayed that into twenty rocking minutes of big laughs off the top, which included a lot of razor-sharp crowd work.

At the back of the room, Dale watched, impressed. Beside him, Hobie took a haul off a pint of lager.

"Goddamn," Dale said, "she's fast."

"I don't know," Hobie sniffed. "They're sort of throwing her softballs."

"Wrong," Dale said. "They're throwing her fastballs and curveballs and sliders, but they don't realize she's calling every pitch. She's totally controlling the room. It's important you figure that out."

"I get it," Hobie said defensively. "She's good. I didn't say she wasn't good."

"You maybe sort of get it," Dale said, "but there's layers to this. Do you know what she's going to do next?"

"Bring me up," Hobie said. "Duh."

"Yeah, but just before that. You know what she's going to do?"

Hobie shrugged, like he couldn't care less.

"She's been killing, the crowd is loving her," Dale said, "so I bet she's going to slow it down. Give them one minute of pleasant, amusing, non-hilarious chit-chat."

"Why?" Hobie asked.

"To cool the room so the next act can follow her," Dale said. "If she kept doing what she was doing, you, or I, or damn near anyone would look lame by comparison."

"I don't need shit geared down for me," Hobie said, his arms involuntarily flaring out at his sides, like a gunslinger. "I'd just go up there and surf her wave and turn it into an even bigger wave. A fucking tsunami, baby!"

"You'd try to. And you'd drown in thirty seconds. There's no—Oh, here she goes . . ." Dale smiled and turned his attention back to the stage.

"You guys are great," Rynn was saying as she placed the microphone back in the stand. "Give me a second here to wet my whistle." She lifted her beer off the stool and took a healthy pull, then said, "'Cause the rest of my act is just twenty minutes of whistling." The crowd chuckled. It was pleasant, amusing, non-hilarious. Dale smiled smugly at Hobie.

"Fuck that," Hobie scowled.

"Watch and learn," Dale said. "She's a pro."

Rynn began her introduction of Hobie Huge, and called him a fast-rising young talent despite her having no personal evidence to support the statement. It was a kindness on her part, a professionalism meant to give him a boost in the crowd's eyes, but Hobie seemed to take it as some kind of patronizing pat on the head, because he leaped onstage with a point to prove.

"Yeah, thanks everybody. How about you give some of that applause to your emcee, Rynn Lanigan." He took a long pull off his pint as the crowd roared their appreciation for her. He set his beer down on the stool and yanked the microphone out of the stand. "She was having a lot of fun talking to you folks, and it made me a little jealous, because that's sort of my specialty," he said, prowling the front rim of the stage and looking at the closest patrons. "So, how about I take a few moments to chat you up, too," he said. "Especially you!" He leered at an attractive young woman in the front row. The woman blushed and smiled and leaned over toward the sturdy young man she was sitting with. The young man put his arm around her. "Whoa," Hobie said, "this guy wrapped his arm around you right away, very protective. Is this your big brother?" The woman laughed and shook her head. Hobie cocked his, feigning confusion. "Well, he's too young to be your dad. Is he your sheepdog? He can't be your boyfriend because he's too fuckin' ugly."

That landed badly. If it was supposed to be a lighthearted jab, it was a thumb in the eye. Every person in the place felt it, except the guy who threw it. But mistakes happen, targets get missed, runways get overshot now and then, even by experienced pilots, and the room seemed to have a collective notion that this had been a misstep. Surely he would understand the error and adjust. Hobie, however, kept walking into the swamp like it was fertile farmland.

"Seriously," Hobie said, pointing to the couple, "he's like an extra off *Hee Haw* and you're like a juicy porn star."

The audience was done with him. The young woman was clearly uncomfortable, and the young man had shifted from sheepdog to Doberman.

"Goddammit," Rynn said, standing beside Dale at the back of the room. "I set a perfect table for him, and he squats over the plate and takes a dump. And I'll have to clean it up, *again*, because it's becoming obvious this idiot doesn't have the brains to."

As Rynn ranted, Dale stood staring at the stage. Riveted. He was angry at Hobie too, yes, but also strangely fascinated. Watching this kid was like watching a laboratory experiment, or some manner of psychological thesis being tested in a live field setting. *What would happen if someone with no comedic ability was hypnotized to believe he was Richard Pryor?* Hobie continued to shoot jagged barbs at the young couple, and a few at the audience as they vocally turned on him. Dale studied the scene like a scientist.

"You know," he said calmly, crossing his arms, "if he had flipped that, it might've worked."

"Flipped what?" Rynn asked curtly.

"If he had said 'porn star' first and ended with 'extra off *Hee Haw*.' If '*Hee Haw*' had been the button, they might have rolled with it."

Rynn gave him an incredulous look. "Really? He's burning the place to the ground and you're analyzing which matches he used?"

After another minute, it was going badly enough that even Hobie began to understand he was sinking. It seemed to be a sudden realization on his part—like he had woken from a nap to see he wasn't in a cozy bed but rather hurtling down a highway on three wheels. As the crowd heckled and booed, Hobie recalled Dale's words from the night before, about taking one for the team. He wanted to do that, to show he was an asset, not a liability. To do whatever it took to turn this around and prove to Dale and Rynn that he was an ally. That he was good. But he couldn't. No mix of prepared material and jovial banter would salve the wound. No jokes could stop the bleeding.

Hobie saw Dale standing near a pillar at the back, waving for him to cut it short, and his heart cracked. He put the microphone back in the stand and left the stage to searing sarcastic applause and taunting. Then he heard the crowd burst into a torrent of warmth and appreciation for Rynn as she stepped onstage behind him.

Hobie walked toward the back of the room, toward Dale, then veered off. He wasn't sure he could face him. The one saving grace he had clung to after the previous night's disaster was that he would have another opportunity twenty-four hours later to prove his worth. When that opportunity had arrived, he instead further cemented the notion that he was a buffoon who had no idea what he was doing, and no business doing it.

He stepped up to the bar to order a drink, but his legs buckled momentarily. He latched on to the edge with both hands to steady himself. Alternating waves of sadness and anger and sadness and anger churned up and over him until he was dizzy. He held on tightly and squeezed his eyes closed. He thought he heard the bartender ask what he wanted, then ask if he was okay, but Hobie didn't answer. He had to stabilize. He leaned against the bar as his large hands began to slide slowly, rhythmically, up and down his pant legs.

The fuck are you doing, boy? Stand up like a man, you little shit.

After an unknown amount of time—ten seconds? five minutes?—the ground beneath him stopped heaving. Hobie opened his eyes again. He could hear laughter. Rynn was onstage, winning the room back. *Goddamn, she really is good.*

He turned and saw Dale, who stood some distance away, waiting to be introduced but looking back at Hobie. Whether it was a look of disappointment, anger, concern or confusion was anybody's guess. Rynn called Dale to the stage, the crowd applauded, and Hobie knew it would be another forty-five minutes of someone else showing the world how bad he was at this. The real spotlight wasn't pointed at the stage, no, it was illuminating Hobie's shortcomings, and it felt like a million-watt bulb. Hobie signalled the bartender that he'd like a beer, and when it arrived he chugged the entirety of its contents without stopping.

Dale was onstage killing the crowd, but he had been handed the reins to a rolling coach and there was little he had to do besides keep it between the ditches. Rynn had, once again, navigated the audience to the perfect place for Dale. She had teed them up so he could blast them over the fence, and even as he was cruising through his material and bringing the crowd to hysterics, Dale was thinking about how much better this run would be if it were just him and Rynn, with no gigantic X factor stabbing sticks into the spokes.

19

Dale came out of the manager's office with empty pockets and a scowl. He worked hard to restrain the anger that was boiling under his skin and keep everything professional as he made his way over to where Rynn was sitting.

"No money again," he said when he got to her table, "so, I don't know . . . maybe Merlin is telling the truth."

"You don't think Merlin is trying to screw us over, do you?" Rynn asked.

"I just don't have a good feeling about this," Dale said. "I mean, I've worked for the guy a few times and there's never been any real problems. A club owner stiffed me on some gas money at one of his gigs, but Merlin covered it out of his own pocket. He's a sick, shifty-looking fuck, but he's always played straight with me. How well do you know him?"

"I learned he was a sick, shifty-looking fuck about three seconds ago," Rynn said, "and that's the extent of my knowledge. Oh, and that he has a fax machine, because I got the show info sent."

"Does it say anything on the fax about how we get paid?"

"No. Doesn't even say how much. Mine's all going to my manager's office first, I assume," Rynn said.

Dale gave her a long look. "Almost twenty years on the road and I'm scratching after every nickel," he said. "You're eight years in and you're so set you don't even care how much you get or when it gets paid."

"My manager arranged all this, is what I'm saying. If I had arranged it, I'd be all over it." She paused. "And now it sounds like I'm telling you you're not on top of your own bookings, and that's not what I meant."

"Well, it should be what you meant because you'd be right," Dale said. "Twenty years of flying by the ass of my pants, it's no wonder I'm in a nosedive."

The two sat quietly for a moment. "You want a drink?" Rynn asked.

"I really, really do," he said, "which means I probably shouldn't."

The vast majority of the crowd had filed out of Vega's. Hobie leaned on the bar, finishing another beer. Behind him, he heard a woman say, "Kenny, let's just go." That was followed by a man's voice: "You get one chance."

Hobie could tell those four words were directed at him. He hadn't heard the voice before but knew exactly what face it was crawling out of. Without looking back Hobie said, "Hee Haw? Is that you?"

"One fucking chance," the man repeated, low and serious.

Hobie turned around. The sturdy young man stood braced, hands low but clenched, while the young woman hovered not far off, looking very concerned.

"Let me guess, Kenny," Hobie said casually. "I get one chance to apologize, is that it?"

"Yeah," Kenny said. "Apologize."

"All right. Absolutely. An apology is definitely in order," Hobie said. "But first, I have a couple questions." He scraped up a few peanuts from a bowl on the bar and popped them into his mouth. "Question one is this: Or what?"

Kenny glared at him through narrow eyes. Hobie clarified. "You said I had one chance to apologize, and that sort of implies there's an *or else*. So I'm curious . . . Or what?"

"Or"—Kenny moved a stool out from between himself and Hobie— "you spend the next two months sucking your food through a tube."

Hobie smiled. He had been hoping for a clear threat. "Got it. Tube food. No one wants that, so one apology coming up." He straightened himself up and away from the bar. He stood taller than Kenny, by three or four inches, but Kenny probably had ten pounds on him. Compact. Wide hands, weathered, looked like he could handle himself in most situations. "But here's the thing," Hobie said. "It *is* going to be just one apology. So my other question is, do want me to apologize to you or to her? It won't be to both of you. And it sure as shit won't be to any of them." Hobie gestured past Kenny to the three stern-looking farm-hands that were rallying up behind him. *The reinforcements might make this interesting.* "One apology. To one person. You? Or her?"

Kenny stared flint-eyed at Hobie for a long second, then said, "One each. To all of us."

"Aw, Kenny," Hobie said, "you could've been a hero."

Dale and Rynn sat talking, finishing up their drinks, when they heard a loud smashing sound come from the bar. They wheeled around to see four men locked in a mass of muscle and denim, heaving amongst a boneyard of overturned stools and tables. A woman was screaming, kneeling beside a crumpled body. A bouncer was rumbling in the direction of the conflict but wasn't breaking any land speed records. Dale and Rynn travelled twice the distance in half the time and hit the pile before he did.

"Whoa whoa whoa whoa whoa," Dale was shouting as he tried to wedge himself between combatants. He knew Hobie's face would be in the middle of the mix, even before he saw it—which he did—beaming with an unnerving blend of rage and elation. A large hand was clenched tight around Hobie's throat, squeezing his windpipe, while a meaty fist slammed repeatedly into his face. After the third punch landed, hard, Hobie looked over at Dale and smiled.

The bouncer hit the clump of bodies like a rhinoceros and the force jarred the pack loose enough for Dale to pull one man away and the bouncer to pull two more. Rynn stepped in, pushing her shoulder into Hobie's chest and wrapping her arms around his middle to hold him back. Hobie held his arms wide and bellowed, "Wooooo! Bench-clearing brawl!"

The owner of Vega's ran out from his office and drove himself into the middle of everything like a UN peacekeeper. "It's done!" he shouted. "It's over!"

"He broke Kenny's nose!" one of the backup punchers hollered.

"I can break yours too if you like," Hobie offered excitedly. "All your fucking noses, so you look like a pack of pug-nosed triplets."

"Shut up, Hobie," Dale snapped. He wanted this finished, not extended into the parking lot.

The owner stepped over to the farm boys. "I'm about done with you guys making trouble in here, Ed. Fuck off and cool down or you're all barred for life."

The farm boys hauled Kenny to his feet. He was still woozy and had a wad of clothing pressed against his face—his girlfriend's jacket, judging by her bare arms—and it was saturated in blood. They were right about his nose being broken. The lads guided their buddy out the door, being sure to leave a trail of threats behind them, promising any and all manner of violence waiting for Hobie if they ever saw his face again. Hobie wanted to let them know he was game, whenever and wherever, but Rynn and Dale kept him quiet.

When Kenny and his crew were gone, Hobie looked to Dale and Rynn with genuine affection. "I can't believe how fast you both had my back," he said. "Looking up and seeing you both there, ready and willing to go toe-to-toe beside me was totally—"

"That wasn't what was happening, you fucking moron!" Dale shouted. "We were trying to keep you from getting killed is all, and we shouldn't have to. One of us could've been hurt. What if it was Rynn's face that was smashed instead of that guy's?"

"I would never let—" Hobie started.

"You're making things difficult when they don't need to be," Rynn said. "All this shit is choices, Hobie, bad choices. Start using your head for more than stirring up shit." She walked away.

"Stop making our life harder," Dale said, getting up in Hobie's face. "If anything like this happens again, anywhere on this run, I'm not stepping in. They can kick the shit out of you." He started walking away and added, "I might even help them out."

As Dale and Rynn moved off toward the back of the room, Hobie stared after them. The choking and the punches he could handle all day, but their words burned like a welder's torch. Seeing their backs turned to him, leaving him behind, ripped at his guts and gouged a cold, achingly familiar hollowness into him. His eyes filled with water. He opened his mouth to call after them, but no sound would come out.

"So," the owner said to Hobie, "should we go do this in my office?"

Hobie wiped at his eyes, watching Dale and Rynn settle back at their table facing away from him as though he was no longer a part of their world, or maybe never was. Abandoned. His face turned to stone. He took a deep breath and said, "Fine." He followed the owner out of the barroom, looking back once toward Dale and Rynn, with hard, wounded eyes.

20

The next morning, Dale called Rynn's and Hobie's rooms at 7:30. He wanted them up and out as soon as possible. The later they delayed hitting the road, the more likely it would be that Kenny and his pals would show up to settle the score.

"Let's be in the lobby in twenty minutes and on the road by eight," he said, in a way that let them know it wasn't a request.

They didn't stop for breakfast until they were over an hour outside Thickhill, and even then, Dale kept asking Hobie if anyone was following them. He felt a little foolish asking, especially as Hobie seemed distant and dour, but he couldn't monitor the situation himself since there were no windows in the van's industrial rear doors. The communication provided Hobie some small comfort, as though he had not been entirely excommunicated. Still, it was clear to him that even if they remained a team, he had been moved to the far end of the bench.

They found a roadside diner and pulled in.

As Hobie and Rynn perused the breakfast menu, Dale stood back near the entrance, punching numbers into another payphone, and soon had Merlin on the line.

"How's she goin'?" Merlin said, chipper and cheesy.

"What's the story on this fucking kid you jammed onto the run," Dale said, getting right to business, "without even telling me?"

"Hobie? He's a good kid," Merlin said. "You know, needs some stage time, some experience. He shows potential, don't you think?"

"Potential inmate at a home for the violently insane, maybe," Dale said. "First night, some drunk dude was heckling a bit, nothing major, and the kid turned into some kind of zombie werewolf and was ready to kill the guy."

"Sounds like he's got your back," Merlin countered. "Good guy to have around."

"Bad guy to have around. Last night he said some horrible shit onstage, almost tanked the show, and ended up in a full-blown fistfight with a bunch of grubby locals."

"Hey, you telling me you never made any mistakes when you started out?" Merlin asked. "You were perfect?"

"Not perfect, but I also never got anyone killed," Dale said. "He goddamn near rolled the van, he wants to punch out the bar owners . . . he's pulling me and Rynn into some very dangerous situations. I have legitimate worries about this kid."

"He's just excited," Merlin said. "It's his first real run on the road, and he's with a big American comic and some international hotshot. He's intimidated."

"Ha!" Dale scoffed. "*He's* intimidated!"

"He'll settle down," Merlin said. "This will all work out."

"It better, and he better, because I'm too fucking old to be getting into scraps and I've been at this too long to be living out of pocket on the road."

"I'm sorry it got set up like this," Merlin said, "but Jesus, you can survive four more days, can't you? Big-time headliner like you?"

Dale hung up without saying goodbye. He pulled out his wallet, counted what cash was inside, then closed his eyes and divided by four.

At the table, Dale declined breakfast again, saying he was too angry to eat.

"Oh, shut up," Hobie said, "this isn't about you being angry, it's about you being short on cash."

"What the hell do you know about it?" Dale said.

"You've been losing your shit over the money since the first night," Hobie said. "You're broke, it's no big deal, I'll buy breakfast."

"Oh, the local whiz kid is going to buy everyone breakfast," Dale said. "How will I ever repay you? Oh, wait, I already saved your ass last night from a half-dozen angry cowboys who were looking to stomp your skull."

"There was four of them, and they were grain farmers, and they hit like children," Hobie said. He took a sip of coffee and looked casually out the window. The waitress stepped up to take their orders.

"Yeah, okay," Dale announced grandly, "maybe I will let you buy me breakfast. I'll have three eggs scrambled, bacon, sausages, and ham, and Texas toast, with an extra order of toast . . . and pancakes." Dale cocked his head at Hobie. "That okay? Mind if I get one of these three-dollar smoothies on top of that?"

"You hear yourself?" Hobie said. "You say 'three dollars' like it's three grand. Have two smoothies. Money's not a thing with me."

"Well hell, must be nice. I'm guessing you don't have a kid going to college then."

Hobie fixed his eyes on Dale. "You got a kid?" he said. "You didn't tell me you had a kid. How old?"

"She's eighteen," Dale said, a little puzzled by Hobie's interest.

"Do you love her?" Hobie asked.

"Does he love her?" Rynn repeated, incredulously. "To be clear, your question to the man is, does he love his daughter?"

"Did *you* know he had a daughter?" Hobie asked her.

"He mentioned it, yeah," Rynn said.

Hobie turned back to Dale. "How come you told her and not me?"

"I was too busy putting out fires you started," Dale said. "Change the subject. You're weirding me out."

Hobie asked Rynn, "Do you have any kids?"

"None that I know of," she said, and chuckled. Then added, "That's a Carol Leifer line, but it's not stealing unless I do it onstage."

They didn't talk about much of anything over breakfast, and not much more over the three remaining hours on the highway to the next town. When they spoke it was cursory surface talk, about the beauty of the flat, open farmland, or the differences between Canadian and American snacks.

"They don't call it Kraft Macaroni and Cheese up here, it's just called Kraft Dinner."

"That's vague. How do you know what you're getting?"

"There's a picture on the box."

That's as deep and introspective as the conversation was allowed to get.

As they were nearing their destination, Rynn said, "You'll enjoy this town's name as well." Dale leaned and looked out the front windshield at the approaching road sign.

WELCOME TO WIRE BEACH

"Ouch," he said. "That sounds inviting, doesn't it?"

A quick consultation of the gig info sheet informed them to be on the lookout for the Brass Lantern Inn, but it was nowhere to be found. They finally stopped at a Husky gas station and asked for directions.

"You going there for the jokes?" the gas jockey asked.

"We are the jokes," Hobie said, and they drove off armed with fresh coordinates: up three blocks then right at the Bubble-Coin Laundry then past the park and past the really old house with the brick well, which is a fake well by the way, and there's a gravel road that turns into a paved road in a bit and the Brass Lantern's on the paved part.

When they arrived and informed the hotel's front desk attendant that they were the comedians and that there should be three rooms there for them, the attendant said, "There's two rooms."

"That's a mistake," Dale said. "There's three of us and there's supposed to be three rooms."

"Don't know what to tell you," the desk clerk said with a shrug. "Says here two rooms. Besides, we only got six rooms upstairs and four of them are occupied. So . . . not much we can do about the math on that." The delivery of the line made it sound sharply sarcastic, although Dale doubted the clerk meant it to be. Regardless, it wouldn't have made him any more pissed off than he already was. Dale took the two keys and stepped away.

"Here," he said, handing one key to Rynn.

"Right. Yeah," Hobie said, "she should definitely get her own room. And I can go sleep in my van, so—"

"You're not sleeping in the van," Dale said angrily. He wasn't angry at the suggestion; he was angry at himself for not being able to let Hobie go sleep in the van. "We can share the room, the guy says it has two beds." He resigned himself to another night of weirdness.

"Yeah?" Hobie said, cautiously. Dale nodded. Hobie nodded back. "That's cool."

"Yeah, super cool," Dale said as they walked toward the stairs. "It'll be like a fun slumber party, only with two grown-ass dudes who barely know each other."

"Well now," Rynn said. "I think we've made some wonderful progress in group therapy today."

A half-hour later, Rynn sat cross-legged on her bed, listening to her opening set from the night before on her small tape recorder. She played a bit, then stopped the tape and made adjustments in her notebook, then played some more.

In the guys' room, Dale lay on his single bed, shoes off, resting his eyes and imagining what he would do to Merlin if he didn't get his money.

In their bathroom, Hobie sat on the edge of the tub. In the dark. He pulled a lighter from his pants pocket and sparked it. He listened to the soft flutter of the flame, watching it jitter and gyrate. He jumped when he heard a distant dog's bark from outside, fumbling to kill the flame in a sudden panic. He held his breath in the darkness, listening.

Listening.

Where the fuck you at, boy?

The dark remained the dark but fifteen years were torn from it.

Shhhh. Shhhhh.

Get the fuck out here, boy.

Shhhh. Don't bark don't bark don't bark. Shhhhh.

You in that fucking pile, boy? I see your eyes!

The dog barked.

Hobie screamed and launched off the tub, slamming against the bathroom door.

Dale bolted up in bed. "What the fuck are you doing in there?"

Hobie couldn't answer. Not for several long, swirling moments. He flailed at the light switch and flipped it on.

"Hobie?"

"I'm good. I tripped."

"Jesus! Scared the shit out of me."

You don't know fear.

"Sorry."

You will be.

21

At eight o'clock the three comedians met in the hall as planned and headed downstairs to the showroom. The Brass Lantern Inn had a substantial tavern off the lobby, which the locals had nicknamed the Brasshole. It had been unchallenged as the community's pre-eminent drinking establishment for three decades, but a couple of years back some competition cropped up in the form of the Caboose Lounge on the other side of town, so this comedy night was an attempt by the Brass Lantern's ownership group to show the good folks of Wire Beach where the good times were still to be had. The good folks had shown up in droves by the look of things, as the comics introduced themselves to the young lady taking tickets at the door. Dale noticed they were actual printed tickets. This was clearly going to be the classiest show of the run.

As the three of them headed inside and met the manager, they surveyed the clientele. Everyone seemed a bit spiffed up and keen for a night's entertainment. One slight red flag did pop into Dale's field of

view, as he saw a long table—three tables pushed together, actually—
with a dozen men parked around it. Their voices and manner told Dale
they had likely been drinking for at least an hour already.

"What's their deal?" Dale asked the manager, gesturing toward
the group.

"That's a bunch of the Loggers," the manager said.

Rynn perked up. "Holy shit. Actual lumberjacks?"

"No. The Loggers are our hockey team," he clarified. "They play in
the Senior Men's Summer League, and they just made the playoffs today."

"They don't look like seniors," Dale said. "They look in their thirties."

Hobie rolled his eyes. "Senior league just means not for kids," he
explained, then said to the manager, "They're not from around here."

"Great. Hockey players," Rynn said to Dale. "Maybe some polar
bears will show up too, to make the prophecy complete."

As the manager went over the show details with Rynn, Dale kept
his eyes on the long, loud table. He wanted to ensure there would be no
extracurricular activities tonight. If Hobie started a battle with a team of
hockey players, there was nothing Dale could do, or would even attempt
to do, about it.

"Hey," Dale said to the manager, "do you have chicken wings or
something like that on the menu?"

"Sure," he said, "chicken wings, chicken fingers, jalapeño poppers . . ."

"Send the team a platter of wings and a tray of the poppers, and let
them know they're from the comedians, who say, 'Congratulations on
making the playoffs.'"

Ten minutes later, as the bar DJ was getting ready to introduce Rynn,
the wings and poppers were delivered to the long table. The waitress
leaned in and said something to the team, and they cheered loudly.

"Aren't you a cagey old so-and-so?" Rynn said with a smile. Dale
doffed an imaginary hat.

The DJ introduced Rynn, and the hockey team led the room in vigorous applause, some even standing. She settled them down, reaffirmed congratulations on behalf of the comedians, and the whole room applauded again. The show was off to a roaring start.

After fifteen minutes of solid laughs from Rynn, Dale knew she would be bringing Hobie up shortly. He looked over to Hobie in hopes of ascertaining where his head was at. *Good luck.*

Hobie looked back, screwed up his face and waved Dale off, as if to say, *Relax, I remember the conversation we had in our room an hour ago. I will give my comedy a chance and I will not start any trouble.* At least that's what Dale hoped the look meant. It could have also meant *Get off my back and stop giving me orders, I'll do what I want.*

"Please welcome to the stage Manitoba's own Hobie Huge!" Rynn said, and she surrendered the stage to Hobie, who hopped up enthusiastically, but not like an escaped orangutan on PCP, as she had come to expect.

Hobie said his hellos and went right into his material. It wasn't cracking Dale or Rynn up—it was a pretty pedestrian and derivative broth of premises—but it was getting a few laughs. Then Hobie moved into more original material, which seemed locally pertinent to Manitoba, or maybe the Canadian prairies in general, neither Dale nor Rynn could tell, and the crowd was really getting into it. He was relating, they were relating, laughs were bubbling around the room. They weren't giant laughs like Rynn had been getting, but genuine, authentic night-out-at-a-comedy-show chortling. Dale and Rynn beamed like proud parents, although no small share of the smiling was fuelled by relief. Dale started to say, "We may actually have a normal—" but stopped. He'd heard a heckle. And it had come from the hockey table.

"I'm sorry, what's that, sir?" Hobie was saying.

"I said bring back the hot chick from Ireland," the drunk said. He was the drunkest of the lot, to be sure. Not sloppy drunk, but while the others looked like they were still in the *isn't this fun* stage of the evening, this goomer with the stitches in his lip had slipped into the *I got shit I want to say and you're all gonna hear it* realm.

Dale was gone. He darted like a jungle cat through the crowd toward the manager. En route he was having the conversation with the manager in his head: *Go talk to the table, tell them not to heckle, the kid is new and he doesn't respond well, this can go sideways very fast,* but when he arrived he saw the manager smiling up toward the stage and chuckling.

Dale looked back to see Hobie interacting calmly with the team and steering the interactions into prepared material he had about hockey, and it was working like a red-hot damn. The crowd was laughing, and the table of players was laughing. Or almost all the players—Stitchlips was still in a mood. But Hobie had backed away from their side of the stage, away from the danger zone, and was directing more written material toward the bulk of the room.

Dale casually asked the manager to keep an eye on the Loggers' table and explained that Hobie was new and sometimes heckling didn't go down well with him. The manager assured him he'd stay on top of it. Disaster averted.

Dale looked at his wristwatch. The kid had done twenty-five minutes. A solid middle-act set, for sure. There were no giant laughs, but plenty of decent guffaws, and even a couple applause breaks for some mildly pandering bits. Hobie said good night and received a lovely round from the audience.

As soon as she hit the stage Rynn coaxed another hand for him out of the crowd. He made his way to the back of the room and joined Dale at a two-top in the corner.

"How did that feel?" Dale said. "I mean, you're grinning like an eight-year-old stumbling out of Santa's workshop, so I'm guessing it felt pretty good."

"Awesome," Hobie said. "It was unreal."

"Well good news," Dale said. "It *was* real. And they were into it. Hey, I had an idea for one of your jokes. If you don't mind . . ."

Hobie beamed. "Really? You want to write with me?"

"Just my two cents, but you know your bit about being hungry enough to eat dog food?"

"Yeah." Hobie nodded, keen and eager.

"It'd be funnier if you said, 'hungry enough to eat Alpo,' or 'to eat a can of Ken-L Ration.'"

Hobie chuckled. "Yeah, that is funnier. Thanks." Then his eyes narrowed. "Wait . . . but why? *Why* is that funnier?"

"Specifics, man," Dale said. "The more specific something is, the funnier it is. 'Buick' is funnier than 'car.' 'Magnavox' is funnier than 'television.' 'Beagle' is funnier than 'dog.' Hell, if you changed the punchline to 'hungry enough to eat the beagle's Alpo' it'd probably get twice the laughs."

"Right, right. I never thought of it like that. Thanks," Hobie said.

"No problem. Good job up there. You stayed in charge, you stayed on point, you never got rattled when that hockey dude piped up—"

"That fucking idiot," Hobie said, the smile dropping from his face like a bag of sand as he turned to look at the players' table.

"No, Hobie," Dale said, putting a hand on his arm and turning him back, "that was pro, dude. Nice work."

Hobie was glowing again. He couldn't recall ever being this happy. Maybe once or twice at his grandma's, but that was a long time ago. This was real and it was now, and he was bathing in it.

Dale and Hobie sat and watched Rynn do her thing. She was riffing some more off-the-cuff crowd work to hone her chops before the Montreal showcase. Dale had always fancied himself as being pretty good at crowd work—and he was—but this was truly Rynn's wheelhouse. He felt like he was watching a masterclass. He wondered why no one had offered her a shot at hosting her own show, then blurted out, "They will."

"What?" Hobie asked.

"Nothing," Dale said. "She'll be introducing me soon. I'm going to get a beer to take up with me." He stood and had only taken one step when he heard Stitchlips piping up again.

"You're a hottie!"

"Well, you're drunk," Rynn said, "and the drunker you get the hotter I'll get, that's how booze works." She turned her attention to his teammates. "Is he new to drinking? He seems new." She leaned away from the table and started delivering some material to the rest of the room.

"I'm serious," Stitchlips interrupted. "I might be falling in love with you."

"That's a sad bit of news," she replied.

"You should blow me in the parking lot," he said.

The room reeled from the comment—a grotesque and unnecessary turn. Dale made a quick move toward the manager but slammed hard into Hobie, who had stood up suddenly, hands coiled into tight boulders, eyes glaring at Stitchlips. Dale could see the zombie werewolf crawling out through the attic window.

"Leave it," he said softly. "She can handle this."

"He . . . won't stop," Hobie said. The words came out slow and broken, like they were pushing through the static of an old radio not quite tuned to the station.

"He's just a drunk asshole," Dale said, "but Rynn's a pro. Look, she's already dealing with it."

Rynn had taken a moment to let the crowd know she thought as much about the comment as they did. That solidified the idea that it was her and them together versus this guy, before she returned fire.

"You love me . . . and I should blow you in the parking lot? Is this your first time talking to a woman? Like a real one, not one you inflate with a bicycle pump." The crowd oohed and laughed.

Stitchlips wrinkled his nose and gave the finger to the room. "Then don't blow me, I give a shit."

"Deal!" Rynn declared. "You drive a hard bargain, sir, but I will settle for not blowing you."

The crowd laughed some more and applauded. Stitchlips could barely be heard, saying "Fuck you" over the noise. It was a final, insignificant volley from a defeated foe. The battle was won—in the minds of everyone but Hobie.

"Leave her alone," he said quietly, his jaw pushing forward into a menacing underbite. "Leave . . . her . . . alone."

"He's done," Dale said. "Look. He's slumped over and pouting and Rynn is back talking to the crowd." He gave Hobie a couple of pats on the back. "It's all good now. Let's have one night where we keep it on the rails, okay?" Hobie turned his head slowly and looked at Dale for a long moment. He was trying hard to focus, trying his best to close the blind on the attic window, but it wasn't easy.

"One night," Hobie managed to say, but was clearly still wrestling internally. Dale kept his eyes on Hobie even as he heard himself being introduced by Rynn.

"It's all good now, right?" Dale said, backing away. "It's all okay." He wanted to stay and talk, to keep Hobie grounded, but had no choice when he heard her say, ". . . from Chicago, Dale Webly." He hurried toward the stage.

Hobie's eyes moved slowly back to the long table and narrowed. Three words whispered low and soft from his mouth: "Leave . . . her . . . alone."

Dale stepped onstage and said his hellos to the applauding crowd. When their clapping subsided, he could hear Stitchlips saying, "Now who's this guy?"

"Exactly, sir!" Dale said. "Who am I? Why am I here? Why does my agent hate me?" That got a good chuckle from the crowd. They were on his side already. But Stitchlips had his own agenda.

"Are you the Irish chick's boyfriend?"

"No, sir," Dale said. "You'll be happy to hear I am not her boyfriend. Which means, after the show, there is nothing to prevent you from blowing me in the parking lot."

An explosion of laughter raised the roof of the Brasshole and the crowd burst into applause. Rynn, who was at the bar ordering a drink, threw her head back and laughed loudest of anyone. In the back corner, Hobie still stood motionless. His face unchanged. *He won't stop*. He fixated on Stitchlips—*won't stop*—who was now receiving playful pushes and jibes from his teammates as Dale proceeded with his material.

"First off, can I take a second to talk to you about the name of this town," Dale said. "Wire Beach? Is there anyone here from the Tourism Board? Because you messed up." The audience was enjoying the show again and Stitchlips was forgotten. Except by Hobie. He glared at the drunk, who sat dejected while his teammates enjoyed Dale's comedy. After a few minutes, Stitchlips stood and pulled his jacket from the back of his chair. Some minor protests from his mates were swatted away as he walked off, but it was clear no one at the table was heartbroken by his departure. The one most interested in his leaving lived in Hobie's attic, and the light in the window was burning red. The hockey player weaved toward the exit.

Rynn received her drink from the bartender and turned around to watch Dale's show, but in the corner of her eye she caught Hobie heading outside. *Now where's he off to?* It was a brief thought before her attention turned back to the stage.

Stitchlips walked through the dark lot, hands rummaging through his jacket pockets to find his keys. As he stepped up to the back end of a grey pickup truck, he heard footsteps in the gravel behind him, and a low, sinister voice.

"You talk too much."

22

Inside the Brass Lantern, Rynn was watching Dale crack up the room, but she couldn't enjoy it. She had an uneasy feeling. *Why would Hobie go outside?* No reason came to her mind that wasn't bad news. Then her eyes drifted to the long table. One of the chairs was empty. The crude hockey asshole had left. *Oh shit.* Rynn set her drink on the bar and hurried for the exit.

She pushed open the door and stepped outside onto the hotel's wooden deck. She didn't see Hobie or anyone else, but the deck and parking lot extended around the building so she moved along the wall and peered around the corner.

The exact moment she saw the two men was the same moment the hockey player lashed out. He grabbed Hobie's shirt with both hands and hauled it up and over his head, bending Hobie forward and using the shirt as a noose to hold him in position with one hand, while the other started landing uppercuts.

Rynn opened her mouth to holler but before any breath could escape, she saw Hobie's arm bolt out between the man's legs. Hobie's other hand latched on to the man's jacket and he stood up in one swift motion, hoisting the man into the air. The hockey player had to weigh two hundred pounds, but Hobie flipped him ass-up like a doll and drove him forcefully back down to earth, headfirst. The man's skull drilled into the ground and bent horribly to one side. His body flopped over limply. He didn't move.

Rynn was jarred by the ferocity, and froze solid when she saw Hobie bend down to the unconscious man. *What is he doing?* Hobie rolled him over onto his stomach, then pulled the man's right arm straight out from his body. He pressed a foot against the back of the arm and leaned forward, pinning it to the ground at the elbow. He raised his head to look around for witnesses, and Rynn saw a contorted demonic version of his face. A monster wearing Hobie's image as a mask. She instinctively ducked back behind the building, then peered around the edge with one eye. That eye widened in horror as she watched Hobie latch on to the pinned arm and yank it straight up.

Rynn was fifty feet away but still heard the bone crack like a bull-whip. Her feet were cemented to the deck. Her hands dug into the rough brick on the wall, reopening the wound on her palm, as her mind reeled like a Tilt-A-Whirl.

Hobie stood, looming over his downed opponent, then looked suddenly toward the hotel. Rynn snapped her head back behind the wall's edge. *Did he see me? Did I just see him kill a man? Did he just see me see him kill a man?* Adrenalin wrenched her shoes free and she scrambled for the door.

She rushed inside and stumbled to the bar in a panic. The bartender looked at her with concern. "Are you okay?" he asked. "Your hand is bleeding."

"Someone is hurt," Rynn gasped, "outside. Hurt bad." The bartender hustled from behind his post and made for the exit.

Rynn pressed a paper napkin against her palm and slumped forward onto the bar, her head pushing into her folded forearms as if she might find a hole beyond them that would let her escape this reality. She caught herself trembling and willed that to stop.

After a few minutes, the bartender returned. "I don't see anyone," he said.

"Around the corner," Rynn said, drawing an invisible path with her hand, "into the parking lot."

"Yeah, I looked. Walked all around the whole lot, between vehicles, couldn't see anyone. Maybe they weren't hurt as bad as you thought. Probably wandered off."

"No way," she said, shaking her head vehemently. "The guy I'm talking about was in no shape to wander anywhere. Come with me, I'll show you."

Rynn stepped outside with the bartender, her wrist hooked through his arm, hauling him along to the wall's edge. She pressed up against the brick and peered cautiously around but couldn't see Hobie anywhere. She pushed her neck out farther and strained her eyes to the spot where she knew, with absolute certainty, Stitchlips had been piledriven into the ground. Only there was no body there. Furthermore, where was Hobie? He hadn't come in behind her, she was sure of that.

"Look, I need to get back inside," the bartender said, a little annoyed. He left Rynn standing alone as she scowled at the spot of the confrontation, trying to make sense of it all. She finally turned and walked back to the door, failing to take note of the empty parking spot where a grey truck used to be.

—

Three blocks from the Brass Lantern, along a gravel road on the edge of town, the truck was picking up speed. There were no buildings lining this stretch, only telephone poles and trees poking up from farmland and undeveloped industrial lots.

Hobie sat behind the steering wheel, buckled in safe and sound, while Stitchlips flopped limp and loose on the passenger seat beside him.

"Didn't like the comedy back there, eh?" Hobie said. "Boy, everyone's a fucking critic." He pushed himself back as deeply into the seat as possible and cinched his chest restraint as tight as it would go. He gripped the steering wheel firmly. "Maybe you'd rather see an impression. Yeah? You like impressions? Okay, watch this." Hobie took a deep breath, braced himself, and rotated his hands slightly. The truck angled off the road, bumped roughly down into the ditch and slammed directly into a thick maple. It was solid contact that crumpled the front end and popped the hood straight up.

As steam and liquid escaped into the night, the driver's door creaked open and Hobie stepped out. He gave his head a shake and rubbed his chest where the seatbelt had caught him, then turned back into the vehicle, grabbed Stitchlips by the collar, and dragged him across the bench seat until the lifeless man was behind the wheel. Hobie propped the body upright and pulled on the pantlegs, tucking the man's feet down near the pedals. With the vignette complete, he leaned in close to the dead man's ear. "That's my impression of you driving drunk. Bang on, eh?" Hobie laughed and slapped his thigh with delight, but when there was no response from his companion, he stopped chuckling and shook his head. "Jesus, you're a tough crowd. Okay then, how about we wrap this up with an old classic?" Hobie grasped a thick handful of hair on the back of the heckler's head and shouted, "Knock . . . knock!," each word coinciding with the man's face being brutally rammed into the windshield. Glass and bones fractured in unison.

"You get it?" Hobie sneered.

He slammed the truck door shut and walked away, back toward the Brass Lantern.

23

Rynn looked at her chunky wristwatch and did a little math, trying to determine how much longer Dale would be onstage. He was supposed to do forty-five minutes, but it was going really well so he might push that and run long. That thought made her stomach sink. She wanted desperately to talk this through with an ally, and Dale was the closest to qualifying. Everyone else within a thousand miles was a total stranger or a violent lunatic. She really hoped to have a discussion before she saw Hobie again—afraid of what she might say to him, and starkly terrified of how he might respond.

This entire event was outside her scope. It was not something real people in the real world had to deal with. A missing body? Was she in the middle of an Agatha Christie novel? If there had been a couple of cops in the room, she imagined she would relay everything she had witnessed, then vomit on the floor to impress the gravity of the situation upon them. At some point, however, something would give her away, and Hobie would know it was she who had seen the altercation and she who had told the police. If he could do that to a two-hundred-pound hockey player, what could he do to her? The thought knotted her guts and the tremble returned. She reasoned a whiskey would fortify her and stepped toward the bar.

Outside, Hobie strode up from the ditch and across the gravel parking lot. As he neared the tavern, stepping onto the deck, his eyes caught a thin streak of colour on the wall. Looking closer he saw what it was: a neon yellow bandage snagged against the rough brick.

Rynn settled against the bar's edge just as the door opened and she saw Hobie step inside. She immediately spun away and pushed herself past some tables, plunging into a dark, remote corner of the room, wedging herself behind a red-and-black arcade game with the words Martian Mayhem stencilled on the side. Her chest heaved but she couldn't quite tell if she was hyperventilating or not breathing at all. From this vantage point she could survey most of the showroom. The stage, the bar, much of the crowd were all in sight.

She scanned the room for Hobie. She saw him walking along the back wall, in her direction, holding a drink, his head twisting about. He was looking for something and it was very probably her.

The panic spread inside her like a network of tumbling dominoes until she felt her entire body shaking. She flattened her hands against the wall and squeezed her eyes closed. *Focus. Get it together.*

The trembling increased as Hobie came nearer. He would have no regular reason to step beyond the ambient light of the showroom into this darkened area, so Rynn knew if he did, it was for purposes beyond their show, and beyond wanting to casually shoot the breeze.

From the moment she first laid eyes on him, days ago—throwing open the grand doors of the hotel with the little round bellman chasing after him—she had considered Hobie to be a very large man, but now he seemed utterly gigantic. The embodiment of his stage name. And he grew bigger with every step, not just as a result of his increasing proximity, but as a by-product of the monstrous nature she now knew lived within him.

He stopped as he reached the unlit void in which Rynn was hiding, and stared into the darkness. He was backlit, so Rynn was unable to see his eyes to determine precisely where they were looking, but his silhouette could not be more squarely trained on her exact position. She wanted to sink deeper behind the red-and-black cabinet but feared any slight motion could betray her, so she remained frozen, even with part of her head and body exposed beyond the game. She held her breath.

After a time, Hobie turned slowly away from the darkness, fixed his attentions back on the stage and took a pull off his drink. Rynn opened her lips and began breathing quietly, cautiously through her mouth, afraid that drawing breath in through her nose might be audible, even though Hobie stood fifteen feet away and Dale was still churning the room with raucous laughter.

She couldn't tell how much time was passing. Seconds and minutes both felt like weeks. She telepathically begged Hobie to leave, to go back by the bar, away from her so she could move. Her leg cramped and her body screamed at her to shift weight onto the other foot, but fear was calling the shots and had kept her system on lockdown. Now, however, the pain and the fear were at a crossroads, and a negotiation had begun. *Just lift your one foot a half-inch off the carpet so it doesn't make any noise as you pull it back under you, then lean against the wall. He's not looking. It won't make a sound.*

Rynn did as her body told her, lifting that one foot ever so slightly from the carpet and drawing it back, slowly, silently—until her heel scraped against the hollow wall of the game cabinet. Hobie's head whirled toward the sound as if it had been a gunshot. He pushed his face into the darkness, like it was a deep puddle of black water, and scanned the depths. Then he stepped forward, immersing himself fully into the shadows with her. Rynn drew in a sharp breath and Hobie took another step in her direction.

"Thanks a lot, you've been great!" Dale's voice bellowed over the sound system. The crowd roared with applause as he stepped back and waved. Rynn launched herself from behind the game like an Olympic sprinter, hurtling past Hobie in a wide berth out of the darkness and into the showroom, running for the front.

As she hopped onstage, Hobie stepped calmly out of the shadows, looking to the spotlight where Rynn and Dale stood shaking hands in front of the appreciative crowd. Hobie lifted his drink to his lips and drained the contents.

Dale left the stage and made his way to the back. From onstage, where she was saying good night and thanking the crowd for coming to the show, Rynn could see Hobie on an intercept course. He would meet up with Dale first, there was nothing she could do about that, and she wondered what, if anything, Hobie would say about what had transpired. She would have to contrive a way to get Dale alone so she could relay her version of events. All these thoughts swirled behind the pasted-on smile she presented to the room.

"Good night, everybody! Drive safe."

Dale settled in at the small table where they had sat before. Hobie stepped up beside him and said, "Strong set, man. That was really great."

"Thanks," Dale said. "How are *you* doing? You looked a little wiggy when I last saw you."

"I did?" Hobie shrugged. "Not sure what wiggy means, but I'm good."

"It means you looked really pissed off and ready to kill that hockey dude," Dale said.

"Pfff . . . that asshole?" Hobie said. "Not worth the effort. No, he just walked out all grumpy and that was the last I saw of him." Then he asked, "Hey, where's Rynn?"

They both scanned the crowd, many of whom were standing and putting on their jackets, and there was Rynn, smiling and shaking hands with some of the folks, while simultaneously shooting furtive glances toward the back of the room.

"Ah, there she is," Hobie smiled.

Rynn was in no rush to head back to where Dale and Hobie sat. She did a bit more glad-handing and chatting with the locals, but as more of them left and fewer remained, it was becoming inevitable. There was simply no sense in staving it off any longer.

"Well, aren't you the belle of the ball?" Dale said as she joined them.

"Just being friendly," she said. "Nice folks. They really loved your show." She shot a quick look to Hobie, who was staring at her.

"Anyone say anything about me?" he asked.

"Yeah, yes they did," Rynn said brightly. "They thought you were really good too."

"Well, that's nice," Hobie said. He took a drink. "What did you say?"

"What's that?"

"What did you say?" Hobie repeated. "When they said I was really good?"

Is this some kind of test? she thought. *Don't be weird. Don't tip yourself. Answer like you normally would.* "I told them you were a pain in the arse," she said with a wry grin.

Dale's eyes darted over to Hobie's, to gauge his reaction to that shot. As far as he knew, Rynn hadn't yet seen what could come out from behind those eyes, and he worried her cavalier comeback might wake whatever creature napped in there. He was relieved to see Hobie smile and lean back in his chair. Hobie slowly nodded as the grin crept wider across his face.

"If you want," he said, "I could be a real stiff pain in that ass."

"Excuse me?" Rynn said, trying to sound offended instead of terrified.

"Dude, that is not—" Dale began.

"Relax, old man."

"You just call me old man?" Dale said, rising to his feet. His pride had preceded his logic. He did not want to lock horns with this big kid, he did not want to rouse that thing inside him, but he was already standing. It was already a challenge, wasn't it? What now?

Hobie didn't stand. He didn't have to. It was a challenge he did not feel threatened by in the least, and they all knew it.

"I *did* call you old man," Hobie said, "and if you don't want me to show you just how old, and slow, and brittle, you'll sit your ass back in that fucking chair."

Dale wanted to sit. He wanted this to end. He wanted to not have his jaw broken and not have his ribs kicked to splinters. But he couldn't bring himself to fold.

"Dale," Rynn said softly, "please sit down. Please."

When Dale heard the pleading pity in her voice, it was clear all three of them knew he was not a serious challenge. His pride sank down to his feet and seeped out his shoes and crawled away across the ugly carpet, maybe for good. He sat down a different man than when he stood up.

Hobie put a big, leathery hand on his shoulder. "I'm sorry about that," he said, with a hint of melodrama. Then he turned to Rynn. "And I'm sorry about what I said to you. The stiff pain in the ass comment. Not my finest work."

Rynn said nothing in return. She no longer knew this person talking to her, if she ever had. She only knew she was scared.

Then another feeling began to rise in her. Shame. She was ashamed of her fear. That shame spurred her eyes to look directly at Hobie, and there she recognized an opportunity.

"If you're really sorry," she said, "you'll go buy a round of drinks."

Hobie looked at her for a heavy, awkward beat. He looked across to Dale, who was staring down and away from the entire conversation, so Hobie looked back to Rynn.

She felt he was studying her, scouring her manner and tone for hints of bullshit. So she doubled down. "Or maybe you don't have as much money as you say you do."

Long moments teetered in limbo. Then Hobie slammed his hand on the table.

"Let's drink!" he proclaimed and rose to his feet. "A beer for my friend Dale, and for you . . . ?"

"Irish whiskey," she said.

"Canadian whisky it is," he said. "In fact, make it Canadian whisky all around," and he strode off toward the bar.

Rynn immediately wanted to open her mouth and pour out the entirety of the grisly scene she had witnessed outside, but she felt certain Hobie would look back at least once as he was walking away. So she sat casually in her chair, watching him go. He did look back at them once, gave a salute, then bellied up to the bar and started to order.

Rynn kept her posture calm and relaxed, in case another glance was shot their way. "Our boy Hobie is a straight up fucking psycho-path," she said.

"Yeah, well . . . ," Dale said, weakly. He was already in his buddy's warehouse, settling into the new job.

"I'm not talking metaphorically," she said. "I watched him go out-side after that heckler."

"He did?" Dale said, coming back to the moment at hand.

"Yeah, so I went out after him, to talk sense into the kid, but it was too late, wasn't it?" she said, her manner beginning to relay some of the terror her mind was splashing through. "They were already into it, and I think Hobie might have killed the guy."

"What do you mean, killed him?"

"That's what it looked like, anyway. Broke his goddamn neck," she said. "But that wasn't even the worst part. As the guy was laying there, limp as a rag, Hobie purposely—" her words cut off as the image tore into her mind and the sound of snapping bones echoed in her ears, making her shudder and gag.

"Purposely what?" Dale asked, not entirely sure he wanted to know.

"Broke his fucking arm. Whether he was dead or just unconscious, Hobie put a foot on the guy's arm and snapped it like a chicken's wing."

"Jesus Christ," Dale said in a whisper.

"And I don't know what to do about it."

"About what?" Hobie asked, stepping up with three drinks in his hands.

"Just . . . my papers," Rynn stammered. "You know, work visa shit."

"You working here illegally?" Hobie said. "Should I call a cop?"

Rynn forced a smile. "Yes, let's do that," she said, then mentally cursed her inner smartass.

"Hey, you gotta do what you gotta do," Hobie said, setting the glasses on the table. "Can't let a few stupid rules stop you."

"Exactly," Rynn said, getting on board with whatever the hell he was selling.

"We all got one life, right?" he continued. "And if you got a dream you go for it. If things get in the way, you figure out a workaround. That's what I did." He took a sip of whisky.

Dale hesitated to ask but wanted to know. "What did you do?"

"Well shit, I couldn't get any stage time in Winnipeg," Hobie said, leaning onto the table. "The clubs didn't like my style. Too edgy, too real. They want it safe, but I tell it like it is. I couldn't even get on open mic night. And the other comics all hated me, wouldn't hang out or write with me. All fucking jealous because they could see what I had. Talent and fire and passion. And it made them feel shitty and small. Which they all are!"

"But you made it happen," Rynn said proudly, hoping to button the conversation before it grew into something unwieldy.

"Yeah, I made it happen. I said fuck 'em all and started booking my own shows. Producing my own comedy nights at different clubs around the city. Goldie's, the Starling, the Red Cactus . . . "

The words stabbed into Rynn's brain like an ice pick. She shot a look to Dale and could tell it had hit him too. They could both see the glaring headline in their mind. "BRUTAL MURDER," it had said. "MURDER AND ARSON."

"Anyway . . . fuck the system!" Hobie declared, raising his drink in a toast. "Am I right?" he said. Then louder yet, with wide, wild eyes, "Who's with me?!"

Dale and Rynn lifted their glasses, hesitantly. "Fuck the system," they said as a weak duet, and downed their drinks.

24

The deep, green water was all around him. Dale floated on his back, facing an endless black sky scattered with stars that he could see even though his eyes were closed. His arms dangled behind him—below him, really—straight down into the depths of the cool, green water. He tried to leisurely paddle his feet but noticed they wouldn't move independently. That's when he realized his lower legs had melded together into one large fish tail. He was a merman, and the idea tickled him. He liked it here in the green water. This made sense. He wanted to arch his spine and knife backward, headfirst into the stillness, flicking his nifty new tail to drive himself down into the cool, green deep. But something kept his back from bending, so he just floated on the surface, smiling up into the night.

Then he heard them. They were shrieking as they carved through the water toward him. The blue bulb-heads had found him again, and they were coming hard and fast, white teeth gnashing at the waves. He tried to roll over so he could better swim away but couldn't. He was caught in a net, helpless. The bulb-heads breached the surface and landed on him, sinking their teeth into his fish tail. He screamed.

He woke.

His breath didn't come for a long moment, but slowly he began to pull in air. Tears welled in his eyes. The dream was getting stranger. Freakier. It was getting harder and harder for Dale to pull out of it, to get his bearings. Especially on the road in strange hotel rooms. He couldn't make out this room at all, it was too dark. He strained his eyes to pan any nuggets of light from the blackness and saw a shape. A face.

"Shit fuck!" he blurted. His pupils widened until he could make out the face. It was Hobie, sitting and staring at him. *Oh, right.* Reality came tumbling into place. *We have to share a room.*

"Hey," Dale said, weakly.

"Hey," Hobie said. "You were dreaming."

"Yeah, bad dream." Dale lay there a moment, clearing the cobwebs. "Same goddamn dream every time."

"In Mexico?" Hobie asked.

"Mexico?"

"You kept saying nachos over and over."

"Nachos? No idea what that's about," Dale said, while all this slowly began to strike him as strange. "You're just sitting there, watching me sleep? That's weird. Go to bed."

Hobie chuckled. "You're a little slow on the uptake, eh?"

What the hell does that mean? Dale scowled and tried to wet his dry lips, but his tongue was dry also.

Hobie leaned closer. "You figure you're all tucked away in your cozy bed?"

The moment he said that, Dale could tell he wasn't. They weren't in the hotel room. *Where the hell are we?* He tried to sit up but couldn't.

He couldn't move his arms or his legs. He felt the bindings on his wrists and ankles.

"What the fuck?" Dale shouted. "What the fuck is going on?"

"Here he comes," Hobie said. "Wakey-wakey."

Dale thrashed, looking very much like a merman caught in a net. He jerked and lurched while Hobie watched, amused. Dale stopped suddenly. "What is happening, Hobie?" he said, with remarkable calm.

"That's better," Hobie said. "You're going to pull a muscle flopping around like that. Or you might smash your head into hers," and he flicked a thumb beyond Dale. Dale wrenched his head sideways and strained to see into the corners, until he saw Rynn, bound on the floor behind him, lying on her side, unmoving.

"Hobie, please tell me what's happening," he said, his calmness beginning to dissolve into a well-warranted panic. "Did you drug us?"

"Well, what's the last thing you remember?" Hobie asked. Dale stared at him vacantly, as memories slid across his vision like a blurry, overexposed slideshow.

"Drinks."

"There you go," Hobie said. "You're getting up to speed."

It was too dark to get a good visual on where they were, but the smell was familiar and definite. "We're in your van," Dale said.

"No stopping you now," Hobie said. "It's all coming together."

"Cut me loose right fucking now!" Dale hollered.

"Stop talking like you're in charge," Hobie said. "If you were in charge, would you be tied up in the back of my van? Probably not. So just relax and shut up for a bit. Enjoy the quiet."

It was quiet. Wire Beach was a small rural town, yes, but there should be some sound, surely, even if it was late. Dale heard absolutely nothing outside.

"Where are we?" he asked.

"We checked out. I checked out for all of us. Nice, eh? Team player, that's me. Told the desk we had to head to the next gig tonight. Instead, I found us a nice spot in the woods."

"But what the fuck? Why are you doing this? Why are we tied up?"

Hobie tilted his head and wrinkled his nose. "I bet if you really tried, you could figure it out," he said. A faint, low moaning rose from behind Dale. "If you can't figure it out, just ask her," Hobie said. "Looks like she'll be coming around any minute. You hungry?" He rose from the velvet captain's chair and moved toward the driver's seat.

"Whatever you have planned, it's not necessary," Dale said. "I don't know what you think the situation is, but whatever it is, this isn't the answer."

"I got some jerky, but not sure if it's beef or turkey," Hobie said from the front. "Got some chips too. Wasn't a lot of choice at the gas station."

"What gas station?" Dale asked.

"Don't get excited. It's an hour's drive back, so about fifteen hours walking. That's if your feet weren't zip-strapped together. And if you knew what direction."

Rynn's voice lilted faintly, "What . . . what are . . . don't . . ." She was trying her best to crawl into the real world, but the path was sticky and uphill.

Hobie jammed a chunk of jerky into his teeth and headed to the back, hunched over at the waist. He stepped over Dale and straddled Rynn. He put his hands under her arms and rolled her onto her back, then lifted her until she was propped in a semi-seated position against one wall of the van. One eyelid half opened as her head clunked back against the metal.

"Easy does it, girl," Hobie said.

"What's happening?" she moaned.

"High drama," he said. "You fucked up back at the Brass Lantern.

Should've stayed inside and kept your nose out of my business. You put me in a bad spot."

"She didn't see anything," Dale said, instantly realizing the stupidity of that statement.

"Oops," Hobie said.

Dale's brain still trolled through a thick mist. Regardless, he began a desperate salvage operation. "So you roughed a guy up," he said. "He was an asshole, a heckler. Why should we give a shit?"

Rynn was dragging her mind into the clear now, her eyes moving more controlled and focused. Fewer and fewer blinks. Hobie still loomed above her, watching her face. When her gaze settled on him, he spoke.

"Did you tell Dale I roughed a guy up?"

She looked him in the eyes. "You did."

"That's true," Hobie conceded. "And what else did you tell him about it?"

"That's all she said," Dale offered.

"You broke his arm," Rynn said, "like a chicken wing."

The corners of Hobie's mouth began to sag. "Maybe you didn't see what you thought you saw."

"Why would you do that?" Rynn asked quietly. "He was already—"

Hobie waited for the words. They didn't come, so he coaxed them. "Already what?"

"Did you kill him?" Rynn asked, as softly and innocently as a child.

Dale, still on the floor of the vehicle, lowered his head and closed his eyes. The more she talked in this dopey state, the less chance they had of getting out of this alive. His mind roared: *Go back to sleep, Rynn. Stop talking. Stop talking. This is not* "—good!"

Hobie looked over to him. "Good?"

"Yeah . . . good, I said! I hope you did kill that mouthy prick!"

"You do?"

"Fucking right. Wish I could've helped."

Hobie's massive frame was still folded in half as he crouch-walked toward Dale.

"And what would you have done to him," Hobie asked, "if you were there with me?"

"Kicked his ass," Dale said, as serious and deadly as he could manage with the torrents of terror churning through his veins.

"Yeah, but details, though," Hobie said. "Like you told me, it's all about specifics. I like the chicken wing thing she came up with. Graphic, but pretty accurate. So what would you have done to the guy?" He leaned in close to Dale's face. "Specifically."

Dale needed to make this count. Whatever he came up with here, he needed it to land in a genuine way that sold Hobie on the idea they were on the same side. His brain, however, was not on board. The after-effects of whatever drug he'd been given, combined with the cocktail of fear and adrenalin that sloshed through his head, had paralyzed whatever lobe or hemisphere or cortex was usually responsible for popping out the creative zingers. He had nothing. But he didn't panic. He had learned long ago to let the silence work for him.

In his early days of comedy, when he was starting to do spots at clubs around Chicago, Dale was terrified of silence. He would blast from set-up to punchline to tag, then instantly rocket into the next joke and begin the rapid-fire cycle again. A lot of young comedians are scared of silence. They think it means they're failing. Or it's giving an opening to a heckler. So they rattle through their act like an auctioneer, barely letting the audience comprehend the words, never mind the concepts. A veteran comedian had taken Dale aside one night and told him to slow down. He told him not to fear the silence. *The silence is exactly as big as your fear. When you're scared shitless, the silence fills the room, but when you're not, the silence sits on your shoulder like a sparrow.* That was the way he had put it—*like a sparrow. And once you get truly comfortable with the silence, it becomes an ally, another tool of the craft to be used as needed, like your parallels, your tags, your takes, your act-outs, your words with a k sound, your words with a double-o sound. A well-timed and well-positioned lump of silence can create an appetite for whatever comes next.*

So there in the back of the van, Dale let the silence simmer, and his mind plucked at a memory.

Many years ago, one hot summer night in Chicago, he and a friend—the one with the warehouses now—were leaving a Thai restaurant near Fuller Park. Dale had let his eyes linger a second too long on a lovely young woman in tight red shorts, and his attentions were noticed by a few neighbourhood guys who began letting him know about it. Dale knew better than to say anything back, and he and his friend kept walking, but one of the threats hurled his way stuck with him. A particularly deep voice had shouted, "I will shove my whole fucking arm down your throat and hook a finger out your asshole and yank you inside out like an old sock!" When he and his friend had made it to their car and had put a few blocks of safety between themselves and the angry young men, they began laughing like lunatics. Dale had never forgotten that threat. It had been so very, very specific.

To most people, the silence hanging between Dale and Hobie would have seemed like a menacing storm cloud. Dale had used it like an artisan and carved out the moment he needed.

"I would've shoved my whole fucking arm down his throat and hooked a finger out his asshole and yanked him inside out like an old sock," he said.

Hobie tossed his head back and laughed loudly. "Well, goddamn," he said. "I asked for specifics, and you brought it! That was awesome!" A warm wave of relief washed over Dale. It was short-lived. "Only thing is," Hobie continued, "I don't believe you."

"It's true," Dale said, his voice rising. "I would—"

"Don't get me wrong," Hobie interrupted. "It's a great line. And you nailed the delivery. Because you're a great stand-up, Dale. I mean that sincerely. It's been so amazing getting to watch you work the past few days. But"—he plopped himself back down into the velvet captain's chair—"being a great stand-up doesn't automatically mean you're a great actor. And that was some shitty acting."

"Leave him alone," Rynn said.

Hobie shook his head and looked up at the van's ceiling. "Jesus, what is it about being tied up that makes people think they can call the shots?" he said. "Every goddamn time."

"Every time?" Dale asked. "You have people tied up in here often?"

"Often enough to notice that particular phenomenon," Hobie said. "Some guy owes a few grand and you slap him around and he's squirting tears and begging and shaking. Then you throw him in the van with his hands and feet tied up and suddenly he's barking orders. You know what it is?" Hobie asked. When he received no reply, he carried on. "Psychology. Like I told you before, everything is psychology, man. Works in weird ways. We may not know how exactly, but that's the shit that's rowing the boat."

"Yeah, psychology," Rynn said. Her voice was stronger now. "Only, you just do the psycho part."

Hobie chuckled. "Not bad. There's those snappy comebacks we all know and love. Well, maybe not all of us. If I'm being completely honest"—he rose from the chair—"I don't love them." He slowly crouch-walked over to Rynn. "I find them to be a little pissy. Sort of shitty and cruel, you know? I mean, yeah, they're fast. But so is a slap. And that's what they feel like to me." He stepped one leg over her lower body. He leaned in closer to her torso, the smile on his face having melted away entirely. "I'm not a big fan of slaps. Are you?"

"Look, I don't mean anyth—"

"A punch, okay, you've done something there. A kick, absolutely, that is significant. But a slap . . ." He was almost right on top of her now. "How do you think that makes someone feel? Would you like to know how it feels?" He rose up, slowly drew back one of his long, powerful arms.

"Hobie," Rynn said softly, "please don't."

"Come on, man!" Dale shouted. "Do not do this."

Hobie's eyes never moved from Rynn's terrified face, even as he replied to Dale. "No? You don't like a slap either?" he said. "You're more like me, you appreciate a good, solid punch. The thing is"—he stepped away from Rynn—"I hate to punch a lady. It's a horrible feeling." He began making his way closer to Dale. "So you don't give me much choice here, pal."

He stopped in front of Dale. His right hand curled slowly into a tight hammer, and his muscular arm pulled back like a slingshot.

Rynn screamed, "What the fuck are you doing?!"

Hobie paused and smiled. "Acting!" he announced, dropping his fist. "That, ladies and gentlemen, is how it's done. Hope you learned something there, Dale. I may never be as smooth at stand-up as you, and I may never be as fast as Rynn here, but if any one of us has raw magnetic movie star potential"—he began dry-humping the air—"it is Hobie . . . fucking . . . Huge! But don't worry, I won't forget you little people when I'm swimming in the heart-shaped pool in my Hollywood mansion!"

He stepped away from Dale to the toolbox on the floor, clicked its metal latch and flipped it open. He fished his fingers past a collection of zip ties, then pulled out a spool of wire and some wire cutters.

"Okay, yeah, that was good," Dale said. "Maybe you do have some acting chops. But why wouldn't we be scared, given the circumstances? I mean, you drugged us and tied us up in the back of your van."

"You're making it sound worse than it is," Hobie said, uncoiling a good length of wire and snipping it free, then doing the same with another length.

"How?" Rynn snapped. "How could it be worse than this?" She immediately wished she could take it back, as her own mind began answering the question for her.

"You're alive, aren't you?" Hobie snapped back. "I haven't hurt you, have I? We're just talking, having conversation, joking around. Is that so bad?" He seemed genuinely wounded by her comment.

"But Hobie," Dale said, "this isn't cool. You have to understand why we'd be upset by this. Why we would assume some horrible shit is going down here. Right?"

"It's just a safety thing. For me," he explained, looping one strand of the wire through Dale's arms, then through one of the van's securing hooks, and twisting the two ends into a knotted tangle. "I need to know you won't go running to the cops about what you think you saw, or what she told you she thinks happened."

"We won't," Rynn said.

"Gotta be sure," he replied as he repeated the manoeuvre on her until she was secured to the van's wall beside Dale.

"Honest to God, Hobie, you're right," Rynn said. "I don't know what I saw, and at the end of the day, fuck that guy."

"Fuck that guy!" Hobie said, settling down on his haunches. "That piece of shit." His head began slowly rocking back and forth, his eyes widening and his vision becoming distant, as though he were beginning to relive the altercation. Dale locked his eyes on Hobie's. He did not want to see the zombie werewolf rising up. Not now. *God, not now.*

"Okay, all right," Dale said calmly.

"So you're not going to hurt us?" Rynn asked softly.

Hobie's head stopped rocking and he looked to her with sadness in his eyes. "When have I ever hurt you?"

How long does this crackpot think we've known each other? Dale wondered.

"Then . . . ," Rynn asked, softer yet, "what are you going to do?"

Hobie turned away from her and replied as though he was detailing the most mundane grocery list anyone could imagine. "I keep you wrapped up in here where you can't cause me any more grief. If you behave yourself and don't do anything stupid, I'll let you go when we get back to Winnipeg." He moved to the front of the van and climbed into the driver's seat.

"Is that where we're going now?" Dale asked him.

Hobie looked at him quizzically in the rearview mirror. "Now? What are you talking about?" He reclined his seat and closed his eyes. "We still got shows to do!"

25

Neither Dale nor Rynn spoke again until they heard Hobie snoring rhythmically. In the fifteen or so minutes it had taken him to drift into that deep state, they had communicated only with exaggerated facial expressions and clownish attempts at mouthing words, which proved utterly ineffectual. So they sat in the quiet darkness, propped up and lashed to the van wall, listening to Hobie's breathing as it gradually slowed, then lowered in pitch as his jaw loosened and he began pulling gravelly swatches of air in through his mouth. Even then, they let long minutes pass before risking any dialogue.

Rynn spoke first, in a breathy whisper. "Is he out?"

"Out of his mind," Dale replied in a whisper of his own.

"What are we going to do?" she asked.

"No idea," he said. "I was hoping you'd have a plan."

"Try not to piss my pants, that's as far as my plan's gotten."

Dale kept an eye on Hobie's head, which was silhouetted against the navy moonlit sky beyond the windshield, and he leaned away from the van wall, testing the restraints. He winced. Whatever wire Hobie had looped through his arms was thick enough to be strong while also thin enough to dig painfully into skin. He leaned back to relieve the strain. Even if he were able to magically snap the wire, his wrists were still bound behind his back and his ankles bound together. What would he do then? Roll across the van floor like a steamroller and crush Hobie underneath him? The situation was ridiculous and hopeless.

"Did he say we still had shows to do?" Rynn asked.

"That's what he said," Dale replied, "but that makes no sense. Is he going to untie us for each gig, then drug us again afterward?"

"You seem like a good guy, Dale, and I wish you luck," Rynn said, "but if he unties me, I'm bolting and running as fast and as far as I can."

"Wouldn't blame you," Dale said, "but I doubt either of us is getting untied any time soon."

"Not very comforting," she said. "So, what? We just sit here and wait to see what happens?"

"Nothing we can do now anyway. Even if we got loose somehow and managed to ninja our way out of the van without him hearing, we have no idea where we are. It's the middle of the night, it's pitch-black out and he's got us parked in the middle of some godforsaken chunk of remote Canadian wilderness a hundred miles from anything. We'd probably be torn apart by grizzly bears or wolverines before we got fifty yards," Dale said. "Probably a fucking Bigfoot staring at the van right now, hoping one of us gets out for a piss."

"I wish you hadn't said that," Rynn whispered. "I really do have to go."

"Better hold it until morning," Dale said. "When the sun's up we'll have a better chance of figuring out our situation. Then we can get a plan together. Until then, let's try to get some sleep ourselves."

The wires that affixed them to the van's wall had been made thoughtfully long enough to allow them to lie down on their sides, so they did and closed their eyes. The quiet was heavy and unnerving, like they were deep underwater or on the far side of the moon.

"Apologies in advance if you wake up in a puddle of my urine," Rynn said.

Neither of them spoke again for hours.

Dale woke to the sound of the van door closing. It hadn't been slammed shut, just pushed closed, but the metal clack of the latch sounded like a rifle shot against the stillness. Footsteps crunched dry grass and snapped small twigs. He looked to the front and saw light streaming in through the windows, and the driver's seat empty. Hobie was up and about, doing something. Doing *what* was anyone's guess. Hopefully not digging graves.

Dale leaned to where he could see Rynn's face. Her eyes were still closed, and he debated whether to wake her. Should he let her sleep through as much of this nightmare as possible, or wake her to give her a chance to focus and prepare for whatever was to come? Their situation was so bizarre, he couldn't determine which was a kindness and which was a cruelty. In the end, he settled on prudence. He tapped at her shoulder with his foot. She didn't open her eyes but whispered, "I'm awake."

"So is he," Dale whispered.

"I know. What do we do?"

"Well, at some point we'll have to—"

The rear doors swung wide open. "Good morning!" Hobie said grandly. "Looks like a hell of a nice day to be on the road."

"Where are we?" Rynn asked, feigning grogginess.

"You're in the business end of Midnight," Hobie said. "I need to brush my teeth. Feels like that beef jerky took a shit in my mouth." He grabbed his travel bag, which lay in the back corner of the van, and unzipped it enough to fit his arm inside. He groped around, scowled, then pulled out a large manila envelope that seemed to be in his way. He reached back in and retrieved a shave kit, removed a toothbrush and toothpaste from it, and, without moving from the rear of the van, went to work. He spit a bubbly white mess onto the ground, rinsed his mouth with bottled water, then repacked the shave kit and stuffed it and the manila envelope back into his luggage.

"Do we get to brush our teeth?" Dale asked.

"Nope," Hobie replied, "you get gum." He pulled a packet of Dentyne from his pocket and popped one of the pieces free from its foil. He leaned into the van and held the piece up to Dale's lips. Dale hesitated to take it.

"No skin off my ass either way," Hobie shrugged. Dale took the piece into his mouth and began chewing. "You?" Hobie offered to Rynn. She nodded, and he popped out another piece. "When you're done with that, I'll feed you some breakfast," he said. "Then we better get rolling to the gig."

"Where are we tonight?" Dale asked.

"Fort Pettiwood."

"Well, that's the least creative town name so far," Rynn said, trying to keep things light.

"That's 'cause we're out of Manitoba now," Hobie said. "Just crossed the border into Ontario, and it's full of uptight stiffs. It's all Fort This and North That, or towns named after crusty old British generals."

He fed them each a few torn hunks of blueberry muffin and gave them some water, then said it was time to get rolling.

"Except we do have one thing to deal with," Rynn said. "I absolutely have to piss. I have for hours and I really do not want to go in my pants."

"I can take you out for that," Hobie said. "I figured it would happen eventually."

Eventually? Dale wondered. *Does that mean he was planning on having us in here for a while?* He admitted the idea provided some pale relief.

"Thing is," Hobie continued, "I'm not unstrapping your hands or your ankles, so you'll have to be okay with me taking your pants down for you." As Rynn considered, he looked at her flatly. "I'll keep my eyes turned away, although, I promise, I've seen beavers before."

Nature and biology were giving her no time to debate; they demanded an answer this instant. "Fine," she said.

Hobie opened the small toolbox and produced some pliers, which he used to untwist her wire binding. He hooked his hands under her arms from behind and slid her on her ass backward to the rear doors, then spun her around so she could lower her bound ankles to the forest floor.

The sharp morning sun gouged into her eyes and she squinted hard. When her pupils had adjusted, she took a quick look around to see if there were any clues as to where they were. *Holy shit*, she thought, *Dale wasn't kidding. Middle of nowhere.* Hobie helped her stand.

"Want to hop or you want me to carry you?" he asked.

"I can hop," she said. "Just to that clump of trees." She jutted her chin toward a small cloister of youngish black ash that seemed to be fighting over the same mound of soil. Hobie held her arm so she didn't go face-first into the dirt as she bunny-hopped the ten or twelve feet over to the trees.

"Hurry," she said to Hobie, as he undid the button on her jeans and slid the zipper down. "Quick, quick, quick."

"All right, Christ," he said, starting to get panicky himself. He tugged straight down on either side of the pants, but they were slow moving.

She wriggled her hips to help him out, and he started tugging one side at a time. "They're too fucking tight."

"Pull!" she screamed. He got them down far enough, apparently, because she suddenly leaned back, pressing against a thin tree, and let loose. Hobie, to his word, stared away at the treetops and watched a hawk circling slowly overhead. When she farted, however, he began to laugh.

"Fuck you," she said. "I'm just as God made me."

Hobie grinned. "Hey, I'm just glad you didn't do that in the van."

"Get my pants up, please," she said, more than ready to get this humiliation behind her. He helped her away from the tree, so she was upright. He bent down to take hold of her pants and without meaning to, came face to face, as it were, with her pubic mound. She saw his eyes taking her in, and she twisted away. He pulled her pants up, went to fasten them, but she hopped away. "Don't bother," she said indignantly.

He guided her back to the van, and back inside, and secured her to the wall once again. Then he looked over to Dale. "You?" he asked. "I'll help, but I'm not touching your dingus with anything but these." He raised the pliers.

Dale sighed and hung his head. "It's gotta happen."

Five minutes of awkwardness later, Hobie climbed into the driver's seat and started the engine. Dale and Rynn braced themselves in the back as the van lurched forward, spinning its way out of some soft, mossy earth. Hobie steered into a clearing, did a three-point turn and followed the tire tracks they had made the night before.

Dale was a little disappointed when he realized they had met up with a main highway after only three or four minutes of slow driving. Perhaps if they had managed to break loose last night, they could have found their way after all. A moot point, regardless, but he vowed to do his best to keep his bearings in hopes of having a better sense of where they were at all times.

There was no traffic on the highway. Hobie roared the van up from the shallow ditch, onto the pavement, and they were off to Fort Pettiwood.

"How long until we get there?" Dale asked.

"Less than four hours," Hobie said.

"Oh, just four hours," Rynn rolled her eyes. "Jesus, the whole of Ireland can fit between the towns in this feckin' country."

"So what do we do when it's showtime?" Dale asked.

Hobie shrugged. "Do the show."

"We're booked for ninety minutes, minimum. Are you going to do an hour and a half by yourself?"

"Not much chance of me pulling that off," Hobie said.

"Then how are we going to work this?" Dale asked, as casually as he could.

"Don't worry about it," Hobie said. "It'll be fun."

"Yeah, but—"

"It will be fun, I said!"

26

The van rolled along the flat, open highway at a little over the speed limit. Hobie didn't want to get stopped by any Mounties or OPP, and he always reasoned that nothing gets a cop more suspicious than seeing a vehicle driving along a dry road on a clear, sunny day right at the speed limit. He figured Midnight was already the type of vehicle that would garner a bit of attention from the cops, and if that was combined with an overt sense of caution, he'd get the rollers flipped on him for sure. Too little caution or too much speed, of course, would get the same result, so he cruised along at what he had long ago determined to be the sweet spot: seven clicks above the posted limit.

From his position on the floor in the back, Dale watched Hobie as he drove. He couldn't see his face, just an occasional fragmented profile, but every now and then it seemed Hobie would be involved in a muted conversation with invisible participants. Sometimes he'd be smiling and enjoying the discussion, but more often it appeared heated and argumentative. Dale wondered if Hobie was reliving old situations, the way we all do sometimes. Everyone has rehashed a past argument with a co-worker or reassembled a confrontation from ten years ago, so it now ends with us making a tremendously salient and witty point. It could've been that. He also wondered if Hobie was just working out new bits for his act. Dale would often do quiet verbal runs of new set-ups and punchlines to test the phrasing, so yes, it could've been that. But there was something about Hobie's manner that made Dale think neither of those explanations told the true story. There was more to those animated moments, he felt. As though Hobie were responding in real time to actual voices. It was a little unnerving to watch it play out, but Dale talked himself out of looking away. Some part of him felt it was important to observe Hobie—to absorb and assess as much as possible about his manner and mind—and file the information away, perhaps to be used against him in the future. It was a scrawny straw to clutch at, but he had nothing else.

Hobie yawned and stretched, arching against his seat and rubbing the back of his neck. When he was done rubbing, he kept his hand there at the base of his skull, propping up his head as if to give his neck muscles a break.

Dale's eyes were drawn to the full-sleeve tattoo on Hobie's right arm. He hadn't paid much attention before, seeing it only as an aggregate mass of colour and swirls without discerning any particular detail. Now he began dissecting the mass into individual artistic components, trying to forage any hints of history or personality from the patchwork.

There were certainly no small number of hokey, unoriginal elements in the mix—skulls, dice, swords, snakes—all bound together by a network of flames, but among them a number of singular and specific items could be noted. The volcano on the side of his neck was most unusual. Time had clearly been spent creating rough texture and highly detailed mounds of roiling lava. It looked three-dimensional. Lower down, on a bicep, a dog's head seemed to have been transcribed with purpose, maybe from a photograph. It was a German Shepherd sporting a dark red collar. Its tongue, also dark red, dangled from a mouth that was drawn back into a contented smile, and the deep brown eyes stared thoughtfully into the distance. There was what appeared to be a fully decorated Christmas tree standing beside a wooden rocking chair. That peaceful vignette was in stark contrast to the image below it, in which a gored matador was being hoisted high into the air on the horns of a bull. At the centre of the montage, in a prominent spot on his upper forearm, was the face of an attractive young woman, winking, and the flames rose up behind her to form a heart. Dale realized there was an almost equal mix of idyllic and tortured imagery. It was like peering through jagged fragments of a cracked window into a madhouse.

The turn signal began to click as the van slowed and drifted toward the shoulder of the highway. Dale and Rynn both strained their necks to see where they were headed but couldn't make out much detail from their low vantage point. They were basically looking up at the sky through the windshield, and the only things they saw were branches of trees reaching out across the roof of the vehicle. Few branches at first, but they were soon passing under an increasingly dense canopy. Hobie was taking them deep into the bush again.

The gravel road became a dirt road, which eventually morphed into a rudimentary grass path, and they carried on beyond that until they were bouncing and reeling along a virginal woodland floor. After ten minutes or so, the van came to a stop. Hobie draped an arm up and over his headrest, twisting around to Dale and Rynn.

"Welcome to Fort Pettiwood! Isn't it beautiful?"

"We're back in the forest," Rynn said. "Why?"

"Busted!" Hobie shouted. "You got me. We're not in Fort Pettiwood. Still a ways to go yet." He rose from his seat and crouched his way into the back. "I'm going to get some water into you both, so you don't dry up on me, and then I have to leave you for a bit."

"Where are you going?" Dale asked.

"Need-to-know basis, buddy," Hobie said, cracking the cap on a fresh water bottle. Dale meant to press the issue, but he soon had the bottle tipping up to his lips, so the conversation stalled. Hobie held the water for each of them in turn to get a few good gulps down, then twisted the lid back on. "Won't be long," he said, and he climbed out of the van.

"You're just leaving us here, alone? Tied up?" Dale called after him. "What if some goddamn poachers or hunters come along? What if they decide to steal the van or kill us, or both?"

"Well then you're fucked for sure," Hobie said. "But good news, we're in a spot no other human has likely set foot on in a couple centuries, so I like your chances."

"How long are you going to be?" Rynn asked.

"Might be thirty minutes. Might be two," he said. "So don't try anything clever." He slammed the door and walked away into the woods.

It was only a matter of seconds before they could no longer hear his footsteps. As far into the underbrush as they were, the ground remained soft and moist, shaded from ninety-eight percent of the day's available sunlight. Nothing grew on the ground except mushrooms, moss, and weird prehistoric-looking ferns.

"Do we seriously just sit here and wait?" Rynn asked.

"I don't know. What's your plan?" Dale asked.

"Get loose and run away," she said.

"Hell of a plan. Count me in. Fax me the details."

"Don't be a prick," she said. "I'm not in the mood. Help me figure something out."

"I've been trying," Dale said, low and sober, "and I have no idea what to do."

They both sat and thought. After a minute, Rynn spoke. "Let me ask your honest opinion," she said, "because you're from a big American city with big American crime, so I figure you might automatically know more about this type of thing than me. What does your gut tell you?" Her face was more serious than at any other point on the run. "Do you think he's going to kill us?"

Dale leaned back and rested his head against the van wall. "I think it depends on whether or not he killed that guy. The hockey guy," he said. "If it was just a beating—even a bad beating with the broken arm and all—it puts Hobie in a much less dire situation. So, let me ask you . . . Do you think he killed him?"

"I want to say no," Rynn mused, "but the images have stuck with me ever since, running non-stop, every time I close my eyes. And I keep coming back to the moment when he pulled that arm up and cracked it at the elbow. The guy didn't react. I don't think someone who was just knocked out could have something like that done to him and not respond in some way. But not a yelp, not a moan, not a whimper. It was like breaking the arm of a mannequin."

"That's not good," Dale said. "If he thinks he's facing a murder charge, or even manslaughter, he'll be desperate."

"He doesn't seem desperate, though," Rynn said. "He's acting like it's all fine. Like drugging us and tying us up in his van is a perfectly rational and reasonable thing that a person has to do with co-workers sometimes."

"That's what scares me about this guy," Dale said. "He seems to have two modes—casual goof and unhinged lunatic."

"That's the other thing I can't forget. His face was full-blown evil. Like a demon's."

"I've seen that face," Dale said, "and I don't want to see it again."

"I think we have to ride his current mood," Rynn said. "Try to keep him loose. Act like, yeah, this is a drag that you had to tie us up, but we get it. Keep things smooth and even-keeled, until we get to Fort Pettiwood."

"Then what?"

"Well, he said we were going to do the show. He said he couldn't do the ninety minutes alone. So whatever his plan is, he'll have to release us at some point tonight."

"I just don't see how he can," Dale said. "He can't pump us full of drugs again before the show. Put us onstage, babbling and slurring and nodding off."

"No," Rynn said, "but he also can't lead us onstage in zip-straps with our arms wired together and try to convince the crowd it's all part of some hilarious avant-garde sketch."

"Yeah, he must assume that neither of us will play along if we ever get in front of other people. That we'll scream our goddamn heads off for someone to call the police."

"Maybe the crowd would think our screaming was part of a sketch," Rynn said. "The more we scream, the more they laugh. Jesus, he could start stabbing us right under the spotlights in front of two hundred people and they'd think it was a rubber knife and fake blood, and we're screaming for help with our dying breaths and they're all laughing and laughing and laughing and laughing . . ." She looked at Dale and saw him staring back at her with eyebrows raised.

"Right . . . well . . . ," he said. "Let's hope his plan is something other than that."

27

As promised, Hobie returned somewhere between two and thirty minutes after he left. Dale's estimate was twenty as he heard the footsteps pressing into the soft mulch right outside the van. He and Rynn exchanged looks of concern and shifted immediately from their state of logical contemplation to a state of high alert. They had no idea where Hobie had been, what he had been doing, or what had transpired, so they didn't know which Hobie would be opening the van door. They both hoped to see a casual, goofy smile.

The driver's door opened and Hobie stepped onto the runner, poking his head inside. "All good?" he asked, casual and goofy as hell. Leaning in, he braced himself against the dash with his left hand. A couple of his thick fingers were looped through the handles of a blue plastic shopping bag. "Both still breathing?"

"So far," Dale replied.

"Awesome. Okay, hang tight in here for a little longer, I'm working on a cool project," he said, reaching for his toolbox. "I think you'll like it."

"Where did you—" Rynn began but was cut short by the slam of the van door.

Over the next while, they could hear Hobie outside, mimicking the sounds of rock-and-roll instruments as he did whatever he was doing. Now and then they would hear the clutter and clank of the toolbox as he presumably switched from one tool to another.

"Did you see what was written on the shopping bag?" Rynn asked.

"No," Dale said, "but whatever store it is, if he was able to walk there, do his shopping, and walk back in twenty minutes, it means the store is less than ten minutes away from here on foot."

"So we're not in the middle of nowhere, where no human has trod in a century," Rynn said. "The son of a bitch was having us on."

"Having us on?"

"It means he's full of shite," Rynn said. "Or shit, if you're still having trouble. He fed us some shit to make us think hollering or trying to escape would be a waste of time."

"And now that he's back, hollering or trying to escape could get us stomped or chicken-winged, or shivved with a screwdriver," Dale said. "He already had my dick in a pair of pliers this morning, and that was when he was doing me a favour. I don't want to relive that scenario when he's pissed off at me."

"We should at least try to loosen or weaken these zip-strap things," Rynn said. "Are they plastic?"

"Yeah, plastic or nylon," he said. "If there was a sharp edge that we could rub them against, we might file through. But I don't see anything like that in here."

"They're strong," she said, "but they don't feel very thick."

Thick enough to be strong but thin enough to dig in, just "—like the wire," Dale said.

"What wire?" Rynn asked.

"The wire he's using to tie us to the wall. It's strong, but thin. And he made them long enough for us to lie down."

"Ah, I get you," Rynn said. "Long enough that maybe I can rub mine against yours and you can rub yours against mine, and yes that sounded filthy but you know what I mean."

"Exactly," Dale said. "If you lean forward so the wire stays taut, I could rub my wrist-straps against it. Maybe it'll cut through."

"Okay," she said, leaning forward, tightening the wire behind her.

"Wait, we have to think about this," Dale said. "I mean, if I get free, then what? I go fight him? I'm no match for that giant psycho."

"You get free, then you get me free, and we tackle him together," she said.

He looked at her incredulously. "We're not Superman and Wonder Woman here. Did you see his face when he was fighting those farm boys? Because I did. There were four of them, each one bigger than you or me, and they were choking him and punching him in the face, and in the middle of it all . . . he smiled at me. He was having the time of his life. I really think if that fight hadn't got stopped, he would have won. He would have beat them all. Probably to death."

Rynn looked thoughtfully at Dale. His assessment was accurate, but still, hearing the prospect laid out so starkly, with no breath spent on the slightest glimmer of possibility, made him seem a little cowardly, and she could not help feeling a pang of disappointment. If that was unjustified or unfair, she felt it all the same.

The discussion died as the rear doors of the van were unlatched and swung open wide.

"Showtime!" Hobie announced.

"What?" Dale asked. "It's the middle of the afternoon."

"Not comedy showtime," Hobie said, furrowing his brow then brightening again, "science showtime! Thought you might like to see what I've been working on."

He clambered up into the back to help each of them swing around to where they had a straight view out the wide-open ass end of Midnight. It was like looking at a framed nature painting—all trees and moss and dappled sunshine with a skiff of sky blue smeared across the top edge.

"You see it?" Hobie asked.

Dale shrugged. "What are we supposed to be seeing?"

Hobie leaned forward so he could share their point of view. He squinted. "Ah, yeah, maybe it's too far away. Hang on."

He trotted over to a birch tree about twenty feet away, stooped down to its base, picked up some dark, lumpy object and hustled back to the van. "Okay," Hobie said, holding it out for them to see. "Big bottle of root beer, right? And here, taped to its neck, a couple shotgun shells. Now," he continued with schoolboy enthusiasm, "you can't really see it, but I scored the side of each shell with a knife and faced the scored side in, toward the bottle. Then, I have this bit of metal taped to the outer side of the shell." He pointed to a three-inch-square piece of steel that looked like it might have come off a vehicle. "So, the outer side of the shell is stronger and the inner side—the side I scored—is weaker. Get me? In theory, if the shell goes off, the bulk of the shot will blast in toward the bottle." He looked at them happily. They looked back with a blend of confusion and growing concern. He pointed next to a small plastic device. "Now see this here?"

"Is that a pager?" Rynn asked.

"It is," Hobie said. "I have a few of my old ones in my glovebox. I used to use different ones for different jobs, but not anymore. I've moved up in the world." He pulled what looked like a red plastic clamshell out of his pocket. "This is the future. It's a two-way pager." He flipped it open, showing them a small LCD screen above a set of tiny alphanumeric buttons. "With this baby, I don't just get messages, I can *send* messages too. Pretty cool, eh?"

"Okay," Dale said.

Hobie pressed on. "See here, I ran a couple strips of copper wire from inside the pager to inside the caps of the shotgun shells. See?" He angled the bottle so they could indeed see the two copper strands. "Now, let's see if I was smart enough to do this right." He jogged back to the tree, where he bent down and futzed with the bottle's placement at the bottom of the trunk, just so, and fiddled a bit with the rigging affixed to the bottle's neck, then made his way quickly back to the van. He sat on the rear bumper and pressed a few buttons on his snazzy two-way pager, then looked back at Dale and Rynn and smiled.

He held up the pager with a thumb perched on a specific button and began to count. "Five . . . four . . . three . . ." Dale and Rynn stared wide-eyed at the bottle at the base of the tree. ". . . two . . . one . . ." Hobie pressed his thumb down, a slim moment transpired, then the air cracked with two sharp explosions in tight succession. The bottle was torn apart in a violent spray of smoke and liquid and foam. Jagged shards of birchbark spiralled into the air and a dozen ravens took flight from surrounding treetops, screaming in protest.

"Woooooo!" Hobie roared. He looked back at them with a face ablaze in emotion—an orgy of elation and pride tangled with a raging righteousness—and his eyes seemed dark and bright at once, like flames reflected in ink. "Even better than I fucking imagined!" he bellowed.

As Hobie ran over to the tree to inspect the damage, Dale and Rynn looked on in dread. Whatever they had just witnessed, it felt like a significant shift in the dynamic. Things were different now. Hobie was different now. His juvenile detachment was no longer an insulation from violence; it rather fuelled it. Justified it. Provided a glib independence from it, so it could spread its wings unfettered. They watched as Hobie laughed wildly, holding up the charred, dripping tatters of the bottle, while the sun slipped behind a cloud, casting a grave shadow across the forest floor.

Hobie gathered his project items and scooped them back into the blue shopping bag. "Better get our asses out of here," he said, jogging up to the rear of the van. "That ruckus might raise some attention." He set the toolbox and the blue bag inside the doors and climbed up. He scooched Rynn back against the wall and did the same with Dale, then hopped out and shut the doors. He raced around to the driver's side, got in quickly and fired up the engine. "I was lying about us being nowhere. There's a town just over there," Hobie said, pointing out the passenger window, "not very far at all. Sorry about that, but I didn't want you thinking you could make a run for it, so I fibbed. You understand, right?"

"Sure," Dale said, giving up any thoughts of ever being one step ahead of their captor.

Rynn lowered her face. She felt a thick blanket of doom being pulled up to her chin, snuffing out any flickers of hope. Then her eyes were drawn to the bright blue shopping bag. The contents jostled about as the van rolled roughly through the bush, and she saw what appeared to be a strip of wide ribbon flopping partially out of the bag. It was not a ribbon, though. It had too much weight, she could tell by how it swung about. A glint of sunlight bounced off one end, and she saw a square metal buckle. She realized she was looking at a dog collar. One that could fit a very large dog.

28

Not much more than an hour later, the van was rolling into Fort Pettiwood.

"We're here," Hobie announced. Dale and Rynn expected to feel the van slowing to a stop soon, and their senses heightened in preparation for whatever was to come. They began leaning this way and that, trying to catch any glimpse of the town. Perhaps they might see a police station, and mentally mark its location in relation to wherever they stopped. They saw no police station, however, nor any other buildings. From their low vantage point, only the tops of streetlights slid by the windows.

They drove on much longer than Dale expected. They must have travelled three miles at least since Hobie announced their arrival. *How big is Fort Pettiwood?*

Shortly, the streetlights disappeared and there was only sky and clouds. Dale and Rynn knew as the van accelerated up to highway speed that they had rolled straight through and beyond the town limits. Their guts tightened.

It was not long, however, before the van began to slow again, and they could feel it make a left turn off the smooth pavement onto some gravel. The sky filled with branches once more as they punched deep into another cluster of trees and bush.

Hobie killed the engine, got off his seat and headed back toward Rynn and Dale. "Won't be long now until it's time to head to the gig," he said.

"So we're still doing the show?" Rynn asked.

"Of course. We can't just not show up," Hobie said. "That'd raise questions and get people out looking for us. Even if we call and cancel, there'll be a shitload to answer. So, as we say in show business, the show must go on! Am I right?"

"Absolutely!" Dale agreed heartily. Perhaps too heartily.

"Don't get excited," Hobie said, smiling cruelly. "This isn't your big chance to take flight."

He grabbed the shopping bag and his toolbox and carried them to the front, where he sat down and went to work. "The way I see it," Hobie began to explain, "if a three-person show is booked and none of them shows up, that's a problem. And if one of them shows up, even if that one *is* naturally talented and charismatic, he's new and can't pull all the time, so that's a problem. But if two of the three show up, and we say the third one is sick but together we'll cover their time, that's no big deal. No one's nose will get out of joint, no one will start asking questions, it's just one of those things."

Dale and Rynn began to see where this was going. At least part of the way.

"So two of us go do the show," Dale said, "while one of us stays tied up in here . . . wearing that thing."

184

"Bullseye," Hobie confirmed. "And if the one who comes with me tries anything interesting, I send a quick message from this"—he waved the red two-way pager—"to this"—he tapped the grey pager taped to the outside of the dog collar—"and these little devils"—he tapped the two shotgun shells that were stuck to the inside of the dog collar—"go boom-boom and tear a big, gnarly hole in the throat of whoever's wearing it." He chuckled. "Might blow their head clean off. I mean, you saw what it did to that pop bottle." When he realized he was the only one laughing, his mood dipped. "Okay, sure," he said, "I can see where you maybe don't find this quite as amusing as I do. But you gotta give it up, I mean, this is pretty brilliant, right?" He waited for them to concede at least that much, but they said nothing. His jaw tensed and his eyes glared. "Come on! It's fucking genius!" He launched himself off his seat right at them, until his face was close enough they could smell his breath. "Give it up for Hobie Huge, ladies and gentlemen! Hobie"—he pushed his face to within an inch of Dale's and raised his voice even louder—"Fucking . . . HUGE!"

"It's genius," Dale said softly, "it really is." Hobie maintained his terrifying proximity, his head tilting side to side, teeth grinding together. "But something can be brilliant and terrifying at the same time, man. We're just quiet 'cause we're scared."

Hobie's head stopped tilting. He stared and seethed for a long, ominous moment. Then he suddenly inhaled deeply as if he were smelling Dale's face, backed off to a reasonable distance and sat down on the carpeted portion of the floor. "Sure, I get that," he said, casually. "So now the question is, who comes with and who stays behind in the headgear?"

"Rynn's a better emcee," Dale said, "and she can work the room for however long you need to cover the time. You should take her and I'll stay behind with the collar on."

Rynn felt her earlier disappointment in Dale being summarily erased. She immediately began to think about how she would play this at the gig.

"All good points," Hobie concurred, "but no. She stays behind."

"Why?" she asked sharply, then wondered if *she* had sounded cowardly.

"Because, no offence," Hobie said, directing his attention to Dale, "I think he'll be easier to control. I've got in his face a couple times now and each time he sits down nice and polite and does what he's told."

"Fuck you," Dale said.

Hobie smiled, then turned to Rynn. "You don't got kids. He does, and he loves her. *He loves her soooOOOoooo much!*" Hobie sneered. "That gives him more reason to play ball." He kept his eyes on Rynn but spoke to Dale. "You want to be around for your little girl, don't you, pal? She is oh so very important!" Dale said nothing. Hobie continued with Rynn. "Plus, I think he cares about you, too. So if you're wearing the collar, it's less likely he'll try any shit. Whereas you, I think you're more of a survivor. More of the do-whatever-it-takes type. I could see you saying fuck it and making a run for it, even though you know it means his head gets blown off."

"Fuck you from me too," Rynn said, and she meant it.

"Hey, it's not a bad thing," Hobie said. "You remind me a bit of myself that way."

"Fuck you even more for that," she snapped.

Hobie laughed. "See? Even scared shitless, you're all but spitting in my face." She hocked up saliva from deep in her throat, but Hobie grabbed her face and turned it away sharply. "That would be a super-bad move, Rynn. So just settle the fuck down and don't make me snap your scrawny neck, okay?" He tilted her head back by digging a powerful thumb under her jawline, then lifted the dog collar bomb, wrapped it around her throat and buckled it closed.

"Not too tight," he said. "You're welcome." Hobie looked over to Dale and gave him the once-over. "Guess you're doing the show in those shitty road clothes. Sorry about that."

A half-hour later, Hobie knelt beside his open travel bag, naked from the waist up, and pulled out a clean shirt. He draped the shirt over the back of the captain's chair, then dug back into the bag for his shaving kit, pushing the manila envelope out of the way. He produced some deodorant, popped the cap and dragged a few hearty swipes along his underarms, then sniffed his pits with two deep inhales. "Like a spring garden," he said, and then looked to Dale. "I'm not rubbing any on your pits, but I can do this for you." He pulled a small bottle from his kit and sprayed a few sharp pumps onto Dale, who recoiled from the mist.

"The hell is that?" Dale said angrily.

"Drakkar Noir," Hobie replied, pumping a final cloud onto Dale's shirt. "You'll have all these Pettiwood babes squirming for you now."

"Yeah, great, thanks," Dale said.

Hobie unlatched the toolbox and pulled out the pliers, then untwisted the wire that fixed Dale to the wall. Dale turned to Rynn, who was sitting rigid with the collar around her neck and a look of desperation on her face. As calmly and directly as he could, he said, "Nothing is going wrong and I'm coming back here. I promise." She nodded with a couple of short, shallow dips of her chin, and a lone tear humped out the corner of one eye and slid down her cheek.

Hobie shoved Dale toward the rear doors. The zip-straps had been cut from his ankles, but his wrists remained bound behind him.

"Don't wait up," Hobie said to Rynn as they slid past, and the two men stood up outside. Hobie closed the van doors and locked them. "Shut your eyes," he said, "and keep them shut until I say open." Dale closed his eyes and Hobie began spinning him around. After a few rotations, he pulled him away, then stopped him and spun him some more. He repeated the actions several more times until Dale piped up.

"Okay, Christ, I'm going to barf. I have no goddamn idea what direction the van is."

"Then open," Hobie said. Dale opened his eyes and they started moving through the trees. "It's about a thirty minute walk," Hobie said. "Be good for you."

29

The once sharp shadows cast by the tall, thin trees were melding now into the dark forest floor. Dale knew it was well into evening, but when he glanced up at the sky he saw it was still mostly blue.

"What time is it?" he asked.

"About seven thirty," Hobie replied.

"What time does the sun go down up here?"

"Later," Hobie said flatly. "Why? You getting a flight plan together? Better be a good one or it could get messy."

"Relax. I just forgot how long it stays light this far north."

"In the summer, sure," Hobie said. "In the winter, it's dark at four in the afternoon. A couple months of that and you're ready to carve your own eyes out with a soup spoon."

Because that's a totally reasonable reaction, Dale thought. As they traipsed along through the bush, Dale wondered if Hobie said things like that casually, as off-handed, comedic hyperbole, or if it was done with purpose to reinforce the idea that he was dangerous and capable of anything. If the latter were the case, it was a waste of time. Dale was already fully on board with that notion. He wouldn't be at all surprised if Hobie suddenly scampered up a tree and bit a squirrel in half.

Dale wondered what creates a person like Hobie, someone so volatile and unstable. Was he born this way? Did his brain develop with two wires touching that weren't supposed to be, or maybe two wires that were supposed to be touching wound up just a hair short? Was it a natural chemical imbalance? Or was he the product of some event or circumstance? Did his environment or upbringing stunt certain aspects of his growth or ramp up others? Dale's mind rolled back to the collage of tattoos that wrapped around the length of Hobie's arms. There was a good chance clues could be siphoned from all that ink, but would it be smart or safe to ask about them directly? It was easy to imagine Hobie happily and casually answering several questions about his tattoos, then whirling around at one question too many—one question that prodded the wrong emotion—and kicking Dale in the guts and ramming his face into a stump. *Maybe I won't ask him while it's just the two of us alone in the woods.*

They marched along for quite some time without saying anything, aside from the odd directional command from Hobie. Dale walked in front, with Hobie following to keep an eye on him, but since Dale didn't know the way to town Hobie would say things like "Angle left a bit up here," or "Head between those trees up there."

Fifteen or twenty minutes passed before Dale saw a light peeking through the woods up ahead and began to hear the sound of vehicles zooming by on pavement. He reasoned they must be close to town and was soon vindicated as more lights began to peck and poke their way through the thinning herd of trees, and he could hear distant voices.

"These woods run behind a small plaza," Hobie said. "We follow along just inside the tree line and out of sight until we get to the corner, then we pop out into the real world and walk a half-block to the gig."

"Okay," Dale said, as though it were no big deal, but he could feel his heart beginning to thump in his chest. He didn't anticipate running, but some primordial patch of survival cells clustered at the base of his cranium and began pumping copious amounts of adrenalin into his system. His ancient ancestors had bequeathed him two options—fight or flight—and were pushing hard for him to pick his poison.

They pressed along inside the nearest file of ash and birch, until Hobie suddenly gasped and leaped sideways. "Fuck me!" he shouted, stumbling backward, wide-eyed, grabbing at a tree to barely keep his balance. Dale whirled his head round to find the source of alarm.

A pair of fat raccoons gawked up at them as if to say, "What the hell are you doing in here? You got roads!" The critters hopped clear of the trees and quickened their pace toward a rusty dumpster behind a restaurant—firing one short over-the-shoulder glance back to ensure they weren't being followed.

Hobie was ghostly pale and his breathing came in rapid, choppy chunks. "I hate those goddamn things," he finally said with a scowl. Dale wasn't a fan of raccoons either, but he found it strange that a man Hobie's size, with his physical and mental capacity for violence, would be so noticeably rattled by the creatures. "Move!" Hobie said, and gave Dale an impatient push.

As the two men drew almost parallel with the far end of the plaza, Dale assumed he would hear Hobie say something like "Okay, step out here and head along the sidewalk," and to that end began veering toward the edge of the wood. But when Hobie did speak, it was something different altogether.

"Well, lookie, lookie here."

Hobie's gaze was fixed beyond the trees toward the far end of the plaza. The shop at the end of the building was a doughnut-and-coffee joint called Jimmo's, according to the red-and-green sign that illuminated the parking area, and there, between some crudely painted lines on the pavement, sat a police cruiser. Two cops were chatting across the hood.

Hobie grinned as he watched them. The younger cop seemed to be on the final stretch of a joke, bearing down on the punchline, and the other one hung on her every word. Neither Hobie nor Dale could make out the kicker, but it doubled the one over like he'd been crotched. He laughed hard enough to spill some hot coffee on his hand and cursed a little, but kept right on laughing.

Dale's attention shifted to Hobie, who seemed tremendously amused by the scenario. Hobie felt Dale's eyes on him. The two stared at each other, each curious to see how the other would react to this new wrinkle.

Hobie took hold of Dale's shoulders and turned him around to face away. Dale expected to feel a gag being dragged across his mouth and wrenched into a tight knot against the back of his head. Instead, he felt the touch of something cold on his wrist. He heard a single metallic *snip*, and the nylon strap popped loose and landed limply on the forest floor.

"Golden opportunity," Hobie whispered into his ear. "Rynn would understand."

Dale looked to the cops, but he wasn't thinking of Rynn. He thought of Vanessa. An album of stills and videos folded open in his mind: Vanessa being born, wailing and wriggling, then calming when he put his pinky finger in her palm. The sensation of her impossibly tiny hand clamping around it. Vanessa throwing handfuls of wet cereal from her high chair. Vanessa on a tricycle, a bicycle, a skateboard. Frustrated at failed attempts to parallel park the car. Tears as she revealed the scratch on the fender where she'd cornered too close to a telephone pole. Her head on his chest as they hugged and agreed not to tell Mom. This was his chance. *Rynn would understand.* Those cops were his ticket back to Vanessa. *Rynn would understand.* They could ensure he would always be there for his daughter. He could see her graduate college. He could see her wedding. Could hear her singing softly, hear her laughing loudly. Could imagine his own screams of terror and desperation as he burst through the trees, flailing toward the cops, begging for help, bellowing about a madman in a purple van. Could hear a bang, could see a flash and a dark red cloud spraying across Rynn's face. Could see her wide, white eyes staring stunned at the carpeted ceiling. Even then, with her throat blown open, she still might understand.

But he never would.

"What time does our show start?" Dale asked.

"Attaboy," Hobie said, and the two of them pressed on past the building, stepping out onto a sidewalk under the pale light of a street-lamp, and walking up the block toward a bar called the Hive.

30

As the sun found its way down to the horizon, the orange and lavender stripes that were smeared across the sky blended into a cool coal grey, but the inside of Hobie's van had dipped further into darkness. Rynn sat against the wall, teetering between openly weeping and nodding off to sleep. The tension of the last few hours and the terror of her situation had dragged her emotions through the dirt, so she found herself balancing on a narrow ledge between fear and exhaustion.

What if something does go wrong? she thought. *What if Dale says one wrong word or makes one sketchy gesture, and Hobie's eyes glaze over into that weird rage and he decides to teach us both a lesson? Only it won't be a lesson I learn, will it? I will be the lesson. I'm the frog that gets dissected while the squeamish kids look away in disgust. I'm the frog that the mean, psychotic kid sticks a firework into and lights the fuse while the other snot-faced kids laugh. I hated those kids. They laughed out of fear, I know. Fear of what would happen if they didn't laugh. Fear of becoming the frog if they didn't play along. But I hated them and their fears. I didn't play along and look at me now—I'm the fucking frog. At least no one is laughing. No one will even see it when my head gets blown clean off. At least it'll be quick, I suppose.*

She began to weep again, but not for herself. *Aw, Ma, you poor wee luckless thing—the only man you ever loved got ripped away from you, and now you're on the brink of losing your only child as well. Why? How can life even be like this? Crueller than any snot-nosed kid could dream of being. You're a cruel, immature, insecure sack of shite, life, and you can go fuck yourself!*

She pushed her back up against the wall of the van. *I'm not letting it end like this. I'm not dying in some stupid purple van because I happened to see a sick kid give in to evil. My ma is not going to lose her daughter because someone wouldn't get the help they need. I'm not missing my golden opportunity and letting my dream get crumpled and pissed on because some nutcake can't keep his oars in the water. I'm going to survive. I'm going to get out of this. And I'm going to be the one who is fucking HUGE!*

She roared, kicking her bound feet, stomping both heels into the floor. She screamed as loudly as she could, a primal, unhinged wail, "HUUUUUUUUUGE!" until her lungs emptied completely, and the van returned to silence.

Then, through a curtain of searing tears her eyes saw the toolbox that sat near the doors.

Dale and Hobie walked up the steps to the Hive and went inside. It was smoky and dim, and well populated. A sheet of posterboard pinned up inside the entrance hall touted that tonight was, indeed, Comedy Night. It featured three black-and-white headshots. One showed Rynn grinning wryly and looking off camera, one showed Hobie making a fist at a rubber chicken, and the third, taped up under the phrase

HEADLINING THE SHOW, was of a smiling dude in a sports coat and skinny tie with the name Jamie Hutchinson emblazoned across the bottom.

"You look different in a suit," Hobie said.

"I booked this run last-minute," Dale said. "I guess that's the dude that cancelled. Or got cancelled."

"Too bad for him!" Hobie said as he moved away into the bar, looking for someone who worked there.

"Yeah," Dale muttered. "Poor guy is missing out on all this." He followed along, and they were soon pointed in the direction of the manager, Percy, a stumpy fifty-year-old with a bad perm, a shirt unbuttoned to his diaphragm, and a ropey gold chain snaking its way through a nasty nest of chest hair. He looked like a guy who had bet the farm on disco fifteen years ago and refused to let the dream die. He was hanging on tight for the comeback.

"You the comedians?" Percy said.

"We are," Hobie replied. "Your poster's wrong, though. Headliner isn't Hutchinson, it's Webly." He wrapped a long arm around Dale's shoulder. "Dale Webly, right here, all the way from Chicago, U.S.A."

"Yeah, I got word about the change a few days back," Percy said.

Hobie gaped at him. "And you didn't bother to change the poster?"

Percy shrugged. "Nobody gives much of a shit. No offence, Mr. Webber. I'm sure you're terrific, but folks just come for comedy. They don't much care who's spouting it."

"You're preaching to the choir here," Dale said. The fact stunk, but it was a fact nonetheless, and its stench had grown familiar to Dale many years ago.

"Where's the gal?" Percy asked.

"Sick as a dog," Hobie said. "Food poisoning, we think, from some truck stop shrimp. Honest to Jesus, who orders seafood at a goddamn truck stop in the middle of the prairie? She can't stop barfing. Might head off right after the show and get her to a hospital, poor thing."

Dale was impressed. Hobie lied so easily and convincingly. It was second nature, like he had been spitting bullshit all his life. Son of a bitch probably *would* do well in Hollywood.

Hobie assured Percy they would not short him on the show—that he and Dale would cover the time and all would be good. Percy seemed satisfied and left the two comedians alone to prepare. Preparing meant getting drinks at the bar, which they promptly did.

"You want me to go up first or last?" Dale asked.

"Both," Hobie said, taking a pull off his beer.

"I'm covering the whole ninety minutes myself?"

"I'll do my time," Hobie said, "but I don't think it's a good idea for me to go up first and set the tone for the room. Do you? I'm too dynamic. So you go up and open the show, get everyone in a good mood. Then you bring me up, I do my time, then you close the show with whatever time's needed to make up the difference. How's that sound?"

Dale shrugged. "A little weird, but we can make it work." He wasn't overly concerned with providing the citizens of Fort Pettiwood with the greatest night of comedy they had ever witnessed. On his mental list of priorities, "quality show" had been shuffled several notches below "stay alive."

Hobie rested his elbow on the bar's thickly lacquered top and scooped a few pretzels from a small bowl. Dale saw the woman again—the pretty winking woman wreathed in a flaming heart on Hobie's forearm. *If I ever want to know that story, now's the time to ask. A hundred people around us and Hobie not wanting to draw attention to our situation. Now or never. Keep it light. Maybe start with some of the other pictures first.*

"Is that a Christmas tree?" Dale said, poking a thumb toward that particular bit of artwork on Hobie's arm.

"Yeah," Hobie said, examining it himself. "Sort of an odd thing to have on a tattoo, I know. I used to spend Christmas with my grandma when I was a kid. Great lady. Some of the best times of my life were just hanging with her. She's dead now. That's why I have the empty rocking chair there." He paused. "Pretty fucking deep, eh?" he said, in what felt like a rare moment of reflective humility.

"That your dog?" Dale asked, waving a finger at the pensive German Shepherd.

"Not really," Hobie said. "Yard dog. But he was a pal. True blue. Looked after me. Protected me." His eyes grew colder as his mind slipped into reverse and rolled backward. "That's what got him killed in the end."

Yard dog . . . ? It seemed to Dale that Memory Lane might not be such a terrific place to go for a stroll with Hobie, but he also felt close to something. Like they might be just around the corner from a snippet that could shine some light onto his captor's headspace.

"That volcano on your neck is super detailed," Dale said. "Nice work, whoever did that. Almost looks three-D."

"I suppose," Hobie said, in a flat tone that relayed no more details would be forthcoming.

Dale looked up at the clock above the bar. It read one minute to eight. One minute to showtime. One minute to Dale having a legitimate reason to step away and get in front of the audience-slash-witnesses. There would never be a better time to ask. *Tread lightly.*

"And . . . who's she?"

Hobie's eyes snapped up from his arm and locked onto Dale's face. Dale's stomach tightened, though he tried not to show it. The heart of flames suggested a fondness for the woman, so he reasoned it might be wise to pay a compliment. "She's pretty."

"That's my mom," Hobie said, "so mind how you go."

"All right," Dale said, raising his hands defensively. "I didn't mean anything. I'm just saying. My mom looked more like Uncle Charlie off *My Three Sons.*"

Hobie's grim stare held firm for several seconds, then he chuckled. "Harsh." He took another swig from his beer. "You said your mom *looked* like Uncle Charlie, not *looks.* She gone?"

"Yeah," Dale said. "Four years ago. Almost five now. Heart attack."

"Mine too," Hobie said. "Not a heart attack, but . . ." The sentence ended there.

"How did she die?" Dale asked, bracing himself for a thunderclap. None came. Hobie quietly examined his beer bottle, scratching at the label with his thumb.

"Probably time to get this show on the road," he finally said, then tipped his beer up and guzzled the rest of its contents.

Disco Percy went onstage to introduce Dale and used the exact phrase Hobie had offered up earlier: "All the way from Chicago, U.S.A.!"

As Dale made his way to the front, his thoughts were on Rynn and how she was coping. How terrified she must be with that evil contraption pressed against her throat. He told himself there was no way he would be able to pull off any kind of half-decent show in this state of mind. But, as experience had shown so many times over the years, any distraction he might be wrestling with in real life would always climb into the backseat and have a nap once that microphone got in his hand and the spotlight hit his cheek.

There had been times on the road when he had such a splitting head-ache, any word over a whisper would jam white-hot needles into his eye, and yet when he got onstage the pain would dissipate for the duration of his show, only to crank up again after he said good night and stepped into the dark. Once, he had the flu so bad he couldn't go fifteen minutes without vomiting and was too dizzy to stand all day, yet he effortlessly pulled off forty-five minutes at the Laugh Resort later that night, then vomited as soon as he was back in his hotel room. One of the best shows of his career happened two hours after hearing his mother had died. He bawled like a baby for two hours before the gig, got an hour of big laughs, then bawled himself to sleep that night.

All comedians seemed to have stories like that. His personal theory held it had something to do with the fact that comedy isn't reality, it's a distorted funhouse mirror reflecting reality in twisted, ridiculous ways. In order to reflect, to bounce something back, there has to be distance. So comedy walks beside reality, just a step or two apart, playing catch. That gap allows it to keep walking for a while when reality stumbles and falls.

Dale saw it happen again that night in Fort Pettiwood. His mind was definitely on the predicament, the volatility, the danger, the fear, but all the while his comedy strolled on ahead, planting set-ups and plucking punchlines and harvesting huge laughs off the unsuspecting locals. If it was comedy by rote, no one could tell.

After twenty minutes, he asked the crowd if they were ready for him to bring up their next act. The audience applauded enthusiastically.

"You're really going to enjoy this guy," Dale said into the microphone as he clipped it back into the stand. "I've been on the road with him for a few days now and let me tell you, it's been wild. He has a very unique way of looking at things and a real original mind, so please welcome Hobie Huge!"

Hobie bounced up onstage and waggled a "hang loose" hand gesture at the crowd. He shook hands with Dale as they traded places and gave him a sincere smile.

"Thanks for the sweet intro, buddy," Hobie said, then leaned in closer to Dale and whispered under the applause, "Rynn wants you to stay where I can see you. Park your ass at the near end of the bar so you're lit by that stupid neon sign and don't fucking move."

Hobie let go, spun away from Dale and snatched the mic out of the stand. "Who's partying in Fort Pettiwood tonight?" he shouted. The crowd whooped and hollered as Dale made his way from the stage to the near end of the bar and sat under a blue-and-white neon sign promoting Wolfmoon Traditional Ale with the slogan "Eat, Drink and Be Hairy."

He watched Hobie jerking around onstage. He was doing all right, insomuch as he had everyone's attention—he was, after all, "dynamic"— but there weren't any real laughs. The audience chuckled in the spots where it was clear they were supposed to chuckle. They were playing along in hopes the cooperation would lead to bigger things. Bigger things were not forthcoming, but Hobie looked happy regardless. He was illuminated and amplified, and every eye was on him. That seemed to be all he needed.

Maybe, Dale thought, while Hobie was busy absorbing the attention, he could formulate a solution. Was there any way he could leave without Hobie noticing? Could he even find his way back to the van? Could he find a cop? Would that even help, or would any of this just get Rynn killed?

Hobie finished a loud, meandering, half-baked thought about smuggling drugs "inside your dink-hole because no one looks there" and punctuated the moronic bit by gyrating his crotch cartoonishly. Then, as if in telepathic response to the very questions Dale was mulling at the bar, Hobie reached into his pants pocket and pulled out his little red two-way pager. "Oops," he said, holding it up and looking over at Dale, a dark, menacing grin on his face. "Better take my pager out of my pants while I'm jumping around up here. Wouldn't want to send a message by mistake." The true message had been sent to Dale in that moment, loud and clear. Hobie kept his eyes locked on him until there was a subtle nod of understanding. "Okay, then," he said. "I'll just set this here within quick arm's reach." He placed the pager on the stool. "In case the Leno show needs to get hold of me."

Dale sat resigned for the rest of Hobie's set. It was difficult to remember a time in his life when he'd felt as helpless. Only one came to mind. It was years ago—1980, to be exact. He had spent almost two straight months away from home, doing shows on the road. He and Brandy were on rocky ground because of his time away, when she called his hotel room one night and a woman answered. Brandy assumed the worst and flew into a rage. Dale tried to explain it was just the other comedian he was working with and they were just hanging out after the show—but Brandy wouldn't hear it. She certainly wouldn't buy it. Back home, his explanations and promises were like tin pellets bouncing off her iron conviction that he had cheated, and the only thing she wanted to hear from him was the sound of his bags being packed and the door of their home closing behind him. She demanded he leave and gave him no option. Vanessa—four years old at the time—was wailing and begging him not to go. He had no choice then, and no choice now. Dale and Brandy had spent almost a year apart before getting back together. Despite their marriage never being fully solid again, it hobbled along for over a decade, until Vanessa graduated high school. Brandy filed for divorce a few months later.

After twenty-five minutes of meandering, convoluted comedy, Hobie said good night and bent into a deep, dramatic bow as though the audience was about to launch onto their feet in hysterics of adulation. Instead, they applauded politely. Dale stepped up onstage and extro'd Hobie, then did another twenty minutes to bridge the deficit on the clock before wrapping up the show and telling the crowd to drive safely.

Hobie was at the bar, taking a drink from a fresh beer, when Dale stepped up.

"We should probably be getting back," Dale said.

"No rush. Let's have a couple drinks," Hobie said. "You know, you and me haven't really got to know each other yet."

"I think we have a pretty good idea," Dale said, a little too sharply.

"Oh. Well, aren't you close-fucking-minded," Hobie snapped. He took another drink. "You think you know about me?" he said, his voice rising. "You think you have any fuckin' idea about who I am or what I think or what I've done?"

"No, no, of course not," Dale said, sitting down beside him and signalling to the bartender. "Can I get a beer over here?" He turned back to Hobie. "I just mean it's been a few days, and . . . look, do you want to leave Rynn alone this long? What if she's gotten loose?"

Hobie's face twisted with disgust. "Wow, you really do think I'm an idiot."

"No, I don't, but no matter how perfectly you planned things—"

"I mean you think I'm stupid enough to be manipulated by your shitty lies. Like I'd believe you want to get back because Rynn might have escaped. Fuck sake. If you really thought that, you'd want to sit down and keep me here for the next ten hours while she high-tailed it." He took a couple of long hauls from his bottle, then burped. "You don't want to hang out with me, fine. Go fuck off and see what happens."

"No, I'm good. Let's have some drinks," Dale said.

Disco Percy approached and whispered in Hobie's ear. Hobie stood.

"Yep," he said, then he gripped the back of Dale's neck with a rough, hard hand. "You're coming with me."

Dale stood, confused, and the two of them followed Percy out of the barroom, into the back.

Percy's office belied his dreams of disco, with hockey sticks, jerseys and other sports paraphernalia framed and hung on every vertical surface. There was also a stuffed black bear standing up in the corner, trying to look as fierce as it could while having a bright Hawaiian lei draped around its neck. Percy was, apparently, a layered individual.

"So . . . we're doing this here? Now?" Percy asked.

"Yeah," Hobie said. "Doesn't matter if he knows, now."

"Knows what?" Dale asked.

"Want me to count it out?" Percy asked.

"Are you ripping me off?" Hobie asked.

"No."

"Then you don't have to count it."

"Wait . . . what the hell is going on?" Dale said.

Percy pulled an envelope out of his desk drawer and handed it to Hobie. Hobie lifted the flap for a quick look inside and noticed Dale leaning over for a peek as well. Hobie shoved it under his face.

"Here! Take a good look!"

Dale saw the envelope was thick with fifty-dollar bills before Hobie yanked it away, folded it in two and stuffed it in his back pocket.

"Nice doing business with you, Percy," Hobie said. "See you around sometime." He pivoted on a heel and shoved Dale toward the door, following along behind him.

31

The two men walked down the sidewalk away from the Hive. When they got to the intersection near Jimmo's doughnut shop, they crossed the street, passed under the streetlamp and sank back into the darkness of the woods. Once they were deep enough that it wouldn't be seen, Hobie pulled a small penlight from his pocket and shone a path in front of them.

"Have you been collecting the money after every show so far?" Dale asked.

"Busted," Hobie said.

"For Merlin?"

"Yeah. He wanted all the money to come back to him, so he told all the clubs to give the money to me and not tell you. We were all supposed to act like it had already been sent."

"Not tell me? Why?"

"Ask him if you're all fired up about it," Hobie said. "He's the booker, he wanted a favour, so I said no problem."

"But if he says, 'Don't tell the headliner,' doesn't that seem a bit odd to you?"

"I'm not going to grill him about his business. Merlin books a lot of shows, knows his stuff, and I was pretty pumped to get the call to go on the road, okay? This is a big break for me. So if he wants me to collect the cash and clam up about it, that's what I'm doing."

"But you could at least—"

"Shut the fuck up about the money!" Hobie shouted. "Jesus Christ, all you care about is money, money, MONEY!"

"I told you, I got a kid who needs—"

"And shut up about your goddamn kid!" Hobie bellowed. "Please and fucking thank you! Okay? I don't want to hear it. Fuck sake. Fuck . . . sake . . ."

Hobie's steps slowed until he had stopped walking entirely. He stood on a rotting mound of leaves and dirt, with his head down, rocking back and forth.

Oh no no no no, Dale began to panic, *not now. Not in the woods.* Fear swelled up from his shins through his thighs into his stomach. He felt like he was being submerged in ice water. He wanted to say something to haul Hobie back, but Hobie was busy rambling on his own.

"I don't even know your kid. Your stupid fucking kid. Why should I give a shit about your kid? Kids have it hard sometimes, so what, suck it up. Can't take it? Suck it up, you baby!"

Dale stood silently. He could tell Hobie was back to having conversations with ghosts, like he had observed on the highway. Whatever discussion Hobie was in now, Dale knew he was no longer a part of it.

"Are you going to cry about it, you baby? Cry your face off, I don't care."

Dale began to back up, slowly, his eyes fixed and unblinking on Hobie. The move was instinctive. It was survival. It was about putting space, even just a bit of space, between himself and the zombie were-wolf. He didn't consider for a moment that he could escape and get to Rynn before Hobie came around and chased him down and strangled him right there in the cold, wet woods. *No one would find me for months. Maybe never. My rotting corpse lying in here like an all-you-can-eat buffet for a bunch of fat, country-ass worms.* No, this was just about getting more than an arm's length away. Dale took another slow step backward and a twig snapped underfoot. Hobie's head wheeled round.

"Where the fuck do you think you're going?" he snarled. Dale began to say "Nowhere" but didn't even get the "No" out before Hobie had surged across the fifteen feet that separated them and driven both hands stiffly into his chest. Dale flew back and landed hard on the ground, his spine and ribs bending brutally across a long, gnarled tree root. The wind rushed out of his lungs and escaped on the night breeze, leaving him gasping and groping in desperate agony.

Hobie landed on top of him, with a knee on each side of his chest, pinning him to the dirt. A crushing hand grabbed Dale's face and squeezed hard—he feared his jaw would break from the pressure.

"Talk me out of killing you right here, right now," Hobie growled.

With the last molecules of air in his lungs, Dale croaked his answer. "Va . . . nessa."

"Vanessa?" Hobie said. "Who is . . . Oh shit, is that your kid? Again, with your fucking kid?"

"Don't kill me. I have to . . . ," he gasped, "for her."

"You have to *what* for her? Be there for her? You said she was going to college," Hobie said. "She don't need you around anymore, Daddy!" He pushed his face closer to Dale's and seethed. "Maybe the kid would be better off without her fuckin' dad. Ever think of that? Maybe I'd be doing her a favour. Maybe a dad isn't always such a shit-hot thing to have around! Maybe she's doing great because you ain't ever around."

"No . . . choice . . . ," Dale whispered. His diaphragm loosened and he pulled in a deep breath, then said louder, "No choice," and louder still, "No choice!" He closed his eyes and tears rolled across his temples and over his ears. "No choice," he said one last time, softly.

Hobie cocked his head and leaned back. He looked at Dale with a curious frown, his eyes narrowing. "You said that to me before," he said. "I heard you say that before, right?" He lifted himself a little, taking pressure off Dale's stomach.

Dale sobbed softly. "I don't know."

Hobie stood. He reached down and pulled Dale up by the shirt collar. "Get moving," he said. He shone his penlight along a trail through the trees and shoved Dale ahead of him. "I want to make some miles tonight."

32

Rynn winced against the pain in her arms, the ache increasing with every minuscule bit of distance she could muster. They bent back behind her at an ugly angle as she sprawled along the floor of the van, stretching her leg toward the toolbox. Her toes pointed like a ballerina's in an effort to maximize her length. If she could hook the hard tip of her shoe under the lip of the lid, she might be able to drag it closer to her. Then closer again, perhaps. And then maybe she could scoop her feet behind it and draw it forward, then roll over to where her bound hands could blindly flip it open to get at whatever sharp, hard and pointy implements lay inside. The plan in her mind toggled between escape and attack, but in either scenario sharp, hard and pointy played a prominent role.

Her teeth gritted and her eyes moistened as the pain increased, but she persisted. She had to be close. She dug her chin into her chest and shot a look down the length of her torso, past her knees, onto her shoes and beyond to the toolbox. It seemed to be almost touching.

Maybe the steep, raking angle was playing tricks with the perspective, but it was right . . . there . . . just . . . a . . . little . . . more. She squeezed her eyes shut and begged another quarter-inch from her tendons. Then contact. She felt the toe of her shoe nudging thinly under the bottom edge of the latch. Would it be enough to hold as she pulled it closer? She began to draw her foot back, slowly, methodically, microscopic progress, but the rubberized floor provided too much resistance and her toe lost hold. Rynn seethed in frustration and lashed out with her foot. Her shoe smashed hard into the face of the toolbox, knocking it farther away.

Well shit, now I'm totally—

She jumped at the sound of a thump from outside. She didn't move, only listened, her heart racing. The thump was followed by faint scratching and a sort of clicking. *What the hell is that? If Dale and Hobie have returned, why would they be bumping and scratching against the van?* She listened more, holding her breath so the sound of her drawing air wouldn't compete. More scratching, scraping—something sharp against metal. A shadow moved against the windshield. Rynn gasped, whirled her head to the front and saw eyes glaring in through the glass. She screamed. The eyes blinked twice and shifted position as two more shadows were draped across the window, silhouetted against a moonlit cloud. *Wings?* They were the wings of a grey owl that had landed on the nose of the van, hooking its claws around the windshield wipers like they were the silvery branches of a garish purple tree. It had likely never seen such a strange beast violating its hunting ground before and had come to investigate.

Rynn stared at the owl, which stared right back, neither less intrigued than the other. "Get help," Rynn said softly. The owl shook its head, which seemed to Rynn like a clear rebuke. "Thanks for nothing," she said.

The owl suddenly cranked its head to the right, shrieked and took flight as a bellowing voice roared, ". . . the fuck out of here!"

Hobie hurled a rock skyward after the owl, missing it by a wide margin as the bird swooped effortlessly along the treetops. He ran to the front of the van and examined the area where the owl had been perched. "Look at this!" he said through gritted teeth. "Goddamn scratches all along the paint. All scratched up from his fuckin' toenails!"

Rynn could see Hobie through the windshield, as she had seen the owl, but where she had felt a sort of wonder at the bird, she now felt revulsion. Hobie squinted and focused intensely into the darkness of the van. She scurried and wriggled back to the wall as he scanned the interior until he made her out. He disappeared from view and three seconds later Rynn heard his keys unlocking the rear doors. They swung open wide.

"Miss us?" he said, with a hard, toothy grin.

She bent one knee to give her leverage and pressed against the van wall, pushing herself more upright. "Not for a second," she sneered. "I was half hoping you'd never make it back."

"Oh, you were, were you?" he said, his head beginning to bob up and down. "That's real nice."

"Well pardon me," Rynn snapped, "but I'm in sort of a shitty mood for some unknown reason." She felt buoyed by a wave of indignation rising in her chest and courage steeled her limbs as she prepared to rip into Hobie about this sick goddamn game he was playing, and how she wasn't going to have any more of it, and how he had better turn them both loose right fucking now, but her crackling internal fire choked itself into a thin wisp when she got a good look at his face.

It was back. The same monstrous demon she had watched gruesomely shattering that man's arm was here now, glowering in at her, half-shadowed against the dim moonlight. It still wore Hobie's face as a mask, but whatever looked out from behind those eyes made her weak with fear. Then it began climbing into the back with her.

Where is Dale? Where is Dale?

"Dale!" she screamed.

"Hobie!" Dale hollered.

She was glad to hear his voice but in no position to feel relief. Dale stepped into view at the rear doors. "Have a heart, dude, she's been through enough."

Hobie continued to glare at Rynn, as he began palming and kneeling his way on all fours toward her.

"Dude," Dale said, "come on. Take it easy."

Hobie continued to crawl toward her, looking less human with every pawing step, until his twisted face was inches from her own. "I'm in a pretty shitty mood myself," he growled, "and the last thing I need when I get back from a hard day's work is a snotty fucking attitude."

"I'm sorry," Rynn said softly. "I'm glad you're both back. Of course I am. I could die out here."

"Yeah," he said. "I could see to it."

"Hobie," Dale said, reaching in and touching his leg, "you wanted to make some miles. Let's just go."

Hobie remained staring at Rynn, but she felt the monster receding, watched the humanity seep into his eyes little by little until he was back. He still wasn't happy, but he wasn't looking to kill anyone either. Not just yet.

"Fine," he said flatly. "We can go. Get in here."

"Come on, man," Dale said. "Let us sit in the seats. We're not going to—"

"You can leave tied up or stay behind buried," Hobie said with cold determination. "I don't give a shit anymore."

Dale crawled into the back of the van and sat against the wall beside Rynn. Hobie reached for the toolbox, but when he lifted the handle the whole top popped open. He frowned as he examined the latch, which seemed to be bent. He didn't recall it being bent before, but it was crooked enough now that it wouldn't catch.

He had bigger things on his mind at the moment, so he resumed the task at hand, pulling out what was needed. He zip-strapped Dale's ankles together and his wrists behind him, then wove the strong, thin wire through his arms, through the metal loop and twisted it closed with the pliers.

"Can you take this collar off me now?" Rynn asked. "Please?"

"No," Hobie said, turning his back to her. He unzipped his travel bag and pulled out the large manila envelope. He removed the evening's show money from his pants pocket and tucked it inside. Hobie stuffed the manila envelope back into his bag, zipped it shut and slammed the rear door. He walked around to the driver's side and climbed in.

"How about we don't talk for a while," he said, jabbing the key in the ignition. "I'm getting a little sick of the both of you."

33

In short order the van was cruising on the cool, smooth pavement of a two-lane country highway at seven clicks above the speed limit.

Hobie hunched over the steering wheel, muttering softly. Dale couldn't tell if the ghosts were giving him a hard time or if it was more of an internal debate about the best place to hide bodies. Whatever the case, it kept Hobie's attention front and forward.

Dale whispered to Rynn, "Remember what we talked about before? Using these wires to saw through our straps?"

"Yeah," she whispered back.

"We should start doing that. Now."

"Okay," she replied, slowly. "But the way you said that sounded sort of ominous. Anything I should know?"

"He's never taking us back to the city," Dale said. "He's not stupid."

"Are we sure about that?" Rynn said. "He's made a lot of bad decisions to date."

"The kid is a maniac and a loose cannon, but he's clearly capable of thinking ahead. So there's no way he's taking us back to the city and letting us go."

"Yeah. If he did," she said, "the very first thing I would do is find a phone and call the cops. He must know that."

"He does," Dale said, "so whatever his plan is, it involves us never talking to anyone ever again. We need to get loose and get lost."

"In that order," Rynn said, scooching her body toward Dale while leaning away from him, until the wire behind her was pulled tight from the wall and closer to him. Dale kept his eyes on Hobie while twisting around so his back was to Rynn, then he wriggled backward toward her until he could feel the thin wire against his hand. He adjusted his arm position so the strap between his wrists rested against the wire, and he began to move his hands back and forth. Back and forth.

After a couple of minutes of steady sawing, Dale was getting discouraged. There seemed to be no progress at all, as the surface of the nylon strapping glided effortlessly, frictionless across the metal wire. He wondered if this was a pointless endeavour driven by desperation in lieu of any practical options. *Is it better to do something, anything, even if it's hopeless, than to accept there is no hope? Is it really better to "rage against the dying of the light" if that amounts to nothing more than a tantrum? Maybe it's not so—*

Then it bit. Dale could feel the nylon had stopped sliding and begun skating. Every motion now would dig the metal deeper. Progress. Hope.

"Choice!" Hobie hollered.

Dale and Rynn both jumped, and the wire staggered free of the groove.

"What?" Dale said, almost angrily.

"You say you have no choice," Hobie said. "I've heard you say it a few times, and it pisses me off. You always have a choice."

"Really?" Dale said. "Doesn't feel like we have much of one at the moment. Feels like we're tied up in the back of a van."

"You had a choice before you were tied up. You could've attacked me when my back was turned. Smashed my skull with a rock or a log. Something. You could have run to those cops back in town when I cut your straps. Saved yourself, but you didn't. Your choice."

Rynn looked at Dale. The opportunity to save himself had apparently arisen somewhere out there on their travels, and she was still alive because of his decision. His choice. She was both warmed and emboldened by the thought and joined in the conversation.

"I'm not sure you know what the word 'choice' means," Rynn said. "'Do whatever I say or I'll kill you' doesn't really constitute choice."

"Bullshit," Hobie said. "Live tied up or die in a fight. That's a choice."

"Great. Point taken," Dale said. "Next time I'll change 'no choice' to 'shitty choice.'"

As he engaged with Hobie, Dale was stealthily guiding his wrists back over the wire until he felt it dig into the nylon groove again, and as the miles churned beneath the van, he and Rynn continued their secretive toiling in the dark. There was no way to monitor progress, since neither could see their hands. They just stared into the blackness and hoped that at some point soon, they would hear the small, sweet snap of release.

Another twenty minutes had passed when Dale and Rynn felt the van begin to slow. The turn signal ticked loudly, and the interior was bathed in bright electric light.

"We need gas," Hobie said navigating to a set of self-serve pumps outside an Esso station. When he applied the brakes, Rynn heard something tumble along the floor and felt it hit her foot. She looked down and saw a small dark cylinder, which had some weight to it, judging by how it had bumped into her shoe.

"Be right back," Hobie said as he popped his door and hopped out.

As soon as the door closed, Rynn gestured with her chin. "What's this thing?"

Dale looked. "That's Hobie's penlight. He must've dropped it when he was climbing in here to get up in your face."

"Our boy could use a feckin' mint, let me tell you. I'm going to see if I can grab it," she said.

"Why?" Dale asked.

"Why not? Better to have it and not need it than to need it and not have it," she said, flicking her toe at the flashlight. "That's what my dear mother likes to say while she's cramming handfuls of fast-food napkins and ketchup packets into her purse."

Rynn managed to roll the penlight up near her hips and leaned over to where she could pinch it between two fingers. She lifted it gingerly, tilted her hand and let the thing fall into her palm. "Jesus, I'm like MacGyver."

"Well, shine the light on my straps, MacGyver, and see how close they are to being cut through," Dale said.

"He might see the light," she said. "Let's wait until he goes inside to pay."

The two of them sat quietly, listening to the whirr of the pump and the gentle gurgling of the gasoline flowing into Midnight's belly. It was a few minutes of that before they heard the metallic clunk of the nozzle turning off and being latched back onto its rest.

"Is he done? Is he headed in?" Rynn asked.

"I can't see from down here," Dale said. "Let me try to . . ." He bent his legs under him so he could roll onto his front and hoist himself upright onto his knees. From this raised position he could peer above the lip of the side windows and the windshield. He saw Hobie loping across the parking lot toward the door of the gas station. "He's heading in."

"I hear other voices," Rynn said.

Dale looked and saw a group of three teenagers walking toward a Mazda hatchback, shoving each other and laughing as they went.

"Yeah, there's other people," Dale said. "Can you get the penlight into my hand?"

Rynn shimmied on the seat of her pants toward Dale and raised herself up as high as she could. He lowered himself down until his butt rested on his heels and his hand met hers. The transfer completed, he hauled himself back up into position.

Dale looked intently toward the gas station. Through its large glass-walled front he could see Hobie casually perusing the aisles of snacks. Dale twisted the penlight on and began flaring it across the van's windows. He kept an eye on Hobie at all times, quickly pointing the light down toward the van's floor anytime Hobie lifted his head, then swirling it back up in the direction of the Mazda whenever Hobie looked away.

"They see it," he said suddenly. "They see the light."

"Are they coming over?" Rynn asked.

"I think so. Oh shit," Dale said. "Now what? Are we getting these kids killed?"

The teens were definitely looking at the van, but they didn't walk over. They climbed into the hatchback and drove it in a slow, wide arc toward the van, rubbernecking through open windows as they came.

The hatchback pulled up parallel to the van, so the two passenger doors were facing each other. The teen in the passenger seat, a red-headed boy of about seventeen with a lengthy snoot draped in freckles, leaned out for a closer look.

Dale saw that Hobie's back was turned, his attention focused on operating whatever swirly frozen drink machine he was standing at, so he flashed the light and screamed as loudly as he could. "Help us! Call the police!"

Rynn joined in. "Help! Help! Call the police!"

The two of them bellowed as loud as they could. The freckle-faced teen opened his door and started to climb out.

"No! For Christ's sake, get away from this van and call the police!" Dale shouted. "For your own safety!"

The gangly teen stopped in his tracks. He remained half-standing, with one foot on the ground and one foot still inside the car. He leaned on his door and craned his neck to see if he could pull any detail from the darkness inside the van.

Rynn sat up as tall as she could and peered out between the passenger seat and the passenger window. Her eyes met the boy's through that narrow gap, and her mind rocketed back to the pig she saw through the slats of the trailer on the highway, on its way to slaughter. She had sympathized with the pig before, but she empathized with it now. "Call . . . the . . . cops!" she shouted as loudly and clearly as she could. The freckle-faced kid stared a moment, then sat back in the car, said something to the driver, and the Mazda rolled away, seemingly in no particular rush.

"Did they hear us?" she asked.

"I don't know," Dale said. "And shit, here comes Hobie."

He was strolling back toward the van, looking at a magazine and holding a full shopping bag and a colourful crushed ice drink. He lifted his head and looked toward the Mazda as it pulled out of the parking lot. He furrowed his brow and looked over at the van, considering, then went back to his magazine.

He hopped into the driver's seat and looked in the back. Dale and Rynn sat beside each other, leaned against the wall.

"Did you get anything to eat?" Rynn asked.

"I'm starving," Dale said. Both looked almost innocent.

"Yeah, I got some food," Hobie said, "but I'm getting us out from under these lights first. We'll stop somewhere a little less conspicuous." He fired up the van and pulled out onto the highway.

After fifteen minutes of driving, Hobie saw a gravel access road leading toward a thicket of trees, and he swung the van in there and brought it to a stop, well hidden from the highway. He killed the engine and climbed into the back with his shopping bag.

"Muffins again," he said, almost apologetically. "Easiest thing for me to feed you. I could have gotten us all sammiches, but trust me, they did not look good. I think we would have been dead within an hour. The meat was the same colour as the lettuce."

Dale chuckled, surprising himself.

Hobie brightened. "Was that funny?" he asked.

"Yeah. Good phrasing. Nice and concise. Caught me on the jaw. You should write that down."

"Where?"

"You keep a notebook for all your bits, right? Ideas and premises, good phrasing . . . so you don't forget."

"Oh yeah. Yeah, of course," Hobie said. Dale and Rynn could tell he didn't. Hobie seemed much happier, having made Dale laugh, and was now in a joking mood. He pulled a muffin out of the bag and peeled it free of its wrapper. He broke a chunk off and fed it to Rynn. "That's yours," he said. He fed a chunk to Dale. "That's yours." He pulled a bag of Nacho Cheese Doritos from the shopping bag. "That's Na-chos," he said. "Get it? Not yours . . . na-chos. Not-chos!" He grinned, but then his smile dropped, and his face turned deadly serious. His eyes went distant. Dale and Rynn both stopped chewing, both terrified to see where this sudden emotional off-ramp was headed.

"I was wrong," Hobie declared.

"About . . . what?" Dale asked cautiously.

Hobie turned to him, an epiphany smeared across his face. "That's where I heard it before. You weren't saying 'nachos' in your dream. You were saying 'no choice.' You kept saying 'no choice, no choice' over and over until it sounded like 'nachos.'"

"Okay," Dale said slowly. "Not sure that makes any more sense, but—"

"Of course it does!" Hobie scowled. "Back in the woods, when I said something about you leaving Vanessa alone, you were blubbering and saying you had 'no choice, no choice' just like when you were dreaming." Hobie sat back proudly and announced, "Your recurring nightmare is about your goddamn kid, I guarantee it."

Dale froze and his eyes went wide. A rush of realization rained down on him.

Rynn watched him, unsure of what was happening, then leaned over to him. "You were blubbering in the woods?" she asked quietly.

"He was bawling like a baby," Hobie said as he stooped his way back toward the driver's seat, "but no shame in that. Psychology is powerful shit, man. It's everything. Fuck atoms and molecules, everything is made up of psychology." He cranked the ignition, pulled a U-turn and roared back onto the highway.

Rynn had been half-joking with her "blubbering" comment before, but she was growing legitimately concerned as Dale hadn't blinked in over a minute. "Seriously," she said, "are you okay? Dale?"

Dale didn't even hear her. He was busy reloading the video in his mind, replaying, rewinding, and replaying the past ten thousand hours of dream sequence footage that had been tearing his nights apart for the past who knows how long. Suddenly he knew exactly how long—it hit him like a clear crack of lightning. Since last August. That was when Brandy filed for divorce. When Brandy told him they were done and she was moving on. That sudden seismic rift must have jarred loose the more distant memory. That crushing memory of when they first split, when their selfish adult actions tore Vanessa's world apart. Dale replayed the moments before he left that first time. Standing on the thick dark green carpet of the hall. He wanted to stay. To dive down into that dark green carpet and never leave. He replayed Brandy handing him his luggage. Then came the screaming, the shrieking of four-year-old Vanessa as she ran after him, the round bulbous blue toes of her slippers rising and falling, churning through the carpet, the white tassels bouncing against the green, then his heart shattering as her fingernails gouged into his leg when she clamped onto him tightly.

"I had no choice," he said softly, with tears flowing down his face.

Even though she didn't understand what he was talking about, Rynn put her head on his shoulder and whispered. "I know."

34

The van rolled on under the endless black sky while the moon pried its way through a jagged ribbon of cloud. Dale stared out the windshield in mute contemplation, while Rynn floated in and out of sleep.

Suddenly Hobie was in a state of high alert. "No way," he said, and not to any ghosts. "No fucking way." His eyes were glaring into his side mirror. Dale was just about to ask what was happening when the lights started dancing across the windows, filling the van with alternating punches of red and blue. Hobie's rage-filled eyes shot up at Dale and Rynn in his rearview mirror. "What did you do? What did you fucking do back there?!"

"Nothing!" Rynn shouted, but her voice was drowned by the baritone roar of Midnight's customized eight-cylinder engine. She and Dale were thrown back onto their sides as Hobie drilled his foot to the floor and the van tore down the highway. The red-and-blue lights were immediately accompanied by a howling siren, and the chase was on.

Dale grimaced as he skidded away from his restraints toward the rear doors before being yanked to a brutally abrupt stop when the wire caught. Rynn had it worse. Being lighter, she was not only yanked to a stop, but tossed partially into the air, then slammed down hard against the protruding metal wheel-well.

"There's never any cops on this stretch at night," Hobie was hollering. "You fuckers did something back there! And you're going to pay for it!"

As dazed and in pain as Dale and Rynn were, they knew with horrifying clarity that if Hobie lost the cops, their lives would end tonight.

The van's engine had been rebuilt for speed, but the cop car was no slouch either and it closed the gap between the two vehicles, pulling out in an effort to pass. Hobie yarded the wheel left, cutting the cop car off and forcing it to swerve and draw back. The cop behind the wheel took a desperate dive at the other side of the van but retreated quickly when Hobie wrenched the wheel to the right. Dale and Rynn tumbled and skidded and pounded against the floor and walls and each other as the van swerved recklessly through its dangerous dance. The cruiser again veered out into the passing lane, and again Hobie swooped to pinch them off, but this time the van's rear bumper clipped the nose of the cruiser. The ass end of the van skidded out and began to fishtail as Hobie steered wildly to recover. The cops backed off a few lengths to see what would happen and watched the van tilt and totter before settling back on all four tires and roaring farther ahead. The cops gunned their engine to keep pace.

Up ahead, Hobie could see a dense wall of woodland pushing out toward the highway. He grinned. "Nobody ditch dives like me and Midnight."

He watched in the mirror as the cops gained ground, then he suddenly slowed, swung the van onto the shoulder and skilfully knifed it into the ditch, bouncing up dramatically onto the field on the other side. His captives were tossed into the air like children's toys and flung mercilessly back down. Rynn landed with a shriek and a grunt, while Dale found himself somersaulting loosely across the floor. When he hit the back of the captain's chair, he looked up to see he was eight feet away from Rynn. He was free of the wire. Then he saw his hands in front of him, loose and independent.

Outside, the brake lights on the cop car turned billowing clouds of white smoke into crimson mist as their tires locked and howled against the pavement. The driver swung the car around and raced back to where the van had left the road. The cruiser shot into the ditch in pursuit—only to grind to a violent stop as its front end carved into the rise on the far side. The purple van roared away across the field toward the woods.

Hobie was laughing maniacally and staring back in his side mirror. Dale knew from the mad glee that there would be no cops riding to the rescue tonight. His heart sank, but only for a moment. He saw Hobie's toolbox splayed open-mouthed on the floor with the bent clasp flapping limply and various tools bobbling loose on the carpet. He dove for a pair of wire cutters and deftly rolled onto his back while bringing his knees to his chest. He reached down and snipped the nylon around his ankles. He was fully loose, if not fully free, and fuelled with a boiling blend of terror and rage.

Hobie skilfully drove the van through openings between trees, finding spaces and files with quick ease. They were soon deep into the woods via a twisting, winding path that had no bearing or frame of reference. Hobie only knew the cops were a long way away and they would have no idea where he had gone. He looked quickly up to the rearview mirror to see what was going on in back. His assessment was brief. Dale's reflection lurched at him with a wrench in hand. The vision disappeared into a blast of colour and pain as the wrench pounded hard against the base of his skull and he slumped forward unconscious.

His dead weight pushed the gas pedal to the floor and the van accelerated rapidly until the front left tire careened up and over a downed tree. The van lifted, airborne, and spiralled a quarter-turn, landed on its side and skidded across the mossy forest floor before slamming hard into the base of a thick tree.

Dale was hurled forward, his head and shoulders driven down into the passenger footwell. But he was conscious, which was more than he could say for Hobie, who sprawled motionless across the console. As Dale pushed himself up from the van's floor he saw Hobie's travel bag had been thrown forward against the seats. He fumbled quickly at the zipper, hauled it open and pulled the thick manila envelope from inside. He jammed it down the back of his pants. Then he heard a faint voice rising up from the dark.

"What did . . . where the Christ?"

Dale scrambled out of the front and crawled to where he could see Rynn, lifting herself off her belly and onto her knees on the floor, which was formerly the wall of the van. Her head was bleeding from a nasty gash.

"Where did . . . what just . . . ?"

"You're okay," Dale said.

"Oh," she mumbled. "That's good news."

Dale scanned for strewn tools and snatched up a pair of pliers. He used the tight joint near the hinge bolt to pinch through her wrist and ankle restraints. He guided her to the back doors, popped the latch and pushed one door open with a shoulder.

"We gotta go," he said.

"Where?" she asked.

"Anywhere but here," he said, and they disappeared into the cover of the trees.

35

They were cold.

Sure, it was July, and the sun could be plenty warm at midday, but this was the middle of the night in the middle of Canada, and it felt like it. Their shivering, however, could not be blamed entirely on the temperature. Both Dale and Rynn were jacked up on a cocktail of fear and adrenalin, and the mix was being stirred by pain. Dale's right kneecap felt like it was cracked in half and the joint was swollen to where it was straining his pants at the seam. The leg was becoming stiffer, weaker, less mobile with every step, and they had taken a lot of steps—even if they had no idea what direction they were walking.

Rynn's left shoulder felt like someone was trapped inside the socket, trying to burn their way out with a blowtorch. She kept looking at it to see if it was, in fact, on fire. It was not, but the arm feeding into the socket was certainly coming at it from a slack new angle. Her brain pounded against the walls of her skull, making each motion a fresh agony. A garish scab had crusted over the wound on her forehead and dried scales of red lined her cheek, blending into the red scratches on her jawline where the buckle of the dog collar had gouged her skin while she was being thrown around. She had desperately ripped the collar off within seconds of leaving the van, and angrily dismantled the evil device affixed to it. She had flung various pieces of it in various directions in hopes of giving Hobie false leads if he should come to and come after them.

As they pressed on, she looked up to the sky as if the stars might hold some insight. "Now what?" she asked, either to them or to Dale.

"Just keep moving," he said. "We need to put distance between us and Hobie. And we need to find a phone."

"But we don't even know where we're going. We might be going in circles. For all we know, we could be walking right back to the van."

"No," Dale said, "we're moving away. We've been angling a little right, and then a little left, but I've kept the moon in the same spot since we headed out."

"How far have we gone?" she asked.

"We've been walking for maybe twenty minutes."

"Shit. Really?" she said. "I thought it was three hours."

Hobie was beginning to stir. Slowly at first, just one elbow rising robotically until his hand slapped flat against the dash and pushed his torso sideways. He dragged his eyelids open and squinted, trying to get his bearings. Nothing made sense. Trees were growing horizontally across his windshield, and he felt like he was being pulled by an invisible force toward the passenger seat. The force was gravity, he soon realized, and his mind began shuffling the available evidence into fragmented memories until the stack made sense. *The van rolled. Midnight is totalled.* His heart suddenly jumped. *Are Dale and Rynn okay?* He heaved himself up and muscled his way into the back.

They were gone. One rear door gaped open. Hobie crawled to the back, out the door and stood. He began desperately scanning the surroundings, tracing back along the skid marks and the tire tracks in case they had been thrown from the vehicle when it overturned. There was no sign of either of them.

An unreasonable amount of time passed before Hobie even considered the notion that Dale and Rynn might have left on purpose. Willingly. Without him. When the notion cemented into a serious possibility, he rushed back to the van and clambered in after his luggage. He saw his travel bag humped up against the seats with its zipper yawning wide. His enormous hands tore into the contents, flinging garments and CDs in every direction, but no manila envelope was found. He ripped up floor mats and clawed beneath the seats before finally accepting the obvious fact—the money had been taken.

He closed his eyes, pulled in a lungful of crisp night air and tried to calm his mind. His brain rebooted and accessed the last image it had processed: *Dale looks mad. He has a wrench. Blackness.*

He opened his eyes. His lower jaw pushed forward, and his eyebrows knitted together into a muscled hump. The pain at the base of his skull was smothered by a rising rage. It was a particular kind of rage—the searing anger that is specifically stoked by betrayal. Hobie had tied them up in his van, held them prisoner, attached them to an explosive device, threatened them with death, and yet their escape felt to him, very sincerely and literally, as a betrayal of their friendship. They had betrayed the team. They had abandoned the tour. They had cancelled the run.

They didn't do their fucking time!

Back at the highway, two police officers stood in the ditch beside their bent cruiser. One of them, a plump man in his mid-forties, chattered angrily into the radio.

"Then wake Rolinson's ass up and tell him to get out here! We need backup, now!"

"Where are you?" the other voice crackled.

"Somewhere past . . . we're east of . . ." He groped to find landmarks, but it was the darkest stretch of the night and everything blended into one homogeneous mash of rocks, trees and sky. "Hang on," he barked into the microphone, "someone's coming. I'll flag them down."

He tossed the microphone onto the seat, stepped out of the ditch onto the edge of the road and began waving his arms at the two headlights of the approaching car. He blinked and refocused his eyes and called to his partner. "Is this two headlights or four?"

"Four," his partner said, walking up beside him.

As the headlights drew nearer and slowed with a low rumble, each seemed to drift about, as though not fixed to anything.

"What the hell is this?" the second cop asked.

The plump cop's face dropped. "Oh shit," he said, and he placed a hand on the butt of his gun.

36

Deep in the woods, Dale's left leg was bordering on useless. He couldn't put any weight on it, and it had become little more than ballast to keep him upright while he hopped on the other foot. Rynn kept pushing on ahead of him, then stopping herself.

"Why am I out front?" she said. "I have no idea where we're going."

"Neither do I," Dale said. "I know you want to move a little faster, I just can't. If you want to go on ahead, I'll understand."

"Oh shut up," Rynn scoffed. "We have little enough chance of getting out of this alive as a team. If we split up, that drops to zero."

"I don't know," Dale said as he hopped along, "if you could race ahead and find help faster, it might increase our chances."

"Between us we have two arms and two legs. That's our best bet," she said.

"But if you—"

"We're staying together," she said, with a grim finality that told him any argument would be a waste of breath.

The moon became a less helpful tour guide over the next while, as it dipped below the treetops and only peeked at them tauntingly on occasion. They kept their talk low and to a minimum, both harbouring a healthy fear that Hobie could leap out from behind a tree at any second with a fresh handful of pain for each of them.

They assumed he was well into the hunt by now, and he clearly had an understanding of this area and its terrain that far outmatched theirs. This wilderness was nothing like the scant, lush shrubbery outside Dublin, and even less like anything you'd find in Chicago. This wasn't some urban park where parents set up a pup tent for their kids to play in for the afternoon. This was a dark and foreboding thatch of horrors where an old, lame timber wolf might crawl off to starve to death and have its carcass stripped of flesh by ravens and shrews. They couldn't get free of it fast enough.

"If we can find our way out of these woods, we should be okay," Dale said.

"With any luck this forest backs right up against a town, or a petrol station," Rynn said. "At the very least, a farmyard, but I'd take that."

It was only another ten minutes of crunching through the underbrush before they began to notice the waning density of trees and the thinning canopy above them.

"I think we're nearing the edge," Rynn exclaimed with hushed excitement.

"We made it," Dale said, hobbling as fast as he could after her.

They rambled and wove through the remaining trunks and branches with breathless anticipation until they shook free of the forest and burst into the open.

The huge, ominous open.

Their excitement sunk into a horrifying abyss as they slowly processed what their eyes were absorbing. If they had been standing on the dark side of Mars, the vista wouldn't be much different. Infinite nothingness swallowed their field of vision. A stark, barren plain of unworked soil stretched between their shoes and the edge of the planet, with the entire width of the horizon stitched to the inky stillness of outer space.

"Jesus Christ Almighty Lord," Rynn said. "There's just . . . nothing."

"If we start crossing this, we're totally bare-assed vulnerable," Dale said.

"Crossing to what?" Rynn asked. "What's beyond this? Dragons?"

Dale pointed suddenly. "There."

She followed his finger and squinted until she saw what he saw. A single white light seemed to rest on the ground about twenty degrees from the tree line to their right.

"How far away is that?" she asked.

"A mile?" he said with a shrug. "Ten miles? Doesn't much matter, we need to get there. It's all there is."

"Okay," Rynn said with a sigh, "but let's limit the amount of time we're out on that open stretch. Let's move along the edge of the wood until we're closer. It'll provide some cover, at least."

"Good thinking," Dale said, then added as a cold afterthought, "although that's where Hobie is."

The two of them began trudging off to the right, parallel to the trees.

Hobie moved through the growth like a jungle cat, with a powerful swiftness that never sacrificed stealth. If they were running, he would catch them. If they were hiding, he would find them. If there had been an observer to his actions, they might think he was the inspiration for Schwarzenegger's Terminator, except that his expression was not cold and calculating like an artificially intelligent cyborg. Hobie looked royally pissed off. Angrily disconnected. A zombie werewolf.

His feet stepped deftly among the roots and rising humps of earth, his eyes raking the ground for any trace or clue. He no longer had his penlight for assistance in the dark, but his vision was keenly enhanced in his current state, with pupils pushed wide by rage and cocaine. He had already collected and carried with him several small discoveries: a wad of black electrical tape, a broken pager, some wire, the dog collar. He had found the items within a shallow radius of the van, suggesting they had been scattered randomly, but deduced that the contraption had to have been dismantled in layers from the outside inward, which meant the collar had been the last thing tossed. He had gambled in that direction for pursuit and had since seen a few promising indentations pushed into patches of moss that resembled footprints.

Bolstered by the tracks and driven by an acrid anger, Hobie gritted his teeth and hastened his pace. He had come to a comforting, clarifying conclusion: *If I can cover Dale and Rynn's stage time, do some crowd work, off-the-cuff stuff, get enough laughs all by myself, Merlin will be super impressed.*

His lips pulled into a chilling smile. All he had to do now was find Dale and Rynn, snap their necks, leave them for the birds and bugs and finish the last couple of shows on his own.

37

Time was moving far too slowly for Rynn, and so was Dale. For every step he was able to take, she could have taken ten, but she stuck near him regardless and hid her growing frustration under a blanket of sarcastic, comedic roasts. "You know there's someone chasing us, right?" she had said once. Then later, "Remember the unstable violent giant who goes nuts every so often? Yeah, he's gone nuts again and he's after us." Another time she had lightly suggested, "Maybe we could use a sharp rock to amputate your bum leg and toss it in a different direction to send Hobie off on a false lead." She followed that with a casual "Something to think about."

Dale had chuckled at each comment. Her comedic instincts were so good, her inherent knack for phrasing so pure, he couldn't help but laugh, even under their grave circumstances. However, his own understanding of comedy ran deep enough to know what she was doing. She was coping—wrestling with the combined weight of a horror, an opportunity and a liability. Her life was in danger, her shot at survival was staring her in the face an undetermined distance away, and she wasn't racing toward it as fast as she could . . . because of him.

Dale tried to grind his way through the crippling pain in his leg and haul himself along at a more practical pace, but the harder he tried, the greater the pain. It was an irrefutable equation that proved itself over and over and would not be erased off the board by force of will. Lesson learned. Class dismissed.

"I'm done," he said, and slumped to the ground. He rolled onto his side and folded one arm up under his head as though he were tucking in for the night.

"Like hell you are," Rynn said. "You're going to get up and get moving. If you need a minute, we can take a minute, but then we're moving again."

"I'm not," he said. "I've thought about this a lot, and you need to go on ahead and leave me behind."

"Don't be daft. What about Vanessa? You want to see her again, don't you?"

"This is one hundred percent about Vanessa," he said. "If it wasn't for her, I'd happily keep crawling along behind you, clinging to your shirt-tails and slowing you down, and whatever happens, happens. But I want to live—for her. I need to be there for her, no matter what. You're not leaving me behind to die, you're leaving me behind to save my sorry ass."

"That's madness," she said.

"Look, if I lie here, I'm hidden by the rise where the dirt and the grass meet. If Hobie even comes by this way, he'll walk right past."

Rynn looked at him, then she looked at the single light in the distance. Despite how long they had been plodding forward, it didn't seem one inch closer. It must still be miles away. She looked up at the stars and said softly, "Maybe we should both stop running."

"No," Dale said. "You're our only chance. Please, Rynn. Please, you can't give up."

She looked down at him with a sour expression. "Who said anything about giving up?" she asked. "I said stop running."

Dale shook his head. "Are you nuts? No. No way. We'd be no match for him at our best. We can't fight him in this condition."

"Maybe not," she said, "if it was a fair fight." She reached behind her with her good arm and fished into her back pants pocket. Dale watched with riveted curiosity as she brought her closed hand forward, palm down, then turned it up and opened her fingers for him to see.

"Holy shit," he said. "You kept the shotgun shells?"

She rolled the two red casings around in her hand. "Better to have them and not need them," she said. "Although I feel like we really do need them."

"I saw the cylinder shape in your back pocket, I just thought it was the penlight," Dale said.

"Nope. But good to know you've been staring at my arse while we were walking, you perv."

They both had a quick snicker at that. Having two shotgun shells in their possession gave them a renewed sense of strength and power. They revelled in it for a few moments, then felt it fading as a realization slowly crept in.

"Only . . . what do we do with them?" Rynn asked.

"Right," Dale said. He considered briefly then added, "Don't suppose you have a shotgun in your back pocket, too."

"I do not."

"A length of steel pipe and a firing pin?" Dale was the one coping now, as hope faded. They sat, trying to think of some way they might practically, actually weaponize the shells, and came to two conclusions.

"We don't have time to dream up some magical solution," Dale said. "Hobie has to be getting close."

"We need to keep heading toward the light at that farm."

It was agreed. Rynn helped Dale to his feet—or foot—and they continued on their painfully slow quest for safety.

Farther back in the woods, very little remained of the Hobie who had picked up Dale and Rynn in his shiny purple van just a few days earlier. In truth, that tailored facade had started to thin and fray on the way to the first show, and it had been worn threadbare since. There wasn't much disguise left in the few sheer tatters that remained draped across him now. The hidden Hobie, the real Hobie, was calling the shots again, and it felt right. He spread his long, muscular arms at the thought of it. Goddamn, it was good to be out of the attic.

He pressed on through the woodland like a juggernaut with a mission and momentum. His eyes burned hot, like the lens of a film projector flaring out his inner thoughts: He was not about to let these false friends, these betrayers, run to the law and hang him out to dry. They weren't going to scuttle his career in comedy just as it was taking off, just when his talents were getting attention from the top booker in the city. They were doing this because they were jealous. That's what it was. He knew it. They had seen him onstage, seen his dynamic natural energy, and got green with envy and intimidated by his talent—just like all the other safe, lame, no-point-of-view, no-edge comedians back home. Jealous and intimidated like that lying sack of shit at the Red Cactus who had cancelled his shows—without even paying him for the ones he had done. *You don't expect payback for that? That's on you, asshole. Good night and good riddance.* Scared and intimidated like that mouthy hockey jock back in Wire Beach, who wanted to be funny without having the guts to get onstage, just wanted to sit safe with his buddies and mouth off from the sidelines. *Not saying very much now, are you, tough guy? Not very fucking funny now!*

Hobie was fuelled and fierce and picking up speed, and God help anyone who got in his way. Three coyotes had seen him coming and paused to consider if he might be breakfast, then scattered when he broke a thick, low-hanging branch off a tree and screamed at them, "Come on!" They wanted no part of that and scurried off to hunt elsewhere, leaving the large, loud human to go after his own prey.

38

There are stories of people crossing the desert and seeing mirages in the distance. A shimmering pool surrounded by swaying palms that cast cooling shade across a green garden. Ancient sailors traversing vast stretches of unknown water told tales of wondrous islands pushing up out of the ocean, with lovely mermaids near the shore, smiling and beckoning them for a respite. All these were wishful illusions conjured by desperate minds, so Rynn rightfully questioned what her own eyes were seeing.

The light in the farmyard remained low on the horizon, yet there seemed now to be vague shapes and shadows sprouting up around it. Buildings, or structures of some sort, forming indistinct angles against the night sky.

She wondered if the shapes were just cruel tricks of the darkness, or if she and Dale were truly closer than they'd thought. Dale had noticed nothing. He trudged along behind her, focused only on her steps and the gut-wrenching pain in his leg. Rynn decided her mind was not playing tricks, but she wanted confirmation.

"Okay, what the hell kind of farm is this?" she asked.

Dale looked up and strained his eyes to pull the image from the dark. He gleaned the hint of a structure from it, yet he also felt he could see sky within the perimeter of the thing. As though it were transparent. "I don't think that is a farm," he said. "I think the light is on some kind of fenced-off area." As they drew nearer, he confirmed it. "Yeah, a chain-link fence around something."

They approached with confusion and caution at first, which gave way to disappointment with the realization that this was an unpopulated set-up, entirely devoid of other humans. They came to a shallow ditch, which they crossed, stepping up on a gravel road that led into a gravel yard. The tall chain-link fence ran around a few variously sized grey metal boxes and cabinets, which were clustered at the base of two metal towers, while a faint hum emanated from within. Wires ran from the tops of those towers to wooden poles that Dale and Rynn could now see jutting up at consistent intervals along the gravel road, disappearing into the distance.

"Some kind of electrical substation, maybe?" Dale proposed with a low level of confidence.

"No idea what that is," Rynn said, "but I'm guessing there's no phone." A brief investigation around the area confirmed the absence.

They both dropped to the ground, leaning up against the fencing for support.

We have struggled and persevered through hunger, thirst and excruciating pain to make our way to "—nothing," Dale said. "There's nothing."

"No offence," Rynn said, "but this run has sucked ass. Shit crowds, barren tundra, psychotic opening act and creepy club owners who don't even pay us."

Dale sat quietly, wrestling his guilt. "Right," he finally said. "We don't even take any money away from this." He went quiet again. The rumpled envelope in the back of his pants suddenly felt thick as a textbook. His words didn't sit well with him, but he had his kid's tuition to pay. Her entire future, he felt, hinged on his silence.

"God knows how far it is to any actual farm from here," Rynn said. "I suppose we could follow this road. It'll have to lead somewhere, won't it?"

"I guess," Dale said, with a tinge of defeat painting his words. "Whatever we do now, we're easy pickings. Honestly, our only hope is if Hobie took off after us in the complete opposite direction. What do you think the odds are of that?"

"I'm going to say slim," she replied, picking up a few pebbles and rattling them around in her hand. "The ground was soft back there, so I bet we left tracks. Besides, we were both too scared to give much thought to strategy. I think we lit out in the most obvious direction."

"So, then," Dale said, "we either walk down that road until we get killed or sit here on our asses until we get killed."

"Sitting sounds good," Rynn said, "but I'm not ready to toss in the towel just yet. I haven't said anything about it, but I'm on the cusp of something big, a literal fecking dream come true that could change my life, and I don't like the idea of losing everything because we got booked on a bad run with a maniac. I may not have a daughter, but I have plans."

Dale didn't ask for any details. "Then we walk," he said. "Only . . . I need a couple minutes' rest first." He lay down on his side and propped himself against the fencing. "I never realized how comfortable chain link and metal tubing could be, but right now this is bliss."

They sat in the quiet, listening to the faint breeze rustling the leaves along the tree line. Rynn stared at the rugged face of those woods, wondering what she would do if she saw Hobie step out of them right now. Or rather, how would she react, because there wasn't actually much to do. They didn't have—

The meandering thought stopped short in her mind, replaced suddenly by another. She turned to Dale.

"Did you say 'metal tubing'?"

His eyes popped open. He understood exactly what she was saying.

39

Hobie continued to stride through the forest and could see the stars were growing noticeably dimmer as their black backdrop dissolved into a cool slate grey. The moon had swung out of sight long ago, but he could see it again now through an ever-thinning shield of timber. He would soon be out the other side and hunting under the pink light of a new dawn. He laughed out loud as he pictured Dale and Rynn trying to outrun him across an open field. He might toy with them awhile, he thought. Then a voice scraped across his inner ear.

No, you won't. You'll finish them and get gone.

"I didn't say I wouldn't finish them," Hobie mumbled. "I might just have a bit of fun first."

Everything is a goddamn game to you, kid. All you want to do is play fucking games.

"What's wrong with a bit of fun?" Hobie's voice was rising. "Would it kill you to have a bit of fun with me once in a while?"

Grow up, already. Quit having temper tantrums.

"Ha! That's rich! You, telling me to control my temper!"

You watch your fucking mouth, boy.

"Just go! Leave me alone! I'm a grown-up now!"

You'll never be a goddamn grown-up.

"Leave me alone! Leave her alone!"

Her . . . ? Jesus, you still screaming about her? Let it go.

"Let . . . her . . . GO!" Hobie shrieked into the night.

His voice had ripped through the air and carried across the country-side. Rynn and Dale looked up from their project.

"He's close," Dale said.

"And pissed off," Rynn said. They hastened their pace on the task at hand.

It wasn't long before those assertions culminated in the terrifying reality they watched unfold before them, as Hobie stepped out from the shadows of the tree line onto the edge of the open field. He hadn't emerged as far back as they had. He stood a scant hundred yards away. Dale and Rynn ducked behind their cover, peering out just enough to keep an eye on him. The hope that he might now wander off in another direction was ridiculous and far-fetched, but they each held it, regardless.

Hobie scanned the depth and breadth of the horizon before him. His head rotated slowly and smoothly, like an automated security camera, starting from his far left and sweeping across the terrain in front of him, carrying on to his right. His head stopped when the fenced sub-station came into his view. Dale and Rynn instinctively pulled back and crouched behind the grey metal boxes at the base of a tower. Rynn repositioned herself so that she could peek through the space that separated two of the metal cabinets. She saw exactly what she expected to see but gasped all the same.

"He's coming straight toward us," she whispered.

"This is it, then," Dale said quietly. "Do or die." He heard his own words and they felt like a kick in the stomach. He hadn't meant to choose a phrase that was so grimly accurate.

With each step that Hobie took toward their location, Dale lost more confidence in their plan. It was simply a bad idea. A sad and desperate idea. The stark reality, however, was this: it was by far the best option available to them. Any and every other option they'd come up with held a zero percent chance of success, while this brilliant gem held maybe two percent. Running more wouldn't get them anything. After the van crashed, it was the thing to do, certainly, and it had gotten them this far, but where was that, exactly? Here, with Hobie bearing down on them quickly. They had staved off the inevitable by an hour or so. Congratulations. At any rate, running was no longer on the negotiating table. Dale's leg had devolved from being merely useless to being a legitimate liability. Hiding was another option, and to the narrow extent it could be done at all, they were doing it. Only their hiding place felt increasingly like a prison—a death trap they had voluntarily climbed into. Still, if fighting was the only option that remained available to them—and it was, aside from surrendering to their certain demise—it made more sense to fight from within the confines of the chain-link fence than outside it. Artillery, like comedy, required at least a bit of distance.

They heard him speak as he approached—still twenty yards away. "Knock, knock. Anybody home? Ding-dong. Yoo-hoo." Fifteen yards. "Uh-oh, maybe you're out. Maybe you dug yourself a hole and are halfway to China by now." He was having his fun. "You know I'll crawl right into that hole after you. Tunnel up behind you and bite your asses." Ten yards. Five yards. "Chomp chomp chomp . . ."

"Never mind biting it," Rynn said, stepping partway out from behind the metal boxes. "You can *kiss* my ass."

"There she is!" Hobie announced with delight. It was meant to sound mocking but had come across at least a little genuine. "Is our headliner with you, or are you doing a one-person show now?"

Dale moved himself into plain view and leaned against the metal box. He hoped it gave him the air of a calm, casual badass, and not a guy with one working leg who needed help to stand. "Yeah, I'm here," he said. "The whole team is back together."

"Team?" Hobie said, recoiling dramatically. "I think we stopped being a team when you two decided to leave me for dead in a rolled van in the woods."

"I think it maybe ended a bit earlier than that," Rynn said. "Like around the time you drugged us and tied us up in that van."

"No, no . . . ," Hobie said, "we were still together, weren't we? Still on tour, still on the run, still doing shows."

"You and Dale were doing shows. You left me hog-tied with a bomb strapped to my neck."

"Oh, well, that couldn't be helped. I had no choice. Or should I say 'nachos,' eh, Dale?" Hobie grinned as he began moving along the fence. "Just like I have no choice but to climb up in there and put an end to this."

He strolled along the wire walls of their cage like it was a day at the zoo. They were doing their best to act brave, and Hobie appreciated it despite not buying it. He had encountered false bravado so many times—on the streets of the city, in the basements of clubs, in the back of his van—he could see through it like a screen door. It entertained him as much as it puzzled him. He was never sure what caused people to act brave in the face of hopeless odds, but he knew that's what it was—acting. And he knew the greatest movie star in the world couldn't pull it off believably when death was actually in the room. When the true, real-world end of the line was crawling right up close, sharing your breath.

Hobie felt that's what would give him the edge when he finally got to Hollywood. He had lived it. Wallowed in it, unwillingly or not, since he was a child. He had been beaten, stabbed, burned, bitten, stomped and dragged. He first faced the end when he was four years old. He kicked its ass then, and numerous times since.

He moseyed along the fence, dragging and drumming his fingers across the wire links. Rynn and Dale shuffled accordingly, keeping at least some portion of the metal boxes between him and them.

"I see you didn't like the collar I made for you," Hobie said, pulling out the remnants he had recovered. "Found the parts scattered all over hell's half-acre. Ungrateful."

"You didn't find all the parts, though, did you?" Rynn said.

He raised a quizzical eyebrow, then looked down at his hand and realized she was right. When he looked back at her, he was looking into one empty end of a long metal tube, which Dale held firm, pointed directly at him. Rynn stood at the back end of the tube, pressing the small end of a bolt against the primer cap of a shotgun shell, and holding a rock in the other hand, poised to strike.

"Well, holy shit. You made yourself a gun," Hobie said. "Jesus Christ, bravo!"

"Never mind that shit," Dale said. "You need to turn around and fuck off or you're taking the blast right in the chest."

"Pretty sketchy set-up, though," Hobie said, craning his neck to see exactly what Rynn was doing back at the far end. "You think it'll work?"

"I know it'll work," Rynn said.

"No, you don't," Hobie said. "That's written all over your face. You're a shittier actor than Dale is, and that's saying something."

Hobie rounded one corner of the fence and made his way along that length. Rynn and Dale shifted and shuffled, keeping the pipe pointed at him as he moved. He rounded another corner and stopped.

"Ah, I see," he said playfully. "This is where you got your shotgun barrel, is it? One of the uprights is gone," he said, then added, with genuine curiosity, "How did you undo the bolt? That couldn't have been easy."

"I owe you a pair of pliers," Dale said. "Now turn around and walk away. We'll all walk away. Forget all about this."

"Oh, well then," Hobie said, holding his hands up in mock resignation, "I didn't realize you were willing to forget all about this. You won't mention any of this to anyone, right? Double-dog pinky swear? No mention of the drugging, or the tying up, or me breaking the scrawny neck of that hump back in Shitsville? That'll all just stay between us, right?"

"Believe it or don't," Rynn said. "Either way, you need to fuck off. Now."

"Or . . . and hear me out," Hobie said, roping a couple of his thick fingers through the chain link at the end where the missing upright used to stand, "I could maybe just come in there and make one hundred percent sure it stays hushed up." He began to slowly push the unattached side of the chain-link fence in toward them.

"Fuck off, Hobie!" Dale said loudly, as seriously as he could. "Or you're dead!"

"Keep it on him," Rynn said to Dale. "If he takes one more step, I'm firing it."

Hobie slid his way sideways through the opening until he was inside the fence. "Uh-oh," he smiled, "fox is in the henhouse."

"You think I won't do this?" Rynn screamed. "After what you did to me? I will drop you cold!"

"You know, I think you just might," Hobie nodded. "Whatever it takes, right? I said it before, you're like me."

"If I thought I was anything like you," Rynn said, "I would put this pipe in my mouth and blow my own head off."

Hobie grimaced. "Jesus, what a shitty thing to say to someone."

"Enough with the fucking games!" Dale shouted.

Hobie glared at him. "And now *you* don't want me to play games, either!"

"What the hell does that—Whoa, whoa! Back the fuck up!" he yelled as Hobie stepped closer. But Hobie continued forward, eyes locked on Dale's, until the pipe was almost touching the centre of his own chest.

"One shot," Hobie said flatly.

"I will!" Rynn screamed, tears swelling in her eyes.

"Do it!" Dale shouted.

Rynn slammed the stone against the end of the bolt.

Stone on metal was the only sound.

"Oops," Hobie said.

It came so fast Dale didn't even blink before the knuckles on the back of Hobie's hand had blasted across his face. Dale reeled backward and dropped into a heap. Blood streamed from his nose and mouth. Hobie picked up the metal pipe, took a step toward Rynn and raised it like a baseball bat. She covered her head and cowered. No blow came. She looked up to see him smiling. He lowered the pipe and brought it to his mouth, holding it like a microphone stand.

"Good evening, ladies and gentlemen," he said into the top of the pipe. He tapped it twice. "Is this thing on?" He pointed up to the tree-tops and shouted, "Can you hear me in the balcony?" An owl hooted. Hobie chuckled. "This guy knows what I'm talking about!"

He held the pipe out to examine it, then tossed it up and over the fence. "I give you credit for the idea," he said. "That was creative. And good on you for having the guts to pull the trigger, even if it wasn't really a trigger. You would've had better luck just winging that stone at my head."

"You knew it wouldn't go off," Rynn said, backing away.

"I did, yeah," he said, moving with her. "Pretty dramatic, though, how I played it, right? You gotta admit, that was a heavy moment, and I nailed it."

"How did you know?"

"Those shells are duds. There wasn't any powder in them. I filled them with dirt," he said. "Probably wasn't even necessary to use duds. The whole pager idea was pretty weak, to be honest. It never would've worked in real life."

"But . . . we saw it work. You blew up that bottle with it."

"Show business!" he proudly declared. "Had to make the audience believe. If you want the truth, I just ran a firecracker fuse into those first shells, lit it and started counting down. About a second before I thought it was going to hit the powder, I pressed a button on the pager. When it went boom, your brain put two and two together and came up with an answer. It wasn't four, but you had an answer. Anyway, when I made the one for your neck, I took the powder and the shot out of the shells."

"Why?" she asked.

He looked wounded by her words. "To be extra safe," he said. "I would never do that to you for real."

"It *was* real, you prick!" she screamed at him. "For me it was real! I didn't know. Every second you and Dale were gone, every second I didn't know where you were or what was happening, was a second of terror for me. Real terror! You did do that to me, you fucking lunatic!"

He didn't like that word. He glowered at her and spoke through gritted teeth. "There are worse things than being scared."

Rynn knew that to be true, and realized this may not be the best time to give Hobie a damn good talking-to. She backed away until the metal boxes were between them, and when he took a step to come around the side, she bolted toward the opening in the fence.

It seemed for a slim fraction of a second that she was going to get there, before her head snapped back. Hobie had a handful of her hair and reeled her in like a trout. He hauled her up and turned her to face him. She saw the rage in his eyes.

"Don't hit me," she pleaded.

"I hate punching women," he said. "It always makes me sick."

He wrapped both his hands around her neck. His grip felt unreal to her. Inhuman. The fingers of a gorilla were crushing her windpipe. Her eyes bulged as he lifted her off the ground, so not only his hands but her own weight was pinching the life from her. His eyes locked onto hers as he studied them like a mad scientist might, looking for the precise moment when her soul left her body.

Instead, *she* saw the moment in *his* eyes when her foot found his crotch.

His grip loosened and she dropped to the ground as Hobie hunched over with a guttural moan. No air had returned to her lungs yet, but there was no time to wait, so she launched herself again toward the opening in the fence. Again she came just short before he had her. This time by the ankle, having flung himself forward across the ground and stretched a long arm out to hook his hand tightly around her leg. It felt like she had stepped in a bear trap. She toppled to the gravel and Hobie began pulling himself toward her. As he neared, she rolled onto her back and kicked the heel of her free foot at his face, multiple times, landing several solid blows, but he was relentless. He heaved himself up above her and went for her throat again, pinning the back of her head against the small stones beneath it. His face was expressionless now. He was truly disconnected. She would be too, in a matter of seconds, as the blackness coiled in and around from the rim of her vision. As her eyes began to roll up into unconsciousness, she felt his grip loosen again, felt his body drop with full dead weight onto her own. She coughed and gasped, her eyes rolled forward and she saw Dale standing above them, holding a large stone.

"Go" was all he said, and she did not have to be told twice. With every ounce of strength she had, she rolled Hobie off her and scrambled for the opening. She hollered once, without looking back, for Dale to come with her, but heard nothing in reply. She shot a quick look as she ran and saw Dale hoist his bad leg over top of Hobie's body, straddling fully above him. Then he raised the stone.

Rynn threw her eyes forward again, not wanting to see what was about to happen.

40

The concept of murder never entered into it. Dale's mind saw this simply as the end. He knelt down onto his good knee, resting his weight on Hobie's stomach, with his bad leg stretched outward for balance. Then, with as much force as he could summon, Dale rammed the stone down hard onto Hobie's head. A jagged gash ruptured across the hairline, producing a torrent of blood. He raised the stone once more and drove it down hard, but it was stopped short. Hobie's hand had shot up and locked around Dale's wrist. His eyes were open and blazing.

"Fuck, Dale, you're always trying to bash my brains out," he said, then rolled violently, tossing the smaller man aside like a doll. "First the wrench, and now a fucking rock . . . like a caveman. Goddamn . . . ," he said, rubbing his skull and rising to his feet as a river of red painted his eyebrow and cheek. "That friggin' hurts, you know."

Dale was still on the ground, pushing himself backward toward the fence. He knew he would need the support of the fence to get himself upright, although he wasn't sure what the point was. Hobie walked slowly toward him, swiping the stream of blood from his eye, smearing it into grotesque streaks. He watched Dale pushing with just the one leg, while the other dragged behind like a bag of cement.

"Got a bum stick, there?" Hobie asked. "Knee looks pretty swollen. Or are you smuggling a pumpkin in your pants?" He chuckled, then leaned over and drilled a fist down like a piledriver directly onto the cracked kneecap. Dale bellowed in pain. Hobie shook his head and said, "Nope. Not a pumpkin."

Dale writhed in agony, alternating between reaching for his knee and arching away from it. He had never experienced physical pain that was anywhere close to what radiated from his leg.

Hobie, meanwhile, casually strolled around inside the fence. "Look at us," he said, "fighting inside a cage, like on that videotape. You ever see that tape, Dale? It was shot in Colorado, I think—*Ultimate Fighting Style*, or something like that. It's wild, and people are making copies of the tape and sending them around. A bunch of fighters, all kinds, they get into a wire cage, like this, two at a time, and fight with basically no rules, to see what's the best style. Boxers, karate guys, judo, jiu-jitsu . . . that's the style that won in the end. This skinny Brazilian dude jiu-jitsued everybody until they gave up. He'd get on the ground with his opponent like this." Hobie squatted beside Dale. "Then he'd worm his way around behind the guy." Hobie manoeuvred himself around until he was seated, spooned against Dale's back, and wrapped a long leg across his belly. "And he'd hook one arm around the guy's neck," Hobie said, as one powerful arm snaked across Dale's throat, "and the other arm locks it in, like this." Dale was entirely at his mercy. "Pretty intense, right?" Hobie said. "And then he'd start to squeeze."

Dale felt the pressure growing, his neck being forced deeper and deeper into the shrinking crook of Hobie's inner elbow. His face darkened as the blood became trapped in his head and the whites of his eyes flushed to a deep pink. Hobie leaned forward and whispered into Dale's ear, soft as a lullaby, "Worse ways to go than this. This way you just go to sleep. And if I hang on long enough, you never have to worry about waking up." Hobie leaned back against the fencing and hauled Dale's head along with him. It was almost peaceful, like he was stretching back on a beach chair while he calmly snuffed the life from another man.

Dale gurgled and clawed at the arm across his neck. Hobie closed his eyes and tilted his head up toward the sky with a tranquil smile. He didn't see the metal pipe feeding slowly past his jaw through one of the diamonds in the fence. The pipe pushed in two or three feet, then suddenly jammed sideways across Hobie's Adam's apple. In a flash, Rynn's other hand poked through the fence and grabbed the free end, pulling it back against the fence as hard as she could. She put a knee between his shoulder blades and hauled back with every muscle in her body. Hobie made a raspy honk like a goose and latched onto the pipe with his left hand, but still squeezed Dale's throat with his right arm.

He tried to lean forward, but with Rynn's entire body pulling him back by the neck and Dale's body weight riding on top of him, he couldn't secure the leverage required. He had no option but to let Dale go. Dale toppled sideways and crumpled to the ground like an empty suit.

Hobie wrapped both his hands around the pipe and pushed forward. Rynn screamed and yanked back harder, trying to redouble her efforts, but she was already at maximum output, with one arm still separated, if not officially divorced, from her shoulder. Hobie forced the bar away from his neck and down to chest level, where his strength and leverage were at their apex, and he shoved the pipe straight out like he was doing a bench press in the gym. Rynn slammed forward, face-first against the mesh, and let go. She instinctively threw herself back and to the side. Those instincts saved her, as Hobie whirled on a dime and harpooned the pipe through the fence. Its jagged end jammed into the compact earth and stuck like a javelin, right where she had been standing a half-second before.

She lit out in full flight, running for her life. She heard the metal fence rattle behind her and knew Hobie had flown through the opening in hot pursuit. She didn't know how long she would be able to stay ahead of him but hadn't imagined it would be less than three seconds. It was. He had erased a lead of forty feet in five fast strides and dropped her with a stiff arm in the middle of her back. She tumbled forward and skidded, bits of gravel gouging into her palms and elbows.

Before she could even try to stand, a powerful hand grabbed her by the back of the neck and yarded her up. Hobie twisted her to face him, and to his surprise she spun around with a clenched fist, hammering it hard into the bridge of his nose. His head snapped back and then righted itself. He blinked as water filled his eyes, and he dragged a knuckle across his top lip. He looked at it and saw fresh blood, then tasted more blood flowing into his mouth. His eyebrows knotted even as the corners of his mouth spiked up into a sinister grin of teeth and plasma.

"Congratulations," he said. "No one has ever been able to break my nose before."

She raised her forearms in front of her, expecting retribution, but the defence was not enough. A giant fist delivered a crushing right cross to the side of her head. Her legs turned to string and her body folded down on top of them.

Hobie gagged and bent away, vomiting onto the ground in a violent splash. He wiped his lips and screamed at Rynn, "Why did you make me do that!? I fucking hate punching women!" He took a step toward her and angrily lifted his boot above her head.

"No!" Dale shouted.

257

Hobie turned to see him dragging himself slowly forward, hunched like a mummy, bug-eyed and covered in blood. He dragged the metal pipe behind him.

"Holy fuck," Hobie said, and began to laugh, lowering his foot beside Rynn's head, "you two are incredible. Show's over. You've both done more than your time, you've given everyone more than their money's worth, but you both keep coming back for encores."

"Leave her alone," Dale slurred. "Fight me."

"I did fight you, buddy. Remember? A couple times. And hats off, I've had bigger, badder bikers begging me to stop. And here you are, you can barely stand, you can barely keep your eyelids up, and you want another round." Hobie walked toward him. "You sure you want to do this?" he said. "I thought you wanted to make sure you were there for your precious little girl. This is a good way to make sure you won't be."

"Fuck it. What's the point of me being there if I'm just going to fold when things get tough?"

Hobie shook his head. "You're an inspiration, Dale. I mean that." As he came nearer, Dale raised the metal pipe like it was a broadsword. Hobie circled slowly. "I'll never forget everything you've taught me on this run, buddy. Never. I'm serious. I'm going to thank you in my acceptance speeches."

"No, you won't," Dale said.

"I promise I will."

"You won't. Because you're never gonna win a goddamn thing," Dale said, then added, with as much conviction and gravity as he could manage, "because . . . you suck."

Those words scalded Hobie like acid. They hurt more than the broken nose, or the kick in the nuts, or the wrench to the head. They staggered him and fractured something inside.

"No, I don't," he said, his bottom lip beginning to quiver. "Take that back, Dale. Take it back."

"You suck," Dale said again. "And . . . you're not funny."

Hobie screamed like a wounded beast and lunged. He grabbed the pipe and flung it away from Dale with ease, then punched him hard in the sternum. Dale felt his breastbone crack and he collapsed backward onto the hard ground. He couldn't breathe and was certain his heart had stopped.

Hobie towered above him, silhouetted against the first purple push of sunrise. As Dale saw the bottom of Hobie's huge boot rising up above his face, he closed his eyes and relaxed. He had done what he could. What he should. Vanessa would be fine.

Instead of feeling the heel crushing his face, however, Dale felt a faint vibration in his back rising up through the ground, followed by a low rumble in his ears. He opened his eyes to see Hobie looking off to the side. The large foot disappeared from view as Hobie turned and walked away, toward the sound. Dale heard him quietly muttering, "What the fuck?"

41

Dale winced and strained, rolling onto his side with great effort, then lifted his head to assess the situation. He could see Hobie moving toward a mass of bright light, which flared out and around his tall frame into a shimmering full-body halo. It reminded Dale of the thin, spidery alien bathed against the otherworldly luminance of the spaceship at the end of *Close Encounters*.

Dale raised one hand as a shield against the brightness. He could then see that the massive radiance was caused by four individual lights. Motorbikes. The low, reverberant growl of the engines told Dale they weren't some kind of Japanese road rockets or European café racers. These were heavy American bikes built for wide asses.

Hobie stepped toward the bikes as their engines were cut, each sputtering to a percussive stop. The headlamps were killed. The biker at the front of the crew rose from his saddle and stood. He was a mammoth. As tall as Hobie but with additional mass.

"Uncle Bull?" Hobie said slowly, softly, as if he might be dreaming.

Bull walked toward Hobie, followed by three large gang members.

"Hey, boy," Bull said casually, like they were meeting up for Christmas dinner. "What the hell are you doing out here in the sticks?"

Hobie was still trying to wrap his head around this encounter. "I'm on tour. I'm supposed to be out here. Why are you out here?"

"Some fucking tour," Bull said, looking around at the terrain. "Telling your jokes to who—skunks and cows?"

"We're playing bars around here, or nightclubs," Hobie said, elevating the run. "Nice clubs. Big crowds. But you still haven't told me what you're doing here."

"You weren't easy to find," Bull said. "I got a list of your shows and dates from that greasy weasel Merlin, so I knew you'd be somewhere along this stretch of road, but still . . . probably would've missed you if we hadn't seen those pigs in the ditch."

"You talked to Merlin?" Hobie asked, confused.

"The pigs said they got a call from some kids about a van with a couple people tied up in the back. I figured that'd be you. Sort of your thing. So we found a side road that led in the direction the pigs pointed."

"Why were you talking to Merlin?" Hobie asked. "How do you even know who Merlin is?"

"Because I'm currently deciding whether or not that little shit-heel lives or dies," Bull said. "Speaking of which, let's have the cash from the shows."

Hobie grew dizzy as pieces of the puzzle clicked into place and the shape of the true landscape began to appear. Merlin's phone call . . .

I've seen you do spots around town, kid. Strong stuff. Raw . . . naturally funny. You show real potential. You just need a bit of road experience and you could become a sharp, original comedic voice. Any interest in going on a run of shows with a couple veteran comics? Wouldn't pay you anything, of course, but it's about the experience.

. . . was all lies. A con. Empty sentences that needed to be said to pull him onto the job.

Hate to put you in this position on your first run, kid, but you'll be doing me a real favour. The other two comics both owe me money. So can you collect all the cash after each show and bring it back to me? And do it without them knowing? I'll let the venues know, so it's all on the sly. Hey, if it's too much to ask, I understand, and I can book someone else—

No, no, I can do that! No problem!

Hobie felt sick, remembering the desperation in his voice. The clumsy, lustful eagerness blinding him into being so easily duped.

"Merlin owes you money," Hobie said to Bull. "That's why I'm here."

"Yeah," Bull said with indifference. "So, where is it?"

Hobie lowered his head and stared at the dirt. He watched in his mind's eye as his future got disassembled like the false walls of a movie set. The picture was wrapped. The lush rugs were rolled up and returned to the rental house, the overstuffed furniture lifted and hauled away by faceless dream-killers who were just doing their job. The heart-shaped swimming pool was drained dry.

"It was all a lie," Hobie said.

"So you're not a clown," Bull replied. "Boo-fucking-hoo."

"Yeah. I know you think my dream is stupid."

"Hey, it was my fucking idea to send you out on these shows," Bull said. "I knew you could keep the money safe, and if you got to do some of your fuckin' skits or whatever, great—maybe you'd be less fucking mopey and testy around work. You got my guys on edge."

"You've never supported me," Hobie said.

"Supported you?" Bull snorted, not even sure he had heard the words correctly. "The fuck I didn't! I took you in, I put food in your guts, I put you to work—"

"You only put me to work when it worked for you. When I got big and strong and when you saw that my head would let me do bad things. Things that made your other flunkies sick. I would do them, to try and make you happy. To make you like me."

"You're sounding a little queer, now," Bull said.

Hobie's shoulders drooped. He took a long, earnest look at the rugged mountain of a man who had raised him. The giant man he had always looked up to, whose approval he would literally kill for, and had, but who now just seemed like an old, crusty, selfish, narrow-minded, backward asshole.

"What the fuck is wrong with you, Uncle Bull?"

"Mind how you go, boy," Bull growled.

"Have you ever thought of anyone other than yourself? Did you ever once think about what I needed? I was just a little fucking kid."

"Oh no," Bull said mockingly, "did you not feel loved? Did you not get enough hugs?"

"Not nearly enough," Hobie said plainly. "A four-year-old could use a few hugs after his mom gets"—it caught in his throat—"his mom dies."

"She wasn't just your mom." Bull pointed a thick finger at Hobie. "Brenda was my kid sister. And I took care of what needed to be taken care of."

"You didn't take care of me. You took me in, yeah, and did what? Left me outside in the salvage yard to live with the fucking dogs."

"You loved those fucking dogs!"

"I loved one of them!" Hobie shouted. "Thor. The one who protected me and kept the other dogs from killing me—which they wanted to do every fucking day!"

"I had obligations!" Bull bellowed back.

"You fucked me up!" Hobie roared, his eyes moistening. "You killed him right in front of me!"

"That's horseshit," Bull said. "You were nowhere around when I shot Luke!"

Hobie froze. He stared wide-eyed. More puzzle pieces began forcing their way into the picture, buckling other bits and popping them off the table.

"I was talking about Thor," he said, "the German Shepherd. My only fucking friend, and you killed him right in front of me."

"Oh," Bull said, as close to sheepish as he had ever been. "Yeah, well, I killed that nasty fucker because he came after me."

"He was protecting me. From your fists. But roll the tape back a second." Hobie stared at Bull with cold, hard eyes. "What did you say about shooting Luke?" Hobie stepped forward. "Uncle Bull? Did you shoot my dad?"

For maybe the first time in his life, Bull took a step backward. He raised his open hands and stammered, "Just, whoa, hold on," trying to get his thoughts together. He had never meant for the boy to know, had always told him that his dad had just left one day, after Brenda had died, and never came back. It was true, in a way. "There might be parts of this story you never knew about," Bull said, "but you know what he did. You were little, but you saw it."

"I saw," Hobie said, trance-like. His jaw pushed forward and his eyes dialed long distance. "I saw. I yelled. Leave her alone. He doesn't hear me. He won't stop hitting. He won't stop. Leave her alone. He won't stop. She's not moving." His voice was rising louder. "Leave . . . her . . . *alone!*" Hobie lurched forward and vomited onto the ground.

Silence draped the scene for long moments, until Hobie raised his head again and said quietly, "I saw."

"I know," Bull said, taking another step back. His men had never seen him like this, rattled, retreating, and they stepped to his side in support as he continued. "I know what Luke did. That's why I had to do what I did. I just didn't want you to know."

"My dad killed my mom," Hobie said. He had seen it, but he'd never uttered the words before. His mind was everywhere and nowhere. He was four, he was twelve, he was alone, he was in a gang, he was forgotten in the dark, he was onstage under spotlights, he was hugging a dog, he was killing a raccoon, he was killing people, he was fighting for his life, he was diapering himself, he was helping Rynn pee, he loved his mom, he hated his mom. His eyes darted in his head, pecking at the images as they flickered past, a waking REM cycle.

Then his eyes stopped darting and they moved to Bull. "My uncle killed my dad," he said bluntly, putting that new peg in its proper hole.

Bull had stepped behind his men, talked over their shoulders. "Better the truth is out," he said. "Now let's go home."

"No."

"Sorry, boy. No choice."

"Nachos."

"What? Look, it's just some business we need to take care of," Bull said, laying it out simply. "You did something bad to a guy at a club. The Red Cactus, remember?"

"He bombed. Zero laughs," Hobie said.

"Well, the club is one of Stacker's. I know you didn't know that, but—"

"I knew."

Bull's eyes narrowed and his voice lowered. "You knew that? You knew it was Stacker's place and you still fucking hit it? Killed his guy? Without asking me?" He pushed his men aside and stepped forward again, his anger throttling any concerns he might have had seconds before. The boss was back at work and he wanted answers.

Hobie looked at Bull blankly. "He said I wasn't funny."

"Jesus Christ, kid," Bull said, "I know you're sort of a head case, and maybe I didn't help that way back when, but this shit has to be made right."

"Made right," Hobie repeated.

"It's restitution, boy," Bull said. "Just business."

Hobie cocked his head at the word "restitution." The zombie didn't know what that word meant, but the werewolf did, and he didn't like it.

"You're handing me to Stacker," Hobie said. His uncle had killed his dad and now it would be him. "He'll kill me."

"Not necessarily," Bull said, calculating a five percent chance Stacker would let his nephew live.

Hobie didn't do the math. The zombie and the werewolf both hated numbers. "I'm not going," he said in a voice that Bull didn't recognize.

"You'll do exactly what I—"

Bull's jaw broke as Hobie's fist cannonballed into his chin. The bigger man buckled at the blow but didn't go down until the second punch, which came a split second after the first and landed hard against his temple. Bull crumpled sideways, blocking the forward motion of two of his men who were trying to respond. It gave Hobie the single moment he required to deal with the third man, which he did by driving the edge of his hand into his windpipe. The man made a sound like a hog at a trough and clutched for his throat in the same instant Hobie's foot crushed his testicles.

Bull was down, Man One was down, and Hobie stepped back to create space between himself and Man Two and Man Three, who were hurling themselves into the fray.

Man Two pulled a knife from a sheath near his boot, while Man Three lumbered forward bare-handed, like a pro wrestler. Hobie got up on his toes, light and quick, bobbing and weaving faster than a man his size should be able to. He held his fists low and danced like Ali, then snapped a lightning-bolt jab into the face of Man Two. It stunned him and he fumbled his knife.

Man Three kept looming, a thick, bearded bear of a brute, and Hobie receded, letting the hairy bastard get some momentum. When the guy had a good four or five forward steps behind him, picking up steam, Hobie suddenly planted his back foot and sent a fist square into the geographic centre of the man's face. The punch fractured several bones behind the wall of whiskers, and Man Three was out on his feet, falling forward unconscious and ploughing a rut in the gravel with his jaw.

Man Two, a lean, muscular thug named Duncan, had his knife back and was blinking through the hot tears that Hobie's jab had aroused. Against another opponent, he might have made some flashy moves with the blade, tossing it side to side or twirling it in his hand, but he knew better than to do that in this situation. Long before this fracas, Duncan had seen Bull's nephew at work. They had been sent out together on a few collection jobs, and if the patsy didn't pay up or tried to act tough, the big kid would put a twisted brand of hurt on the poor son of a bitch that had, on occasion, turned Duncan's stomach. He knew some fancy knife moves would neither impress nor intimidate. It would just offer a sliver of opportunity, and that's all this kid ever needed. So he stayed focused.

"I'm gonna gut you, Howie," the man said, "like a fish."

"Like a fish?" Hobie repeated. "No, no, Dunc, if you want it to sound good, it has to be specific. Gut me like a salmon, gut me like a tuna, something like that. They have to believe what you're selling. It's the same in comedy, Dunc. Specifics! 'Buick' is funnier than 'car.' 'Pop-Tart' is funnier than 'breakfast.' Ya see? Try another one."

Dunc gritted his teeth, but it did nothing to hide his abject fear. "This ain't no joke, Howie. This is real life, and yours is about to end."

Hobie dropped his hands and started laughing. "Oof, Dunc. That is some bad dialogue. Maybe you should just be an extra who doesn't say anything. One who comes at the hero with a knife and gets one of these—" Hobie launched a foot up like a missile and caught the man under the chin. He then dove forward and threw one arm around Duncan's shoulder, landing in a vise-like headlock, while the other latched on to the wrist of the knife hand, bending his arm until the knife was pointing back at the man's own face. Duncan struggled but was still dazed by the kick in the chin. Hobie's bulging arms squeezed together like a trash compactor, drawing the point of the knife and the man's face ever closer.

"Don't . . ." was all Duncan could muster.

"Don't what?" Hobie asked. "Don't say some cool line like 'stick around' or 'it's been knife to know you' or 'fuck you, Dunc, I never liked you and you always had rank BO and stunk up my van'?" The face and knife were rammed together, and as the man screamed, Hobie broke his neck.

He watched the body slump to the dirt. "Oh, forgot to tell you," he said. "I ain't Howie no more."

A low, guttural grumbling pulled Hobie's attention, and he saw Bull rising. Even on one knee and wobbly, the man still looked dangerous. Hobie headed his way.

As he neared, Bull reached down and pulled a handgun from the holster strapped to his boot. He pointed it at Hobie, who just kept coming in a straight line. He either didn't see the gun or didn't care.

Bull was shaky, and one eye was filled with blood, punctured by a fractured orbital bone, so his first shot missed by a good margin. He recocked the hammer, bore down on the job and steeled himself. His second shot tore through flesh in Hobie's lower torso and burst out the far side. Hobie twisted, stumbled, and dropped to the ground. He clutched the wound and roared, then heard the small mechanical click of Bull's gun being cocked again. Hobie bled and his gut burned but he rolled over in a flash onto all fours and sprang forward like a leopard. Before the gun could be fully raised for a third shot, Hobie had the barrel in his hand and twisted it backward, breaking two of Bull's thick fingers in the process. In the same fluid move Hobie hammered his elbow hard across Bull's already broken jaw and dropped him to the dirt again.

Hobie stood, towering above his uncle. His breathing was heavy but shallow, burdened more by emotion than exhaustion. He pressed a hand against the bullet hole in his abdomen and took several seconds before speaking. "Give me a smoke," he said, and he reached into Bull's vest pocket, pulled out the pack and a naked-lady lighter. He popped a cigarette into his lips, lit the end and took a drag. His face screwed up and he coughed a little. "How the fuck anyone finds that a treat is beyond me."

He leaned down near Bull's head and said, "Maybe you're right, Uncle. Maybe it is time for some restitution." Hobie stretched out to retrieve the handgun from the gravel and stood up with it. He cocked the weapon and pointed the muzzle at Bull. "This is for my dad, shit-sack that he was," Hobie said, and he pulled the trigger. The flash and blast synchronized with Bull's scream as a bullet pounded into his right shoulder. "This is for my mom, warts and all," Hobie said, and he squeezed again, sending another explosion of fire and lead into Bull's left shoulder. Another roar of anguish. Hobie lowered the gun and took a drag off the smoke, then pulled it from his lips and exhaled across the ember, blowing until it glowed a crackling orange. "This is for a six-year-old me," he said, and he dropped a knee onto Bull's chest, pinning him, then pushed the red-hot cherry tip into the flesh on Bull's neck. The big man bellowed again and bucked like a stallion, but Hobie held him flat, grinding the cigarette in deeper. "Take it!" Hobie shouted in Bull's face. "Show me your mettle!" Hobie crushed the cigarette until it sizzled and snuffed out against Bull's skin. "That looks nasty," he said, examining the burn. "Like the mouth of a goddamn volcano. I know a guy who can cover that up for you."

Bull writhed in agony. Hobie stood up and silently watched his uncle suffering. He didn't take the pleasure from it he'd hoped he would, but every part of him was glad it had been done. It was freeing somehow, even as it killed some part of him inside. Maybe it was a part that needed to die.

Bull looked up at his nephew. "Boy," his voice rattled, "we can work this out. I can make this good."

"So can I," Hobie said. "It's not complicated business, it's just simple debt." He raised the gun and pointed it at Bull's forehead. "This last one's for Thor. He sends a big, furry 'Fuck you.'" The barrel barked and a bullet punched a hole in Bull's skull, settling all accounts.

42

With a lifetime of pent-up horrors let loose into the night, and his four most formidable opponents sprawled across the clearing, Hobie looked back to where he had last seen Dale. He wasn't there. At least not in the exact spot.

In the time it had taken Hobie to deal with his uncle and his gang, Dale had made it all of ten yards, dragging his smashed leg and using the metal pipe as a very ineffectual crutch. If he put any weight on the pipe at all, the rough, jagged rim would gouge into the earth and send Dale tumbling.

Hobie felt a little bad for him, hobbling away for his life. Still, there was a job to do. Gigs to finish. *I'll show you who's funny.*

Dale could hear the large feet crunching into the gravel with an ominous methodical rhythm, legs swallowing yards of space with every stride. The logical centre of Dale's brain told him to stop, turn around, prepare, fight, however pointless it would be, but the fear centre just kept throwing coal into the furnace.

Dale was shoved forward onto the ground by a boot in the back. He dropped the pipe to break the fall with his hands, then rolled over to see Hobie swooping down at him like a hawk. Two huge claws dug into the front of Dale's shirt and hauled him vertical. He was pulled close to Hobie's face.

"Maybe *you* suck," Hobie snarled. "You ever think of that?"

Dale blinked a slow blink and said weakly, "I think that all the time."

"Well, then," Hobie said, "let's give you the red light so you can say good night and get offstage." Hobie's left hand released Dale's shirt in exchange for his throat. His right hand did the same, and both began to tighten. Dale's hands hooked limply over Hobie's wrists but offered no real resistance. There was no fuel left in the tank. As his throat constricted, Dale's vision blurred and gave way to colourful sparks that danced on his eyes. He felt the small bones in his neck begin to give way. Then he felt something sharp scrape against his cheek. He felt the pressure on his neck wane and disappear. He felt a single puff of Hobie's breath drift across his forehead.

As the sparks extinguished and his vision returned, Dale could see Hobie's face—eyes wide but motionless, mouth gaping open in wonder or confusion. He looked down and saw the metal pipe, tainted with narrow ribbons of red, the jagged edge protruding through Hobie's chest. The pipe had been pushed through from behind, far enough that the rough rim had scratched the side of Dale's face. Hobie dropped to his knees, slumped sideways to the ground and lay still. Rynn stood there, shivering and sobbing.

"I had to," she said, tears flowing down her face. "He was going to kill you. I had no choice."

Dale whispered hoarsely, "Where did you find nachos?" Then he plopped down heavily onto his ass. Rynn laughed, coughed and sobbed simultaneously, and dropped herself down beside him.

They sat quietly for a long minute, doing little beyond trembling and replaying the events of the evening, and the past few days, in their minds.

"Hey . . . ," Dale said weakly, "I've got something for you. In my pants."

"Jay-zus, does pain make you horny, you sicko?" she said.

He smiled a swollen, bloody smile and leaned forward, pulling up the back of his shirt. Rynn saw the thick manila envelope tucked into his jeans. She pulled it out, lifted the flap and strummed the layers of cash.

"Horny and resourceful," she said.

"Fifty-fifty?" Dale offered.

"That's up to you." She tossed the envelope onto his lap. "The split's between you and Vanessa."

Rynn surveyed the cache of large bodies strewn across the gravel yard, then looked beyond them. "Would you happen to know how to drive one of those things?" she asked.

"Would you?" Dale replied. "I might know how to sit on the back and hang on."

"Let's find out," she said, and she hauled herself up. She helped Dale to his feet and the two of them walked slowly toward the motorbikes, each using the other for support. "On a side note," Rynn said, "I don't suppose you've seen my fecking purse?"

43

The summer ended and autumn came, to no one's surprise, but when winter followed, Dale Webly did learn something new. His cracked kneecap, which had been surgically pinned and fused and otherwise generally healed, began informing him in explicit terms that it did not like the cold Chicago wind that spilled off the shores of Lake Michigan. It was a binary agreement; any temperature above freezing was all right, but the moment the air dipped below freezing his knee sent a harsh memo up to head office.

That had become the daily vernacular in Dale's new life: memos, emails, inventory reports, conference calls with other managers of other warehouses in the network of commercial storage facilities owned by his childhood pal. It wasn't a bad way to make a buck. The pay was pretty good and promised to get better, while the fact he knew exactly how much he was making and exactly when had given him a foundation of security he hadn't known in adulthood. The provided benefits—medical, dental—were a fresh and welcome wrinkle he had never enjoyed as a stand-up who drifted across North America getting paid in crumpled twenties out of bar registers. He was also home every night and every weekend, which would be absolutely ideal if Vanessa had still been living there and not in the dorm on campus in Wisconsin. Still, this new arrangement and new routine comforted him. It grounded him. And he just plain liked it.

Dale swung his previously-owned-but-new-to-him 1993 Pontiac Grand Am into his designated parking spot near the front door of the warehouse and went inside. His secretary, May, handed him two small slips of pink paper as he passed by her desk on the way to his office door. They were "While You Were Out" telephone messages, and once inside his office he set down his briefcase and looked at the first one. It made him smile.

He dialed the phone and heard it ring twice.

"Daddy?" Vanessa said.

"Now how do you know it's me calling and not one of your dopey boyfriends?" he asked.

"Wouldn't be them," she said. "They're all here in my room."

"Don't even joke," Dale said. "That is my new nightmare."

"What do you mean, 'new'?" she asked.

"Never mind. But the old one was about you, too, so I guess my overall point is stop giving your old man nightmares. Anyway, what's up? You called."

"Yeah. Did you say you were getting a new folding computer for work?"

"I did. It's called a PowerBook. Why?"

"Any chance I could have your old one? I could use it for school, for writing assignments. They have some great computer classes here and I just, I don't know, I think computers are the future," she said.

"You're probably right," he said. "Another ten years and everything about us will be on these stupid things. Sure, I guess you can have my old Tandy. Hey, how about I drive it up there after work this Friday and we can hang out for the weekend?"

"Well, I sort of have other plans," she said. "Any chance you could just ship it?"

He smiled. *Wow, it's a good thing I made sure to be here* "—for you," he said, "no problem, baby girl. You should have it by next week." He told her he loved her, and she echoed his words—but not just the words. The meaning behind them rang honest and true for the first time in forever.

When he hung up, Dale looked at the second pink slip and his smile grew wider. He picked up his phone and starting dialing.

In a television studio in Los Angeles, California, Rynn Lanigan stood on a dark blue patch of highly polished vinyl flooring that reflected the colourful lights hanging above her on a suspended metal grid. She held a script in her hand but read aloud from a large cue card gripped by a young intern just below the lens of the main camera.

". . . and the man had the nerve to complain that his wife was overdue for a facelift. He actually said that. Meanwhile, his own face looks like the underside of an alligator."

She stopped and looked down at the script in her hand. "Did I read that right?"

The floor director, wearing a headset microphone and holding his own copy of the script, said, "Uh . . . let's see . . . yes, 'underside of an alligator.' That's the line."

"It probably shouldn't be the line," she said. "Do you think? I mean, that feels soft."

The man shrugged. "Alligators are pretty wrinkly."

"That's sort of my point, though," Rynn said. "Pretty straight-ahead. Not much of a twisteroo there." She looked out past the lights, up into the empty bleachers. "Is Vic or Gail out there?"

"On our way," came a man's voice, and the dapper executive producer, Vic Zayne, and Rynn's manager, Gail Beering, approached centre stage. "What are you thinking?" Vic asked.

"Well, not to be indelicate," Rynn said, "but can we say 'nutsack' on this show?"

"Not sure," Vic said, raising one eyebrow. "Believe it or not, that question has never come up before. Let me make a call," and he stepped over to a white telephone perched on a rolling cart.

"While that's getting sorted," Gail said, "why would you want to say 'nutsack'? On TV or anywhere else?"

"I think it's just a bigger surprise for the audience. A sharper left turn. It's a bit puerile, maybe, but it's got a better bite. And we're on late at night."

Vic returned. "I'm told you can say 'scrotum' without any issue."

Rynn scratched her head, then sounded it out. "His face looks like an alligator's scrotum." She tried again. "An alligator scrotum." She wrinkled her nose. "It's not great." She thought again. "Crocodile scrotum. That'd be better, I suppose. The hard 'c' sound helps, and it pings off the 'c' in scrotum."

"If you say so, Shakespeare," Gail said, walking away.

"Try it out and see how it feels," Vic said. "I'll go back and watch on the monitor."

Rynn ran the line quietly a few times to herself. "Crocodile scrotum . . . crocodile scrotum . . ."

"Going again from the last line of that last joke," the floor director hollered, then pointed a finger to Rynn. She began again.

"Meanwhile, the guy's face looks like a crocodile's nutsack."

Every crew member on the floor burst out laughing. So did Vic. Gail turned to him and said, "She should say it her way. Her way is really good."

"It *is* why I hired her, isn't it?" Vic said, then made the call for all to hear. "Nutsack is in!"

A production assistant approached the floor director with a message, and he, in turn, relayed it. "Rynn, phone call for you. We'll take a break and get the nutsack change in the script."

At a long production table, a multi-line phone sat with one light blinking. Rynn picked up the receiver and pushed the flashing button.

"Hi, Rynn here."

"Hello, my name is Dale Webly, and we were almost murdered together. Do you recall?"

"Ah yes," she said, "it's a vague recollection. I've forgotten the face but remember the voice."

"How the hell are you?" Dale said. "I got a message you called."

"I did, yeah," she said. "It's been a while since we talked and maybe you're busy and everything, but I wanted to run something by you."

"Shoot," he said.

"My show goes into full production in a week. And I'm swamped with a million details, and it means I can't focus on the monologue jokes as much as I'd like. So I want to hire you to be the head writer for the monologue. Oversee which jokes get picked, shape the flow of the set, make sure the phrasing is good, all that stuff."

"Really?" Dale said. "That's . . . wow. But why me?"

"Because you happen to be really good at all that, and I trust your taste and your sensibilities, and it would let me focus on other things and not worry all day every day that the monologue is going to suck."

"But there must be some fantastic joke writers in L.A.," he said.

"Probably. Somewhere," she said. "But I trust you. I'd rest easy knowing you were in charge."

"That is an incredible offer, Rynn," Dale said, "and I'm very flattered you thought of me, but I just can't drop everything and move out to Hollywood. I made a commitment to this job. I can't quit."

"Did I ask you to quit?" she said. "I remember very clearly you telling me that if you took that warehouse job you could write at night."

"You mean you'd let me write for your show from here, from Chicago?"

"You got a fax machine there, don't you? Welcome to 1995, Grandpa!"

"Well yeah, I mean . . . I still do spots at a couple clubs here in the city, just to keep my hand in. I could run the material in front of a crowd and then shape it and edit it, try different—"

"So that's a yes then?" she asked.

"Yes. It is a yes," Dale said.

"Fantastic! Thank you, Dale. I really appreciate this. Someone from production is going to call you with a contract and all the details. You won't believe the fecking money. It's mad what they think a joke is worth in this town." Then she said, "We'll talk more later. I have to get off the phone now. I'm being flagged down for an interview with . . . guess who."

"The news?" he said.

"Yes!" she squealed. "*Entertainment Tonight* is here to chat with me, of all fecking people!"

They said their goodbyes and Rynn was scooted away down a hall into a boardroom where the small crew and on-air interviewer from *Entertainment Tonight* were set up and waiting.

Rynn sat on a stool as a lavaliere microphone was clipped to her collar and some quick powder was puffed onto her forehead and under her bottom lip. The interviewer asked if she was ready, and she nodded, so the camera rolled and the chat began.

"I'm here with Rynn Lanigan, who is the host of *Friday Raw*, the new sketch and variety show that makes its network debut in March, is that right?" the interviewer asked.

"That is exactly right," Rynn said. "Your sources have not failed you."

"Tell us a little bit about the show."

"Well, it's sketch and variety, as you said, and there will also be some stand-up and celebrity guests, so it's really all over the map and we have no idea what the hell we're doing," Rynn said. "But that's what makes it fun, and believe me, we're having an insane amount of fun putting this together."

"Who are some of the celebrity guests you have lined up?"

"I'm not yet allowed to say who has or has not confirmed appearances on our show. It's all very hush-hush," Rynn said. "I can therefore neither confirm nor deny that Keanu Reeves has agreed to do a sketch. I can neither confirm nor deny that Sheryl Crow has signed on to do three songs. If you ask me if Stephen Fry makes an appearance in the first episode portraying a mercilessly cruel theatre critic who gives scathing reviews to middle-school productions, I can legally only shrug in response while giving a coy wink. I can also tell you that I'm flying my ma over from Dublin to be here for that one."

"That sounds amazing." The interviewer beamed. "Now, you were chosen as the host of the show because of your skills as a comedian and emcee, and how you blew everyone away at the Just For Laughs festival, despite—it should be noted—having just come off a rather horrible and traumatic experience on the road. Do you want to tell us about that?"

"Not really," Rynn said. "You used the words 'horrible' and 'traumatic,' right? That's pretty bang on, so no need to dredge that all up and have me slip into a catatonic state right here on camera."

"Understood," the interviewer said. "But for those of our viewers who are not aware of your story, I'll just briefly give them the broad strokes." The interviewer turned to the camera. "This woman right here, Rynn Lanigan, was on tour with another comedian when they were captured and tied up and beaten, and she saved them both when she was able to escape and kill their captor. It's a heroic story of courage and strength that is truly inspirational."

"Well, listen," Rynn said, "if you want to call me heroic who am I to argue? But just as a point of clarity—a rather big point—I managed to *stab* our captor so we could escape, but I didn't actually kill anyone. Just to be clear."

"I'm so sorry," the interviewer said. "I guess my sources did fail me on that one."

"I guess they did," Rynn said. "And now I get to sue you, right? God bless America. And listen up, America." She looked right down the barrel of the camera. "Watch for *Friday Raw*, coming to your TVs this spring. Check your local listings."

44

Seventeen kilometres south of Winnipeg, Manitoba, the stony grey walls of the Flatwater Federal Penitentiary pushed up from the prairie, jutting in defiance of the otherwise ceaseless horizon. The ominous grey perimeter was crowned in a wreath of razor wire punctuated by three brooding guard towers that overlooked both a medium-security and a maximum-security prison. The first had a genuine and benevolent mandate to rehabilitate and reintegrate the occupants into society. The other focused on keeping unrepentantly violent individuals locked away from the rest of the world. Iron bars, steel doors and thick concrete were the meat and potatoes of the place, but increasingly over the past decade that recipe had been augmented by a desire to study and understand the violent mind.

In her drab, utilitarian office, Dr. Jean Larence sat at her desk reviewing notes she had made on a small yellow pad. After some time studying the ballpoint scribblings, she picked up a hand-held cassette recorder, pushed the one red button and began to speak into it.

"February 17, 1995. Case 1844 regarding inmate 306873, Howard Henski, male, twenty-three years of age. Mother, Brenda Henski. Father, Luke Deller. Parents unmarried. Note: inmate will not respond to legal name, although acknowledges that his legal name is Howard Henski, insists on being called Hobie Huge. Hobie Huge, being an informal pseudonym, has not been changed legally. Lists his occupation as professional comedian and actor, although no evidence is provided to support that assertion. When asked how long he has been a comedian, he responded only with 'long enough.' The claim is likely dubious, or at least exaggerated, although I have not yet pressed further.

"After two sessions, inmate demonstrates a mostly cooperative attitude toward evaluation. Keenly cooperative, in fact. Has verbalized his belief that, quote, psychology is everything, end quote. Has apparently had psychological or psychiatric assessments in the past, although at present have not been able to determine with which professionals. Again, have not yet pressed that issue. Important to make independent evaluation before reviewing any previous diagnosis. Third session with inmate is about to take place. Notes for transcription will be dictated after session and will follow immediately on this same tape."

The doctor clicked the recorder off, gathered her yellow pad and pen and left her office.

Three minutes later, Dr. Larence stood in front of a thick green door that had one narrow window running vertically along the upper half. The window was not glass, but two layers of robust Plexi that sandwiched a panel of wire mesh. She waited to hear the buzz of the lock release, then turned the handle and pushed the door open.

"Hiya, Doc," Hobie said, giving a slight wave with one hand. He was seated on a metal chair, and she saw his ankles were shackled together, and his wrists were clamped into a set of handcuffs linked by chain to a metal loop in the floor.

"I'm sorry, Hobie," she said, stepping inside. "I told the guards you didn't need to be restrained like that."

"And I appreciate it, Doc," he said, "but I may have done a couple things recently to make them think otherwise."

"Oh? Do you want to talk about that?"

"I had a violent response," he said, rather cheerily, "but it was in response to a violent situation, so I feel like that shouldn't count against me. Besides"—he poked a finger toward her yellow pad—"there's plenty on my plate to deal with already, am I right?"

"Very well," the doctor said, settling into the metal chair opposite. "Let's go back to where we left off last session. Is that okay?"

"Sure. I know I had a few stops and starts last time, and I turned my nose up at a few of your questions—maybe wasn't as forthcoming as you'd like. But I've been thinking it over. I have big plans for the future, and if you can help me get all my wheels on the track now, that'll help me down the road. Especially in the movies. Good acting requires tapping into deep moments, dark moments. Gotta be willing to pick at the scars and scabs to get an honest performance. So I'm going to be open with you here. Pop my top and let's look inside."

She flipped back a few pages on her pad. "In our last talk, you spoke about your uncle killing your dog."

"My friend," he said.

"Your uncle was hitting you?"

"He was going to. So I was hiding."

"Right. And you said you had seen your father hurting your mother."

"Watched him beat her to death, yeah," Hobie said, nodding casually as though she had just read his address back to him.

"I'm sure you understand," the doctor said, "experiences like those, especially for a child, can have deep, long-lasting effects. Do you recall if there were any other instances when you were young that might qualify as childhood trauma?"

Hobie forced a smile. "Just a few, yeah."

"Do you feel up to discussing that further?"

"Sure. Let's dump the bag out on the table." He took a deep breath. "As far as trauma goes, the earliest thing I remember is being four years old and bundled up and taken to a party. By my mom. Party was out in the woods in some old, abandoned farmhouse or cabin. Mom was pretty gooned on whatever, but felt she should bring me along, I suppose. Look after me. But she didn't do much of that, she just plunked me down in a corner and while everyone was getting fucked up, I sat there and drew. I always carried a scribbler around with me, and two pens. Red one and a blue one. I drew all the time as a kid. Wasn't bad at it, either. I should pick it up again."

"Did something happen at the party?"

"Don't know. I fell asleep after a while. I remember being cold. The cabin had no windows, the glass had been all busted out, it was just open holes for the wind to whip through, so I crawled under my blanket. Laid there quietly and had myself a snooze. When I woke up, I was alone. Everyone up and left, and I guess my mom had imbibed in enough liquids and powders that she sort of . . . I don't know . . . forgot I was there. At least I hope she forgot."

"Do you recall how you felt when you saw you were alone?"

"Confused, I suppose. Scared for sure. Wandered around inside the cabin a bit to see if I could find my mom, or anyone else. Couldn't, so

I picked up my book and pens and decided to walk home. Turns out four-year-olds don't have a terrific sense of direction."

"Was it still nighttime?"

"Yeah, dark as hell. I remember thinking Mom might be mad at me for being out past my bedtime. And that was the first time I killed anything. So that'd leave some emotional scars, right?"

"I'm sorry. You said you killed something?"

"Yeah. And at that age, makes sense it would sort of mess me up. Don't you think?"

The doctor waited for him to provide further detail, but he seemed to be done.

"Hobie," she said, "I think you've left something out of the story."

He scrunched his face and looked up into the corner of his eyes. Then his eyebrows lifted. "Jesus. I skipped right over the whole thing," he said. "Fuck, that's weird. I'm being straight with you, Doc, I didn't even realize. God as my witness, I thought I told you the whole story just now." He shook his head. "That is fucked up."

"Do you want to take a moment? Consider what you missed?"

"No," he said, "I know what I missed. I missed the whole trauma part."

"Well, being left alone in the woods when you're four years old would constitute trauma," the doctor said.

"Okay," he said, "but that'd be the soup before the steak."

"All right." She nodded. "Would you like to tell me about the steak?"

He shook his head again. "I seriously thought I had. Weird. Anyway, there I was, walking along in the woods. I was scared, so I was being real quiet, and I guess I unintentionally snuck up on a raccoon. Startled it. Big, fat fucking thing, bigger than me. Like a grown man facing a bear. I remember thinking it was cute. That was short-lived.

Fucking thing attacked me. I tried hitting it, but that did nothing. They're all teeth and claws, but their body is loose and flabby, the skin just slides around on top of it like an oversized sweater while they're biting and scratching you." He paused. "Fucking things," he added, quieter, frowning at the floor.

"Can you tell me what happened next?" the doctor asked.

A long moment passed. His own memories seemed to be slowing him down.

"Killed it." He didn't elaborate.

"How were you able to kill it?" she asked. "I just wonder, because you were a small boy, it was a wild animal—all teeth and claws, as you say. How did you kill it?"

His eyes stared emptily at the light grey flooring, watching a memory flicker across it like an old film. A horror movie. Shaky hand-held camera with choppy, random cuts.

A child in diapers, screaming. A wild animal biting and tearing pudgy pink flesh. Screaming. A desperate little arm flailing at the beast. Hitting thick fur, having no effect as the clawing and biting continues. The screaming. The pain. The terror. That animal face. Filling the frame. Flooding the memory. That fierce, wild face matted with the boy's own blood. Hitting that face. Panicked punches bouncing off a hard skull. Glancing off an angular muzzle. Then sticking. Sinking in. A feral shriek wailing from that animal face, screeching past that mouthful of razors. Half the length of a red pen sticking out from one eye socket. Convulsing. The beast vibrating on the forest floor as if electrical currents were pulsing through it. The pen hurts it! My pen will save me! The small hand pulling the pen from the creature's eye and jamming it down again. And again. The point piercing the face. The neck. The face. The neck. Writhing. Shrieking. Screaming. Crimson fur. The vibrating stops. The kicking stops. The breathing stops. The stabbing does not.

"Hobie?" the doctor's voice was soft, gentle, but enough to break the film. "Do you remember how you were able to kill it?"

Hobie's eyes rose slowly up to meet hers.

"Maybe it just ran off."

Hobie had promised to be forthcoming and share everything, and had been sincere in the intent, but as the discussion extended beyond the raccoon story, Dr. Larence saw him growing distant again. Other examples of abuse were touched upon, but his answers were truncated and cursory. She felt this was not the time to push him deeper, so ended the session. The patient was making progress, she was learning more, but this would take time. Fortunately, they had a surplus of that available. Somewhere between twenty-five years and the rest of Hobie's life.

Back in her office, Dr. Larence switched on her recorder.

"February 17, 1995, second entry." She looked at her watch. "Three ten p.m., third session with inmate 306873 complete. New recollections by the subject in this session, when added to previous, suggest a possible pattern. Four particularly traumatic events from subject's childhood share a common element, beyond extreme violence. One—he had been sleeping quietly under a blanket when he was abandoned by his mother in the woods. Two—he had been walking quietly through the woods when he startled a raccoon, which attacked him. Three—he had been quiet, hiding from his uncle, which led to a beloved dog being killed. Four—when he watched his father beat his mother to death, he had tried to shout out but his voice was too quiet. These episodes of graphic and horrific violence were all preceded by moments of quiet. Moments of not being heard or seen. If subject's mind has associated quiet with trauma, it may have led to a form of athazagoraphobia. That is, subject may have deeply rooted fear of being forgotten or ignored. Fear of not being heard. Perhaps this subconscious need to be noticed is what draws the subject to stand-up comedy. Spotlights to be seen. Microphone to be heard. Hypothesis needs more examination. Much, much more. As does the depths to which past violence triggers current violence."

The doctor clicked off the recorder, tore some pages from her yellow pad and placed them into a tan file folder, which had the name HENSKI typewritten on a white label, and under that, handwritten in red marker, the word HUGE.

45

The clinking of Hobie's chains echoed against the walls as he was led down a hard, beige corridor by two beefy prison guards.

"That shrink is good," Hobie said to one guard. "She knows how to root out the rotten bits, that's for sure."

"You're too far gone," the guard sneered.

"You'd be surprised," Hobie said, taking no offence at the ignorance of the statement. "A good psychologist can get in there and round up all your ducks and figure out which ones are wounded, pluck them out, fix them up, and next thing you know they're all in a row and ready to fly."

"You ain't flying anywhere," the guard said.

"Sure of that, are you?" Hobie asked, looking up at the grille on a vent as they walked by.

They rounded a corner and started down another hall, this one lined on their left with holding cells. Inmates sat behind bars, reading or sleeping their years away. As they passed one cell, a large, bald man with a thick moustache hollered out, "You're dead, kid."

Hobie kept walking, pushed on by the guards, but hollered back, "You keep saying that, Fritz, but you never do anything to make it happen. Dreams are good, big man, but you gotta take action."

"I'll be seeing you soon," the bald man bellowed.

"Okey doke," Hobie yelled back, "but do your push-ups, Fritz. Your boy Smitty wasn't strong enough when he tried it. Did they have his service yet? Was it nice? Were there snacks?"

"Keep laughing, funny boy!" the bald man's voice boomed down the corridor. Hobie chuckled.

Fifteen yards farther down, the guards pulled Hobie to a stop outside his cell, unlocked the door and pushed him inside. When the bars clanged shut, Hobie turned and alternately held up his wrists and ankles so his shackles could be removed. That done, the guard gave a couple sharp yanks to make sure the door latch was secure.

"Nighty-night, asshole," the guard said. "Get comfy, 'cause you're going to be here a long, long time."

"Ha!" Hobie laughed. "Now *that* is funny!"

The guard folded his arms. "You seriously think you'll find some way out of here before you get killed by one of these other animals?"

"Either way"—Hobie shrugged and lay back on his bunk—"you're gonna miss me when I'm gone."

ACKNOWLEDGEMENTS

Writing certainly looks like solitary work. Maybe great, sweaty chunks of it are. But it's a fairly arrogant fool who bypasses the opportunity to get an entirely different brain in an altogether different skull to chew over the prose and offer up some notions about how it could be better. I've always been open, even keen, to get input from others. Perhaps growing up in a house with nine people, as the youngest of seven kids, I had that concept develop organically *(see: "had no choice")*. I've also spent a couple of decades writing scripts for television, which is very much a team sport, even if one person's name is credited onscreen. So, when I had finished the first draft of this book's manuscript, it was both natural and important for me to seek input from others. Even more so as I'd never written a novel before. I have been honoured with, and benefitted greatly by, input from some people who I truly admire and respect. I will always be grateful for their having taken the time to read a draft and provide their thoughtful and incalculably constructive notes. To that end, I send HUGE (get it?) amounts of gratitude to Meredith Hambrock, Linwood Barclay, John Rogers, Joel Walmsley, Lance Storm, Rachel Talalay, Charles Demers, Beau Smith, Craig Northey and Ed Byrne . . . with an *extra* special bit of thanks to Ed Byrne for not only reading an early draft, but also having patience enough to school me on the proper use of "feck" in hopes of at least mitigating the degree to which I come across as an ignorant doofus. Much appreciated, pal!

Enormous thanks also goes out to my wondrous and wise long-time (trophy) manager, Elizabeth Hodgson, the diligent and razor-sharp George Caetano, the bright and brainy Arthur Evrensel, who keeps reminding me he is my "lawyer" not my "legal guardian," the team at Cooke McDermid—especially my literary agent Ron Eckel who actually believed I wrote an actual novel—Tim Rostron and everyone at Doubleday Canada for accepting the notion that "TV joke boy" wrote a serious, dark (maybe even a little bit scary) thriller and to Colin Oleksyn, an all-around good egg and my first real writing partner, who many years ago blew wind beneath my wings when he uttered the phrase, "I'm not thrilled about saying this, but you're a decent writer." Of course I send tremendous love and life-long thanks to my family for having a ridiculous and probably unwarranted amount of faith in me for a hell of a lot of years now. I was haywire lucky to land in amongst you.

And to Nancy, who is simply the love of my life; thanks for your belief, patience and understanding. And for loving me back, because . . . I mean . . . that has *really* worked out great!

I also give a very special, knowing nod to every stand-up who ever suffered along a chunk of road with some knobby arsehole who made the journey more difficult than it needed to be.

Lastly, I send sincere and heartfelt thanks to every one of you who picked up a copy of this book. Truly. I appreciate your support more than you could know.

Thank you.

For more from Brent Butt, sign up for his free newsletter at
brentbutt.com/bulletins

Instagram and Twitter: **@BrentButt**
Facebook: **officialBrentButt**